LARAMIE
MOON

CLARE MCKAY

TRIFECTA PUBLISHING HOUSE

First Printing: 2016
Print Book
ISBN -13: 978-1-943407-15-6

Trifecta Publishing House
1120 East 6th Street
Port Angeles, WA 98362

TRIFECTA PUBLISHING HOUSE
Contact Information: Info@TrifectaPublishingHouse.com

Edited by Eilis Flynn
Cover Art by Rae Monet, Inc. Design.
Formatted by CyberWitch Press

For Bob —
Always in my heart

Laramie
Moon

For Joni
Enjoy the hotness!
Clare McKay

chapter one

Laramie, Wyoming

The drums pounded out a merciless rock beat. The deafening twang of electric guitars was underscored by the persistent hum and crackle of the neon beer signs and droning commentary from competing sports channels on the big screen TVs above the bar. Jim Winter's temples throbbed from the noise and the overpowering stench of stale beer and vomit, sweating bodies, raw sex, and the noxious artificial odors that humans felt compelled to slather on themselves.

Out of the corner of his eye, Jim saw a flying punch about to connect with its intended victim. He stepped in, catching the clenched fist in his huge hand before it landed. He understood it was just rowdy high spirits, but on principle he stared down the subdued fighters.

"Sorry, Jim." The cowboy's sheepish grin signaled that the barroom brawl wasn't serious. He and his partner dropped their eyes and held up their hands in surrender and also as a gesture to show no fangs or claws were involved.

"No harm done," Jim said, but he wasn't finished putting out fires yet. The first scrap had set off another, so he turned his attention to two cowboys still grappling on the floor and yanked them up by their collars. The fight went out of them as soon as they saw who'd intervened.

"Boys, I think you've had enough fun tonight. Daniel, dump some cold water on these boys and get 'em a ride home." Jim passed the whole bunch off to his ranch foreman who pushed the boys toward the door with an irritated "Harumpf." Jim knew Daniel enjoyed a good fight, and hated to have his entertainment, or his beer, interrupted.

Jim strolled back to his spot at the bar. With a beer in hand, he acknowledged friends and neighbors as they moved past him. It was a typical Friday night at the County Line Roadhouse, loud and crowded.

The bar was packed with a mix of college students, ranch hands, and people from town. Young to old. Hipsters, as hip as you could get and still be in Laramie, cowboys, and nerds. There was even one professor type looking uncomfortable and out of place in a just-out-of-the package plaid cowboy shirt and stiff new jeans. He appeared to be taking notes on his phone. Jim made a mental note to have someone check him out. He could simply be doing a study on the mating habits of drunk college students, but these days threats could come from anywhere. Mixed in among all the regular folk were Werewolves. *Werves*, that's what humans were calling them these days. His Werves. His responsibility. They looked as human as anybody else, but Jim knew their true natures were never far beneath the veneer of humanity they showed to the world.

Jim scanned the wide open room. One end had long, picnic-style tables congested with noisy groups celebrating the weekend.

In a dim corner nearby, he noticed a few quiet couples paired up to share a romantic moment, oblivious to the chaotic atmosphere. At the other end of the room, a band banged out a mix of country and rock tunes for the enthusiastic dancers. If there was any trouble, it would come from that end of the room. The pounding rhythm and overheated bodies pressed close created a perfect storm of hormonal aggression that could quickly turn violent, considering the situation.

Jim felt the moon's pull deep in his bones. It set him on edge, but he'd learned to ride it out. As Alpha of the Laramie pack, he had more control than most. Some of his pack, younger Werewolves mostly, were in the bar, and he was there to keep an eye on them. He didn't always shepherd them this closely, but it was the eve of the full moon.

Alcohol wasn't the problem. Weres metabolized liquor so fast they could only get drunk if they were seriously trying, and some of them were. The problem was hormones. Shifters felt prickly and irritable as the full moon approached. It was like being over-caffeinated and having the hives at the same time, and it wouldn't get better until they could shift and run off their aggression in a hunt.

Fights between pack members were inevitable. The younger Weres competed for their place in the pack, scrapping to see who came out on top, and some of the older ones just liked to fight, so Jim was there to referee and see that their battles didn't get out of hand or spill over into the human population.

Tomorrow night's run would ease a lot of tension. Then they'd all settle down for another month, but they had to get through tonight first.

Jim was jerked out of his reverie as he sensed two of his pack enter the bar. He was always aware of his pack around him, but he'd been waiting for these two, one in particular. Randi Harris led the way in a skintight dress and stilettos. Not appropriate for this venue, but Randi could pull it off. It was the one who came in next that had his full attention—Sissy Hunt, Daniel's daughter.

Sissy's given name was "Sarah," but to Jim's recollection, no one had ever called her that. She'd always been Sissy. She was tall for a female at just under six feet, and Jim took in every inch of her as she walked toward the bar. Lean and trim, she moved with a fluid grace that took his breath away. Unlike Randi, who was decked out in one of her Friday night "Make 'em drool" outfits, Sissy was dressed like most of the men in the room, in dark jeans and boots.

But there was nothing masculine about Sissy. The fit of her jeans cupped her very feminine behind, and the burgundy western-cut shirt hugged her compact breasts. Her sun-streaked, blonde hair was pulled back in her usual ponytail, and her hazel eyes glinted in the low light with luminous streaks of brown, gold, and green. Jim's gaze settled on her full rose-colored lips that seemed to be permanently drawn into a scowl, at least whenever he was around.

Daniel joined Jim at the bar. "Good evening, ladies."

"Hi, Daddy." Sissy rose on her tiptoes to give Daniel's cheek a quick kiss. "Jim." She acknowledged her Alpha with a nod before she turned and greeted some other members of the pack.

He was busy watching Sissy walk away when an elbow caught him in his ribs. Daniel grinned and gestured with his beer toward a ruckus on the dance floor.

Jim spotted the trouble. Two guys were squaring off, and a crowd was forming around them. Jim couldn't see who it was, but odds were likely that a wolf was involved on a night like this, and he had to make sure it didn't get out of control. If it was a wolf-on-wolf problem. Jim could simply order them to back down, but a wolf versus human conflict could get ugly fast.

By the time Jim reached them, the crowd was cheering them on with a "Fight, fight, fight" chant. One of the young, unmated Weres from the pack was facing off with a drunk college student, apparently over rights to a pretty Werewolf female named Julie, a beta in the pack.

"Figures," Jim muttered. He wasn't surprised to see who was causing the trouble. It was a cocky young alpha named Adam, who'd earned a reputation as a hothead, always trying to challenge for rank. Jim had called him down before for being a bully.

Adam pushed Julie behind his back and kept her out of the college kid's reach in a taunting, keep-away move. The kid weaved and grabbed at her, ignoring the very solid obstacle of a pissed-off Werewolf who stood between them. Stupidly, the kid didn't look like he was going to back down. There was no doubt who'd win in this matchup. The Were was bigger, stronger, and faster than the human.

Adam dropped the college boy with one punch. Not satisfied with the easy win, he jumped on the dazed kid and got in a few more blows before Jim broke into the ring and yanked Adam off the human amid a chorus of boos.

Daniel sauntered over and took charge of crowd control, shooing away the complaining onlookers. "There's nothing to see here. Show's over," he shouted. He pulled the college boy to his feet and gave him a gentle shove toward a group of his friends. To make sure they got the point, he flashed them some cash. "Why don't y'all go on and have a beer on me?"

As the college kids dragged their friend away to the bar, Jim used his powerful body to block Adam from following his opponent. In Adam's heightened state of arousal, the Were considered the retreating student as prey, and his instinct was to give chase and take him down. Not a good situation.

Adam tried to push Jim out of his way, but the Alpha caught his arm and growled so low only Adam could hear it. The younger Were's head popped up, and he boldly matched Jim's stare for a few seconds before he dropped his gaze with a sullen snarl of his own.

"Daniel, take Adam out of here. Make sure he's headed home." Jim never took his eyes off of the overgrown pup in front of him. Adam bowed his head, but he was shaking with pent-up fury.

"Jim, I'll take care of him." Julie stepped forward and stood beside Adam. "It's my fault. I shouldn't have danced with Brad," she said, indicating the drunken student who, despite a black eye and the fact that he could barely stand on his own, still leered in their direction from the bar.

Jim weighed his options. Adam was following orders, at least for now, but he was still riled up, and Jim didn't trust that Adam wouldn't take out his frustration on Julie later on. She was a sweet girl but a beta, and she was no match for a frustrated alpha with a bad temper. "Did you come with Adam tonight?"

"Yes, sir," she said, studying the floor.

"I'm going to have Daniel find you another ride home."

"Make sure they leave separately," Jim added to Daniel. He allowed himself a sigh. It was strictly forbidden by pack law to challenge humans. It was a law that kept them safe and off the radar, and it was absolutely necessary for their survival, especially in this part of the country where wolves of any kind were considered nuisance predators that had to be eliminated.

He'd have to openly punish Adam at the next pack meeting. This was one part of being Alpha that Jim hated. Punishments weren't pretty. But that wasn't for two more weeks, in the middle of the moon cycle when emotions were more low-key, so he'd either have to chain him up in a holding cell or keep an eye on him during tomorrow night's full moon run. Adam was going to be a problem either way.

"HEY, LADIES, THAT was some ruckus, huh?" A tall cowboy stepped up to Sissy and Randi. "Sissy, you want to dance?"

Lost in thought, Sissy didn't notice the young man standing in front of her until Randi tapped her on the shoulder. "Oh, hi, Johnny. No, I'm not dancing tonight," Sissy said, flashing a weak smile.

"I'll dance with you, Johnny. Sissy's on her period. You know how that is." The cowboy turned bright pink, and Randi gave Sissy an evil grin as she led her partner onto the dance floor. After a quick two-step, Randi reclaimed her spot at the bar.

Sissy was fuming. "Why did you tell him that? It's not true, and now half the guys in here will be sniffing me up. Gross."

"I know, but it's the quickest way to brush off these cowboys without a long, detailed explanation. Would you rather I told him, 'Sorry, Johnny, Sissy won't dance with you because she's busy pining away for our Alpha who's currently got his eyeballs glued to a really trashy human'?"

Sissy glanced over at Jim then followed his fixed stare back out to the dancers.

AFTER THE RUN-IN with Adam, Jim didn't think there'd be any more trouble. He could hand things off to one of his more levelheaded wranglers and head back to the ranch. He wanted to just take one more look around before he left to make sure.

Oomph. He turned and walked right into a curvy platinum blonde.

"Hmm, hard body," she purred, boldly skimming her hands up his chest.

Jim caught her wrists. He'd never seen her before, but her scent was all heat and his cock jumped to full alert status. He could hear her heart racing, and his own heartbeat sped up in response. As he brought her hands down and released them, he stepped back. "Excuse me, miss."

"No problem. It was nice bumping into you. Maybe we can try it again sometime." The woman smiled flirtatiously and headed for the dance floor.

Jim inhaled a few deep breaths, trying to bring his heart rate, and other physical reactions, under control, but it wasn't working. His whole body was lit up like a Christmas tree. His gaze sought out the blonde among the dancers, and she wasn't hard to spot.

Her dress left little to the imagination, and neither did her dance moves as she ground her pelvis against her partner, a preppy frat boy. She deliberately looked back over her shoulder to see if Jim was watching. When she caught his eye, she smiled and turned her back to her partner to give Jim the full view, showing off ample breasts barely contained in a skimpy halter-top dress. The frat boy threw his head back and held on to her hips for dear life as she rocked her ass into his crotch, her eyes locked on Jim.

Riveted, Jim watched as the tease swept her tongue over her bottom lip, leaving it wet and inviting. She brought her hands up to cup her face then blatantly traced them down her body, caressing her neck and skimming down the sides of her breasts in a classic Marilyn Monroe move. Her hands met over her bare stomach then pushed lower until they pressed at the apex of her legs.

Jim's jeans strained uncomfortably, and he shifted his weight to relieve the discomfort.

"Somebody's gonna get lucky tonight."

Jim tore his gaze away and turned to see Daniel grinning at him. "Well, it's not going to be me."

Daniel Hunt was not only his ranch foreman. He was Jim's Second, second-in-command in the wolf pack. He'd been Second for Jim's father as well, and Jim had known the older man all his life. He was tall and lean like his daughter Sissy, but his wiry frame was covered with hard muscle, and his usually serious, weather-worn face was framed with shaggy gray hair and a ragged three-day stubble. "Aw, come on. She's a hot one, and she sure wants you. I can watch the boys while you have some fun."

Jim shook his head. "Not my type."

Daniel grinned. "She's female, isn't she? How're you ever gonna find a mate if you don't even try?"

"If my mate's out there, she'll have to find me."

Daniel pointed to the wriggling blonde. "That one there's trying. I guess next she's gonna have to come over here and grab you by that hard-on to get your attention."

"I'm not interested." Jim frowned. His body was plenty interested. "Anyway, she's human."

"That doesn't mean you can't scratch a little itch, you know."

Jim shook his head. Daniel was always trying to set him up. That was nothing new, but this time was different. It was like his head and his body were out of sync. He couldn't understand why he'd become so aroused by just watching the dancer. She wasn't anyone he'd normally be attracted to. Just a trashy little human. But he couldn't take his eyes off of her.

With pack business and the ranch, he didn't have the time or the inclination to properly woo a female, but as Daniel had said, this female didn't need any wooing, and she was a human, so he wouldn't have to worry about the mate issue. A smile slowly crept across Jim's face as his cock got the better of his brains. *It wouldn't hurt to blow off some steam, and she's definitely not playing hard to get.*

SISSY HUNT WATCHED the bleached tramp put on her show for Jim. She'd seen that kind of thing before, but she didn't have to like it.

Women were always coming on to him, and it wasn't hard to guess why. He was the epitome of Alpha maleness. At six and a half feet, he was usually the largest man in the room. His broad shoulders filled out his western shirt, and she knew his upper body was all ripped muscle. His jeans hugged his long, muscular legs all the way down to well-worn boots.

Jim was handsome in a rugged way. His dark hair flopped over his forehead, always looking like he'd missed a haircut. His deep brown eyes dominated his face. Hooded by dark brows, his intense stare could command a man or animal and melt a woman to her core. And he knew it. As Alpha of his pack, that was part of the job. His mouth was often drawn into a hard, thin line, but on occasion, a smile softened his face. He was smiling now.

Sissy couldn't hold back a threatening growl.

"Your wolf is showing." Randi shoved a beer toward her. "You need to chill out."

"What I need is for our fearless leader over there to keep his dick in his pants."

"I wouldn't mind if he took it out, maybe waved it around a little. I bet you wouldn't either." Randi smiled a dreamy little smile.

"Yeah, well that's not going to happen. He seems to prefer human sluts. When's the last time he looked at you like that?"

"Never."

"That's what I mean. He never gets with anybody in the pack."

"I'm sure he hooks up every now and then."

"Only with humans, it seems." Sissy scowled.

"I hear he likes the chase, but he doesn't want to get caught." Randi gave her friend a slow once-over. "Seriously, you'd have a better chance if you dressed like you were interested."

"I can't watch anymore." Sissy turned away and took a long drink of beer. "What's he doing now?"

"Still watching and maybe drooling a little, and he's got a whopping boner I can see from here."

"I'm getting out of here." Sissy hated the way things were with Jim. They used to be so close when she was younger. He'd been her big brother's best friend, and he'd always made her feel special. She loved the way his eyes lit up and his smile spread clear across his face whenever he saw her, but now that she was grown, he practically ignored her. Tonight, he was eye-fucking the human, but he'd barely given her a second look.

"He's too old for you anyway." Randi said. "He's practically ancient, like forty or something."

"He's not that old, but it doesn't matter," Sissy said. Under her breath she added, "It doesn't matter to him what I do at all." She turned from her friend, afraid that the other girl would see the tears in her eyes. "I'll see you later."

THE SONG ENDED, and the crowd on the dance floor regrouped. As soon as Jim lost sight of the blonde, he came back to his senses. He shook himself like a wet dog, but the unsettled feeling was still there. His reaction felt all wrong, and he wanted to get out of there before he did something stupid.

He glanced around the room for Sissy. He wouldn't leave until he knew she was in good hands, even if they wouldn't be his. Daniel's daughter was off-limits to him, and anybody else, as far as he was concerned. The thought of someone else touching Sissy made his teeth hurt. He held back the urge to let his fangs fill his mouth.

He spotted Randi. She had a couple of lovesick cowboys hanging around her, as usual, but Sissy was nowhere to be seen. She'd probably gone home. She usually didn't stay late. He'd just check with Randi to be sure, then go on home.

"I saw you watching me."

A sultry voice whispered from right behind him. The human blonde. A hand traced the muscles of his back. "Mmm. Nice," she purred. "How about you buy me a drink, and we can get to know each other?"

Jim burned as her light touch melted through his shirt and into his skin. Pushing down every primal instinct, he turned and faced the human woman. "I don't think so. I'm just heading out."

"Fine with me. We can skip the drink and get right to the getting to know you part. I'm Debby. You know, like from Dallas." Her tongue slid from her lips and ran a slow circuit across her plump bottom lip again before coming back to the top and giving a little flick.

Jim followed the tip of her pink tongue, mesmerized by its lazy journey, and when it disappeared, he sucked in a deep breath. For a moment, he couldn't think of one good reason not to drop and fuck her right there.

Damn the moon. "Sammy," he called to the bartender. "Get the lady a drink."

chapter two

Debby smiled and turned triumphantly toward the bar. Jim pivoted and headed for the door. He made it outside and into his truck in record time, but before he could clear the parking lot, he saw her in the rearview mirror. Bathed in moonlight, the little minx was standing with her hands on her hips.

Jim was sweating and had a raging hard-on by the time he pulled up in front of his ranch house. Normally, he had perfect command of his body and his emotions. As a mature, dominant Alpha, he could shift at any time, but even under the influence of the full moon, he retained rational thoughts and control.

Some of the lesser wolves, young alphas and most betas, reverted mostly to their animal natures when they shifted. All of their senses were ramped up and primal instincts competed with social conventions. That was what made the pack so important. One of the main functions of pack life was to train young shifters to manage their instincts.

The ability to control their passions was what made their

kind different from the legendary beasts in stories and movies. They didn't run out of control through the streets of Laramie, ripping humans to shreds. That kind of behavior would get them all killed.

As the pack's Alpha, Jim was responsible for guiding them and handling problems both in their wolf and human forms. He took the duty seriously, which was why his loss of control at the bar puzzled and irritated him. He'd managed to handle a large, angry male Werewolf, but a sexy human female had him panting like a hound.

He needed to decompress. Instead of going inside the ranch house, he slipped into the darkness, stripped off his clothes, and shifted.

As he dropped down on all fours, dark, thick fur smoothed over his body in a wave of tactile sensation. Each hair caught the vibrations of the air and transmitted them down to his skin. He felt his bones and joints reforming, his body contorting into his new form, that of a huge mahogany brown wolf. Called by the moon, the change was involuntary for most shifters. It could be excruciatingly painful for some, but Jim could shift at will, and he'd always had an easy time slipping between shapes.

He loved the feel of his powerful animal body. His muscles worked effortlessly, and his senses were keen. Although the waxing moon was almost down, he could still see clearly in the dark. He could smell the wranglers in the bunkhouse, all of them pack members. Those who were still awake likely sensed him running in the dark. Pack was like that. They were connected. Some more than others.

He heard the horses in the barn shuffle and snort nervously as they caught his scent. They were used to being around Weres, but having a fully grown wolf nearby still set off their instincts. As he loped through the night, he could scent and sense all of nature around him on the expanse of his property. He could hear the wind blow through the tall grass and the prairie dogs chirp as they scurried away at his approach.

Jim broke into a full-out run. This was what he needed. City joggers, human joggers, who ran around an asphalt track had no idea what they were missing. Four perfectly coordinated legs pounding across the land, claws gaining purchase in the sandy soil, and powerful lungs pumping clean oxygen into his blood, all while he could feel the land around him.

He ran and ran until he was panting with exertion. Finally, he trotted down to the river and took a long drink of cold water before he plopped down in the cool grass.

Tomorrow night the moon would be full and the whole pack would gather at the ranch. They'd change and most would run together. They'd take down a deer and share in the kill, but it would be noisy and Jim would have to remain alert and watchful so that no one got hurt. Life was good, but not perfect.

After a while, Jim padded back toward the house. He shifted back to human form and picked up his clothes. He grabbed his boots, checked that his wallet and watch were still stuffed inside where he'd left them, and headed to his ranch house.

He wasn't surprised to see Daniel kicked back on a rocker on the long porch. He didn't appear surprised to see Jim naked and carrying his clothes. Clothing didn't remain intact through a change, so casual nudity was a fact of life, at least on the ranch. Jim pulled on his jeans and joined Daniel on the porch.

"Good run?" Daniel offered Jim a cup of coffee from his Thermos.

Jim shook his head. "Yeah, I guess I needed it."

"Is everything all right with you?"

"I'm okay."

Daniel smiled. "I know you're okay, but something's not right. You didn't stay to cash in on that little gal who was shaking her ass at you?"

"No, it was too weird. She's human, but she was giving off signals like a female in heat. She wrecked my control. It took everything I had to resist her."

"Why'd you want to resist her? It sounds to me like you've gone too long without a female." Daniel leaned back in his rocker. He and Jim often disagreed on pack issues, but his primary job was to take care of his Alpha and the health of the pack, and as far as he was concerned, nothing was off-limits.

"You don't take females from the pack, and now you're refusing a pretty human who was throwing herself at you. You studying for the priesthood?"

"No, it's not that. Something was off." Jim paused as he thought about it. "My reaction was too strong, too urgent."

"Well, it ain't gonna get any better until you get some release. Tomorrow night there's gonna be plenty of females out here for the run who'd be more than happy to spend a little time with their Alpha. Just pick one. It's that easy."

"It's not that easy," Jim muttered as he stalked past the old man into the empty house.

THE NEXT MORNING, Jim headed into Laramie. He liked to get all of his business out of the way before the full moon. He ran into the Albany County sheriff outside the bank.

"Frank." Jim nodded to the officer. In years past, he would have offered his hand to his old friend. They had played high school football together and had shared the usual teenage adventures, but now their relationship was strained.

As a young officer, Sheriff Frank Murray had responded to a disturbance call to find a drunk cowboy having a howl by the light of the full moon, and he'd watched, horrified, as the cowboy shifted from man to wolf. Jim's father, the Alpha at the time, had arrived in time to keep Frank out of harm's way and had convinced him to keep his mouth shut. Now, as sheriff, his first priority was the safety of the community, and Jim knew that the man was conflicted about keeping his knowledge of the local pack a secret.

Werewolves and other types of Weres had been outed to the public about ten years previously, but the military and the government had known for much longer. Over time, Were genes had made it into the general, human population, enough to be medically and scientifically noticeable. Some packs went public, but some of the Alphas had decided that it was safer for their packs to remain hidden.

There had been a lot of negative reaction to the news, mostly based on Werewolf stories and myths. Humans were afraid of being attacked or bitten and turned into Werewolves even though experts had assured the public that couldn't happen. They had explained that Weres were a species, and they were born from Were parents, but that didn't allay the public's fears and had even fired up questions about the rights of non-humans living among humans. As a friend, Jim had tried to explain all that to the sheriff, but a rift had grown between them.

"Jim." Frank kept his distance. "I heard there was a ruckus out at the Roadhouse. I assume you took care of it."

"I did. It wasn't serious, but I made sure it wasn't more," Jim said with more confidence than he felt. Adam was going to be a problem, and he was going to have to deal with him. "Just like I always do," he added as he entered the bank.

The encounter with Frank Murray was still on Jim's mind as

he left the bank, so he was surprised to find Debby, the brazen blonde from the night before, waiting at his truck.

"Hi, cowboy," she drawled. She was draped over the truck grill like a juicy hood ornament.

"Is that the best you can come up with?" he said, irritated. He made a point of not getting too close to her.

"Oh, I can do a whole lot more than that." She eyed him head to boots and came back to rest her gaze on his crotch.

"I'll bet, but I'm not interested, so please get off my truck."

She hopped down, and he saw she was decked out in some western-style Daisy Duke outfit, with another skimpy halter top, short cutoffs, and red boots. She must have thought he'd find that sexy. He didn't. She just looked desperate.

Jim had plenty of experience avoiding unwanted come-ons. Like any Alpha wolf, he liked the chase. But something smelled different about this woman. Something that made him wary.

Despite his brushoff, she advanced on him as if she were the predator. With a smile, she trailed her hand down his arm, and his response went from zero to pure lust in record time. In one smooth movement he could have shredded her tight shorts, dropped her to her hands and knees, latched his teeth onto the nape of her neck, and sunk himself deep between those rounded hips. Classic wolf mating behavior. The type of behavior he'd always denied himself.

Her scent flooded his senses and kept him rooted in place, fighting his instincts. Perhaps sensing victory, she leaned in seductively and palmed his erection right there in broad daylight on the sidewalk.

"Well, big man, you look interested now."

Her touch seared through his jeans, and when the shock cleared his head, he jerked away. In a voice thick with lust, he warned, "Lady, I don't know what you think you're doing, but you'd better back the fuck up before I bite off your pretty little arm."

The woman released her grasp and stepped back, smiling. "I just thought we could take up where we left off last night."

"You're right about that." Jim stepped around her and opened the door to his truck. "Last night I left you standing on the curb."

Her smile instantly changed to a scowl. "You bastard!"

WHEN HE WAS in town, Jim always checked in on Maggie, one of his oldest friends. Maggie Hunt had a small art gallery tucked into one of the historic buildings along Second Street in Old Laramie. He'd known her since they were children, and she'd been mated, and married, to his best friend Lucas, Daniel's son. When Lucas had died in the military, Jim had taken responsibility for her and helped set her up in the gallery. She could take care of herself now, but he checked in with her whenever he was in town.

Maggie was Sissy's sister-in-law, and she'd practically raised the younger woman, who worked part time in the shop. Jim rarely passed up the opportunity to see Sissy, if only for a few minutes. He knew it was masochistic to tempt himself, but if a casual meeting in the shop was all he could allow himself, he'd take it.

The bell over the door tinkled, and Sissy emerged from the back of the shop. "Oh, it's you," she offered without enthusiasm. "Maggie, Jim's here," she called over her shoulder. "I'm going to go get some coffee."

As she passed Jim, he snagged her elbow. "What's up with you, baby doll?"

Sissy sniffed in his direction. "You smell like slut." She yanked her arm from his grip, and stalked toward the front door. "And don't call me baby doll."

Maggie emerged from the back. "What'd you do to her?"

"She doesn't like the way I smell."

Maggie stepped up to him and took a deep whiff. "Well, she's got a point. You smell like you got tangled up with a female in heat."

"Damn it. That's what I told Daniel last night." Jim told Maggie about his strange encounters with the persistent blonde.

"Sounds like you've got a stalker," Maggie said matter-of-factly. "I've heard if you look hard enough, you can buy illegal wolf pheromones over the Internet. She was probably drowning in them, hoping you'd find her irresistible."

"I don't know. There were a lot of other wolves in the bar last night, but I was the only one reacting to her. If she was using pheromones, there should have been a stampede to get at her."

Maggie leaned against the counter, frowning. "I don't know how they work, but it seems like they're always coming up with new ways to get at us. Maybe you were targeted in some way. Like she was trying to lure you out."

Jim shook his head. "That's ridiculous. There's no way she could know I'm a Were. I've never seen her before."

"Ridiculous or not, you'd better alert the boys at the ranch," Maggie said. "She might be more than she seems. Remember that boy in Idaho."

"Yeah, I remember." It had been all over the news. A young man had been found dead about ten miles outside of Idaho Falls. He was naked and a wolf skin had been draped over his body. He'd been shot several times with a high-powered rifle. The Idaho Falls pack wasn't out to the public either, but somebody had found out about them and hunted them on a full moon run. It had been covered up as an unsolved murder, but the packs all knew what it was. "You're right. I'll get the boys to beef up security. When are you and Sissy coming out—assuming Sissy's even speaking to me."

Maggie smiled. "She'll get over it. We'll be out early to help set up."

"Okay, I'll see you then." Jim gave Maggie a peck on the cheek, then left. Spotting Sissy on the sidewalk outside the gallery, leaning against a lamp post, he grinned and called, "I'll see you tonight, baby doll." Jim only received a growl in return.

SISSY STOOD IN the gallery's doorway, watching Jim as he headed toward his truck. She couldn't help it. She loved the way he moved. He had an effortless grace that was surprising for a man his size. She watched his muscles flex and relax with each step. It amazed her that regular humans couldn't see Jim for what he was. His wolf nature was never very far beneath the surface.

Surreptitiously, she studied his face as he slid behind the wheel of his truck. She knew every line and angle—his straight nose, his strong cheekbones, his square chin.

He met her gaze through the glass and flashed a broad smile before he pulled away.

She blushed. "Baby doll," she muttered. That name, like "Sissy," was a holdover from her childhood. She'd outgrown her name and had even considered asking everyone to call her Sarah now, but when Jim said "baby doll," it still melted something inside her.

After calling out to her sister-in-law that she was back, Sissy slid behind the counter. She'd been helping out in the art gallery since she was a kid. It was just a small shop, but the business had grown steadily over the years. Maggie carried local artists, mostly paintings. The aesthetic was purely Western, ranging from landscapes and animals to cowboy and Native American themes. She represented some of the artists as their agent and had placed some of their work in prestigious galleries across the country.

Sissy was always amazed by the number of orders they

received from people in big cities like Boston and New York. *I guess it's hard to resist a cowboy,* she mused. *But I don't seem to have a problem resisting them, and at least one of them has no problem resisting me.*

She turned to her favorite painting. The gallery's most popular artist was a pack member. He painted beautiful wildlife scenes—eagles, bison, deer, but mostly wolves—and they were hot sellers. But this one painting wasn't for sale. It had a special meaning to the artist, and he retained the right to approve the buyer. He didn't want it to go to just anybody. After refusing to sell to several out-of-state buyers, he had finally given it to Sissy, knowing she appreciated it more than anyone else ever could.

The painting displayed a magnificent wolf standing in the snow under the full moon. It was a portrait of Jim in wolf form, and the artist had captured him exactly. His thick fur was the color of rich, dark chocolate, only slightly lighter on his chest and his muzzle. His powerful muscles were tense and ready, but he was perfectly still. Golden eyes rimmed with white looked out— the leader watching over his pack.

Another Were would easily recognize it as a portrait of a dominant male, but ordinary humans just saw a beautiful wolf. Often, when Sissy had her back to the painting, she could feel his eyes on her. She was comforted by its presence, more comfortable than she was around Jim in real life. When he was close, her body took over and her brain melted into sappy goo and she ended up either angry or babbling, sometimes both.

Jim had always looked out for her, but he only saw her as Lucas's baby sister, and she wasn't a baby any more.

THE DAY OF the full moon was always busy, and Jim strode around the ranch compound, checking on all the preparations. The livestock had to be moved out of the path of the run. The pack buildings needed to be cleaned and set up.

More outbuildings had been erected since Jim took over. He'd built changing barns with lockers and showers for the men and women where they could store their clothes and valuables. They even had bunks and rooms for whoever wanted to stay over. Most of the pack lived around Laramie, but some had to drive hours and opted to stay over.

He'd also put up a large outbuilding for the kids. Werewolves didn't begin to shift until late in their teens, so Jim had established a special place where parents could safely park their younger kids. He stocked it with everything they could want: cribs and baby toys, playscapes, TVs, video games and movies, and a pool table for the older kids. Non-Were spouses and younger teens took turns as babysitters.

A huge barbecue was set up to feed everyone beforehand. They'd hunt and kill a deer, maybe an elk, during the run, but that was mostly symbolic. The kill wasn't really dinner, and shifting burned up calories.

Jim always had security patrolling the ranch during the runs, but after his incident with Debby, he was concerned. He didn't want any stalkers near his pack.

"Hey, Jim." Clint, his nephew, waved him over. "I ordered some new communicators, and they just came in. They work a lot better than your old two-ways." He'd been briefing some of the men, and he showed Jim the small digital devices. Clint had recently returned from a tour of duty in Afghanistan, and Jim had put him in charge of security. Clint was tall and powerfully built, and he had the dark Winter good looks. Not many people, human or Were, would mess with him.

Since Clint had come home, he'd been training some of the wranglers and other pack members for security duty. Most of the hands on the ranch were Werewolves, but a few were halves, the children of a mixed Were and human couple or even spouses. Some halves had all the traits of a full Were, but most of them didn't shift, and those who kept their human form took care of details during the full-moon runs.

"We're going to keep a tight perimeter tonight, right, men?" Clint said. "There's not much chance that any outsiders will get in."

Jim tipped his hat back. "Well, you boys keep your eyes open, and be careful. This particular threat is a sexy little blonde, and if you're not careful, she'll have your jeans around your ankles before you know what hit you."

The men chuckled and one of them said, "That doesn't sound too bad."

"No, but we don't know what she's up to or if she's alone. Just because she's small and female, don't assume she's not dangerous. We think she may be using illegal wolf pheromones." Jim saw Maggie's pickup pull in, so he slapped Clint on the back and moved off to meet her.

chapter three

Jim felt better after talking to Maggie in town. He always did. Maggie, Lucas, and Jim had grown up together. Daniel's family lived at the ranch, so the young boys were constantly together, running wild. Especially Jim. He was always headed for an adventure or looking for a fight. Lucas was quieter, more thoughtful. He didn't start the trouble, but he never hesitated to back up his buddy.

Maggie Conner was a little younger than the boys. The Conners' ranch adjoined the Winter property, so she was over there as much as she was at home. Boys being boys, as much as they tried to ignore her, she managed to insinuate herself into their partnership. She was the third piece of their puzzle. Maggie was the peacemaker, even tempered and funny.

It had been clear early on that Lucas and Maggie would be mates, and Jim had no problem with that. When Lucas died, Jim and Maggie leaned on each other. He'd helped her buy the gallery, and since he was unmated, she'd become the matron of the pack, taking on the duties that the Alpha's mate would usually handle.

"Where's Sissy?" Jim asked after giving Maggie a quick hug. "Why isn't she here?"

"Don't worry. She'll be out in a while."

People liked to come out early in the summer so they could socialize. Pack life was all about being together. Trucks and cars would start arriving late in the afternoon. Kids ran all over, playing with their cousins and friends. Parents kept one eye on their children while they caught up with their friends. The older folks visited and played cards or dominoes. It really wasn't much different from a church social, except for the turning furry part, and that would come later, when the full moon rose.

Jim moved between groups, greeting them and listening to their news or complaints. As Alpha, his role included being advisor, elder, and protector, but ultimately he was the lord over his people. For them, pack law superseded human law, and the Alpha's decision was the last word.

Hierarchy was instinctively a part of the pack's wolf nature, but Jim had never been comfortable with the absolute authority that came with his position. Alphas had often abused their power over the centuries, demanding subservience and even breeding rights over the females in the pack.

Jim realized that a lot of the power afforded an Alpha came from the Weres' long history of surviving in a hostile world, but he was determined to assimilate the pack into the human world by behaving as much like humans as possible. This issue had become a point of contention between Jim and Daniel.

Eventually, most of the folks settled around the picnic tables. Somebody hooked up speakers in the back of a truck, and country music floated through the hot summer air. A circle of trucks created an impromptu honky-tonk. Jim strolled over to watch the dancers, but when he spotted Sissy twirling gracefully with a tall cowboy, he cut across the ring and tapped on the young man's shoulder.

Sissy's eyes widened as she stared at Jim looming over her dance partner.

The cowboy was also surprised to find his Alpha crowding behind him. "Oh hey, Jim. You want to dance with Sissy?"

Get lost. Beat it. Take your hands off her. "Yeah."

SISSY DIDN'T SAY a thing as the cowboy handed her off to Jim, and he smoothly pulled her into his arms. Sissy's shoulders felt stiff, and her hand barely touched his back as her eyes searched his. She'd always danced with Jim when she was younger, but then he'd quit asking, and she'd gotten too old to come begging for a dance.

Instead of making small talk, Jim tucked her cheek against his shoulder and pulled her closer. Sissy's body settled in against his, a perfect fit. As George Strait sang "I get carried away," they lost themselves in each other.

They meshed flawlessly, her body anticipating his moves. She buried her nose in his soft chambray shirt, breathing in the scent she loved. To her, he always smelled like pine smoke in the woods. His muscles shifted under her hand. The heat of his body burned against her chest. His hand slid from her shoulders down to her lower back, pressing her closer. He guided her around the circle, his knee slipping between hers with every step.

She'd danced with Jim a million times in the past, but it had never been like this. They swayed together, like lovers alone under the stars.

Drowsy heat suffused her muscles and emptied her mind of anything but the feel of Jim's body against hers. Her legs moved to the music's rhythm. Her breasts ached for his touch, her pebbled nipples chafing against the thin cloth separating her from him.

With each step, their thighs rubbed together, their heat creating enough friction to start a campfire. His hard response pushed against her abdomen.

And then it was gone.

Jim mumbled, "Fuck. I'm sorry, baby doll," in her ear and left her standing alone.

Sissy staggered out of the circle on shaky legs. Hopefully no one had noticed that Jim had shot away as though she'd stung him. She stumbled to her truck and climbed into the cab before she allowed the hot tears to fall.

After a few minutes, a manicured hand reached in her open window and handed her a pink bandana. "You want me to kick his ass? If we all ganged up, I think we could take him." Randi perched on the running board of the truck, leaning inside with both elbows.

"Did everybody see?" Sissy asked, not looking at her.

"I think there are a few people in the state of Wyoming who didn't notice, but not many. It was pretty hot. I thought you were going to do it right there in the dirt."

"Oh, God."

"Yeah, you were wrapped around each other, and just about every cowboy out there sprouted wood watching you two."

"Enough." Grabbing a tissue from a pack next to her, Sissy blew her nose. "Why did he leave me like that?"

"'Cause he's a stupid-ass man."

FUCK, FUCK, FUCK. What am I doing?

Pressed against Sissy, Jim came to his senses. His erection was sandwiched between them, pressing against her soft belly and itching to go lower. His senses were swamped with the scent of her arousal. Abruptly, he peeled himself away from her and fled into his house to the privacy of his study. He didn't need the lights to find the decanter of whiskey.

He'd lost it again, and this time with Sissy. Wishful thinking suggested it was just another reaction to the illegal pheromones, but that didn't explain it. He was fine around all the other females. It was pheromones, all right, his and Sissy's. They'd tangled up together and lit up the night, then he'd cut and run like a coward. And now he had to go out there and lead the run.

As the night closed in, the light social atmosphere changed into anticipation. Parents got their kids settled with the babysitters. Some folks moved off to the changing houses, while the less modest just stripped and left their clothes in their trucks. But they all began moving away from the ranch compound toward the pack's meeting circle. They came together in a large open space ringed with trees where they could watch for the full moon.

As Alpha, Jim had shifted already and taken his place on top of an outcropping of rocks, overlooking the entire pack gathered around. Together they watched as the moon rose bright and yellow on the horizon, and he began the howl.

Some of the pack members shifted immediately into full wolf form, ready for the run. Jim watched as the others who found the process laborious and painful shifted more slowly, but eventually they each found their form amidst the chorus of howls.

Jim leaped down and took his place at the head of the pack, and Maggie came to join him. Maggie and Sissy always ran by his side, but tonight Sissy was nowhere to be found. Jim finally spotted her a distance away, in the midst of a group of unmated females. She was so beautiful in the moonlight. Her sleek coat was a luminous silver, almost white.

He wasn't surprised she'd chosen to run apart from him after that stunt he'd pulled. It was just as well. He couldn't trust his wolf around her. It was only natural that she'd find her own place in the pack. He was never going to claim her, but it hurt like hell to let her go.

Following Jim's lead, the pack all set out together, but they soon split into smaller groups and ran at their own pace. He didn't care as long as everybody stayed on his property and kept away from the livestock. He'd be able to keep track of them all through their howls.

When the group of females Sissy had joined broke off from the pack, they were immediately followed by a group of unmated males. Jim growled and turned to go after them when Maggie bumped into his side. She gave him a look that clearly implied, *Leave them alone.*

He watched Sissy heading into the woods, away from him, and his wolf cried out to her. His howl cut through the night and Sissy froze. She turned and met his eyes, just for a second, before she ran and caught up to her friends.

The rest of the run was long and tedious for Jim. He'd decided to let Adam run with the pack, so he stayed near the young alpha's group, keeping an eye on them. Adam took the lead and set a grueling pace, clearly challenging Jim to keep up. It wasn't a problem for Jim, but some of Adam's pals would be hurting.

When they returned to the compound before dawn, amid the pack shifting back into human form, Jim left Daniel in charge and vanished.

HOURS LATER AFTER everyone had been fed and headed home or settled down, Daniel found Jim at the kitchen table, surrounded by empty beer cans and nursing a near-empty bottle of Jack Daniels.

"What bit you in the butt?" Daniel asked.

"Nothing. I just didn't feel sociable."

"I can see that. The hooch helping you any?" Daniel nodded toward the field of empties.

"It's not hurting."

"You're not being real talkative this morning."

"If I'd wanted to talk to anybody, I'd have stayed outside." Jim grabbed a fresh bottle off the counter and stood up.

When Daniel heard Jim's bedroom door slam shut, he went out on the porch. Maggie was basking in the early morning sunshine, her eyes closed.

"He's got it real bad, Maggie," Daniel said, sitting in a rocker next to her.

"Yeah, but I don't think he even knows what 'it' is."

"The boy's pretty dense sometimes. Can't you do something?"

"Me?" Maggie opened her eyes and smiled. "He's been carrying his guilt about Lucas's death for so long that he doesn't know how to do anything else. Right now he's torturing himself because he thinks what he's feeling for Sissy is wrong. And nothing any of us say is going to change that."

JIM DIDN'T EMERGE from his room for twenty-four hours. He came down with his rifle and a duffel bag and headed out to a large building set behind the barns. He unlocked the doors and slid them open, surveying what lay within with satisfaction.

The small Bell helicopter gleamed in the daylight. He and Lucas had been pilots with the 160th Special Ops and he missed flying, so when he'd seen it for sale, he couldn't resist the chance to get in the air again. It wasn't a Black Hawk, but it worked just fine for his needs.

He moved the copter out into the open space and started it

up, keeping an eye on the propellers and listening to the engine. Jim's ranch was huge, one of the largest in eastern Wyoming, and he used the helicopter to survey the livestock and pasture land. He loved to fly in low and herd the stock from the air. Well, that had been his excuse for the purchase.

Truth was, he also used the chopper to get away. He'd fly out in the hills alone and hunt or fish as a human or just run by himself as a wolf until he felt ready to rejoin civilization.

This time he was gone for five days, but he couldn't shake the restlessness that consumed him. He stayed busy helping the wranglers move the bison herd further out into the hills for the summer pasture. He checked on the hay fields and the barns and inspected the horses, generally getting in everybody's way. He even leafed through a stack of breeding journals he'd put off reading, but he couldn't concentrate. There was only one type of breeding on his mind, and he was doing his damnedest to forget about it.

Pining after something that was never going to happen was a waste of time, and it was unfair to Sissy. Lucas was dead, and Jim owed him a debt, and that debt didn't include seducing his friend's sister. End of story.

He knew Sissy had feelings for him. She'd rejected almost every male in the pack, and as happy as that made him, it wasn't right for him to let her think there was ever a chance for the two of them. He loved her. He wanted her. But he had to let her go.

Jim had managed to avoid town for a couple of weeks. He'd made his decision, but he had no idea how to break it to Sissy. He headed toward Laramie running possible scenarios in his mind. No matter what he said, it was going to hurt.

He was just a few miles from town when he spotted a car that had run off into a shallow ditch beside the road. He pulled over and took a hard look. The vehicle was late model, with rental plates. The air bag had deployed. He smelled blood in the air and traced the scent to a woman sitting in the shade of a nearby tree. The driver, Jim assumed. She looked shaken up but not afraid as she watched him approach.

"Thank you for stopping." She sounded relieved, and gave him an uncertain smile.

"Are you all right, ma'am?"

"I'm fine, just stuck. I had a blowout, and I ended up in the ditch. I called the county sheriff's office, and they're sending somebody out."

Jim walked over to her as she was speaking. She was a pretty human woman, mid-thirties with ivory skin and thick red-gold hair. He extended a hand to help her up, but as she rose, she wobbled and fell against him.

"You better stay down for another minute." Jim took both of her hands and lowered her back to the ground.

"I guess I hit my head."

"Let me see that." Jim brushed her hair away from her face. "You've got a little blood here in your hairline." He gingerly felt around on her scalp until she winced. She smelled nice, warm and spicy, like apple cider with a touch of fresh blood.

"You've got a bump and a little cut. It doesn't look too bad, but you should get it checked out anyway. Do you want me to call an ambulance?"

She shook her head. "I just need to sit a minute. Do you have anything to drink?"

"I've got some water. How about I take you into town? I can take you by the emergency room and get them to take a look at your head."

"But the sheriff is coming. I should stay until he gets here."

"I'll give him a call. You don't need to wait. I'll get a tow truck out here to pick up the car, and they'll bring your things." Before she could protest, Jim swept her up and deposited her in his truck. He gave her a bottle of water and made some calls before he slid into the driver's seat.

"I guess we should have some introductions," he said, extending his hand. "I'm Jim Winter. I have a ranch about thirty miles from here."

The redhead smiled. "Hi, Jim. I'm Crystal Chandler. I was on my way to Laramie. Is it far?"

"Just a few miles. We'll be there in no time. Do you have someone in town you want to call?"

"I don't actually know anybody there. I've got a research grant at the University of Wyoming, and I've only talked to the department chairman. He's supposed to have set up some housing for me. I was going to go there first."

"Nope, you're going to see the doc first. Then you can call the university, and we'll get you settled."

Crystal gave Jim an embarrassed smile. "You're being awfully kind."

"It's nothing. I could hardly leave a lady in distress out on the road."

The ER doctor saw Crystal quickly, patched her laceration, and assured her she didn't have a concussion. Then they swung by the garage and Jim gathered up Crystal's bags while she called the university.

"Thank you so much for stopping and taking care of me." Crystal held out her hand. "I can take it from here."

"Nonsense." He took her hand between both of his. "I've got all your stuff loaded in the truck already. Do you know where you're staying?"

"Are you sure it's no trouble?"

"No trouble."

"Well, the university confirmed I have an apartment. Do you know where this is?" She handed him the address. He did.

After a quick drive, Jim picked up her key from the apartment manager and carried her bags in for her. While she went off to freshen up, he checked out the kitchen.

Jim called toward the back of the apartment. "You don't have any food."

"I can take care of that. You've been so nice, Jim. How can I repay you?"

"I told you, it's nothing. But seeing as how your pantry's empty, you could let me take you to dinner."

"I'd like that. You could pick me up later, about eight. Right now, I'm just going to lie down for a while." Crystal put her hand on his arm to go up on her tiptoes. Her breath fanned his cheek before her lips brushed his skin. "Thank you, Jim Winter, for coming to my rescue. I'll see you tonight."

chapter four

The light kiss was just what he needed. Providence had dropped a beautiful woman right in his lap, the first one who'd even remotely interested him in a long time.

His desire for Sissy had put his love life on hold for a long time. He could flirt with the best of them. In earlier days, he'd been quick to follow up on his charm with a roll in the hay. It had earned him a reputation as a ladies' man, a reputation that still lingered.

But his life was missing something.

He'd thrown himself into running the ranch and the pack until they occupied most of his time. He had been so absorbed that he hadn't even noticed that Sissy was coming of age.

Nobody else had claimed his attention or his heart. If Sissy saw him getting serious about someone else, she'd stop waiting for something that was never going to happen. It was the right thing to do for both of them.

He tried to get some work done, but he couldn't concentrate.

After a few hours, he gave up and went for a swim in the Olympic-sized pool behind his house. He made about thirty laps before he pulled himself out to dry off in the sun.

He heard footsteps approach. Familiar footsteps. "I've been looking all over for you," Daniel said. "Taking the afternoon off?"

Even Daniel's sarcasm couldn't put a dent in his optimistic mood. Jim didn't open his eyes. "Yeah. You should try it some time. It might make you a little less sour."

"Yeah, and it might make nothing get done, which is what's happening now. You go off to town and then you come back and disappear. What happened? You meet the love of your life or something?"

"Maybe." Jim dove back in, making sure to splash Daniel. "I've got a date tonight with a pretty lady," he said when he came back up, noting with satisfaction Daniel's slight dampness.

"Anybody I know?"

"Nope. She's new in town." Jim gave Daniel the short version of the day's events.

Daniel listened, a frown on his face. "What happened to your 'I don't have time for a woman' attitude?"

"I've changed my mind. I've got to go get ready."

AS SOON AS Jim left, Crystal sat down and pulled out the research report her assistant had forwarded to her and confirmed a suspicion. She grabbed her briefcase and headed to the university, making a couple of calls first.

She found the molecular biology building, and made her way to the chairman's offices. He was waiting for her. "Dr. Chandler, we're so pleased to have you join us," the white-haired man said, his eyes beaming behind his spectacles. "I've read some of the papers you've published, very cutting edge, but I'm hoping to hear more about the project that brings you here. It's all very hush-hush. I have to admit I'm intrigued."

Crystal smiled reassuringly. "I'm sure you're curious, and I appreciate the university cooperating, but this is a sensitive government grant. This project requires a great deal of discretion, so I can't share any of our findings. As my assistant and I are being funded completely by the grant, I'll be reporting directly to Washington. We will no doubt be publishing when our findings are complete, and the university and your department will of course receive credit for accommodating us so generously."

They had reached the locked door of her project area. It was, as she had requested, at the end of the hall on the first floor and had a more discreet outside entrance for her research subjects. Crystal noted her name freshly painted on the frosted glass of the door. The chairman handed her a key card and lingered. "I understand your assistant, Dr. Weston, is already here," he said, clearly angling for an introduction and a peek into the new lab.

"Yes, he came ahead to set everything up. I'm sure you'll run into him soon. Thank you for making us welcome." Crystal keyed the lock and extended her hand for a quick handshake before opening the door and ducking inside. Her generous federal grant was supplemented by a side grant from Gen-Chem, a major pharmaceutical company, all of which covered a newly remodeled research suite with a private office, interview and treatment rooms, and a small lab with first-class equipment, not to mention allowing for her to bring her assistant from Seattle so she didn't have to rely on local lab assistants.

As soon as the lock clicked behind her, she surveyed her new kingdom. She was in her element here. "Weston, are you here?" she called out.

A tall, pale twenty-something young man in a baggy lab coat

emerged from one of the observation rooms. "Dr. Chandler, welcome to Laramie," he said, waving his arm at their new space.

"It'll do. First of all, please have my name taken off the door, and get us some secure locks, maybe biometric scanners. It would be better if we're as anonymous as possible. Anybody could get in here with these key cards." She glanced at the one in her hand with distaste.

"I'll take care of it. What happened to your head?"

Crystal touched the bandage. It didn't hurt anymore, but it still wasn't comfortable. "It's a long story, but this bump on my head may have been very fortuitous. Now, tell me what you've accomplished so far."

The young man brightened. "I think you're going to be happy with the latest developments. I've been running detailed genetic profiles of athletes from the area high schools. I've found Werve markers for most of the better athletes. Not enough to consider them true Werves, but enough to account for their superior physical performance and general health."

She shrugged. She wanted more than anything to don her own lab coat, but knew there wasn't time to dive in quite yet. "That's not much of a stretch. A lot of people have some Werve genes. That's how we learned about them in the first place."

Werewolves and other Were species were thought to be variations on a genetic strain that had evolved alongside regular humans from the earliest hominids. Through gradual interbreeding over time, enough Were genes made it into the general, nonshifter population to be picked up in lab tests. Genetic studies in the 1970s and 1980s had alerted the world to their existence as a scientific fact rather than a myth.

"They've been studied for years now by geneticists and the military," she reminded her assistant. "It's not rocket science to assume that the larger the Werve contribution, the greater the physical enhancement. We've got to take our project farther than that."

"I know, and here's the good part," Weston said eagerly. "While I was taking some preliminary samples in the athletics department here at the university, one of the student workers gave me a lead on a young man, a local, who tried out for sports but was disqualified genetically. She said his Werve genes were off the charts, but he still thought he'd have a chance to play. Since NCAA rules have prohibited Werves from competing, he's probably a nonshifting one quarter- or even half-Werve. He may not even know his heritage. I've scheduled an interview with him."

"You got him to agree to come in?"

"Well, he didn't want to talk to me, but I told him if we did more testing, I might be able to get him into athletics."

Crystal nodded. "He could be our link to the local pack. I picked Laramie, and the University of Wyoming specifically, because this area has statistically lower incidences of disease, particularly cancers, low childhood mortality, a slightly longer life span, and a very healthy recovery and healing rate. I suspect the local Werewolf pack has been interbreeding with humans in this area for a long time, probably a century or more.

"We're here to prove there is a correlation between the local pack's genetic contribution and the general good health of the locals. This could mean life-saving genetic therapies. You know what you have to do, don't you?"

Weston nodded. "I have to get the subject talking."

"Yes. Maybe he can turn us on to some of the other locals. We've got to find a way into the pack."

Weston frowned. "Why is this pack so secretive? Werves have been out of the closet for a while now. The Seattle pack is completely open to the media and research."

"Which makes them useless for our purposes, but the Laramie pack is unstudied. Wolves and ranchers have a long history, especially around here. True wolves are federally protected, and the ranchers resent it. They certainly weren't happy to find out about a new species of predator, one that might be living among them. There have been some unpleasant incidents."

"And the western packs keep a low profile because of it, which makes it hard to get test subjects," Weston concluded.

Crystal paced the room. "Yes, but that also means they've probably kept apart from humans, maybe interbreeding but only marginally interacting with human society over the last century, so their genes will be less diluted. I know they've been here for a long time. The numbers prove it. And we're here to find out which Werve genetic markers in particular result in what we're looking for."

"Don't forget the pheromone project," Weston reminded her.

Crystal shrugged. "That's not really part of my research, but it was tacked onto the grant by Gen-Chem, so we have to get them some results if we want the money to keep flowing."

"We didn't get the reaction we'd expected with our first field test, but that doesn't mean it didn't tell us anything," Weston said. "The tactilely released pheromones we developed in Seattle worked perfectly in the lab, much more efficiently than aerosol or liquid delivery. The tester can go through a room of subjects, subtly touching them all to differentiate the Werves from the humans or target one particular subject without soliciting a response from other Werves that may be within inches of the tester."

Crystal frowned. "So, what was the problem in the bar?"

"We got results, but they were inconclusive. I observed

positive arousal markers from several subjects. The problem was in the delivery vehicle. She was too overtly seductive, so it was unclear if the reaction was to the pheromone or to the tester herself. I was closely observing her behavior, and she was turning on half the men in the bar, most of whom she didn't even touch."

"But you noticed one in particular," Crystal guessed.

"I did. His powerful build and apparent command of others in the bar gave me reason to believe he might be a high-ranking Werve. He seemed very interested, but in the end he left her. She reported that she tried again the following day after she spotted him in the street, and he rejected her again. If the pheromone was effective, he shouldn't have been able to resist."

Crystal leaned against a desk and nodded. "That would be a fair assumption, but we may have underestimated the control of a mature alpha Werve," she said thoughtfully. "Today I met your subject from the bar. At least I assume it was the subject. His name is Jim Winter. I recognized him from the photos you sent. I had a car accident, and he came to my rescue. I think you were right in your assessment. He is almost definitely a Werewolf, maybe *the* Alpha."

"Then why didn't the pheromone work?" Weston asked incredulously.

Crystal mused. "I think it did, but you shouldn't have trusted the test to that particular delivery vehicle. I think he probably responded but was able to resist the effects. We'll refine our testing protocol, and I think we'll get the results we want."

"And the funding we need," Weston added.

"Meanwhile, concentrate on the athlete. I'll be in early tomorrow, but I need to get back to the apartment now. Tonight, I have a date with a Werewolf."

JIM PULLED UP at Crystal's apartment right on time. He'd taken special care getting dressed, even passing up his jeans for a pair of dark gray slacks and a white dress shirt.

Crystal let him in. "I'd ask if you wanted a drink, but I haven't been to the liquor store yet, so I don't have anything to offer you."

"That's okay. We'll get a drink at the restaurant." Jim noticed the bare white walls. "Are you going to get settled in here?"

"I really won't have much time. If the project doesn't get the results we need, I may only be here for three months. I'm waiting to see if the research grant gets renewed."

"Well, we'll drink to your success then and see if we can't keep you in town."

Over dinner, Crystal told him about her work up in Seattle, and the research grant that had brought her and her assistant to the University of Wyoming. She explained she was working on a genetic testing program that would keep her in Laramie for at least three months, if not longer. In turn, Jim told her about his ranch and his breeding program for the bison-cattle hybrids.

"I guess we're into the same thing," she said.

Jim shot her a quizzical look.

"Genetics, with my research and your breeding program."

"I guess you're right." Jim liked the conversation, nice and easy. Not forced, like some of the first dates he'd had.

"So tell me about Laramie. What do you like to do?" she asked.

"I love the outdoors. I hunt and fish. Do you ride?"

"Not unless you count pony rides as a child, but I'd be willing to give it a try. I have fished." Crystal smiled.

Jim felt himself relaxing. "Of course, the university has some museums—rocks and insects, even art. My friend has an art gallery just a few blocks from here. She probably knows more things that you'd enjoy than I do, but I'd be glad to show you around."

"I would love to see Laramie through your eyes. I can tell you love it."

It was one of the best dates he'd had in a long time. It might not have been what his heart wanted, but it was exactly what he needed.

They were both quiet on the ride back to Crystal's apartment. When they arrived, Jim came around to the passenger door and opened it, easily lifting her out of the tall truck. She rested her palms on his chest, and he pulled her in close. She was so small. He leaned over and touched his face to her hair. Her warm cider scent enveloped him.

Jim tucked her in under his arm. He let her walk up two stairs in front of him, then pulled her to stop and turned her toward him. Her face was finally on the same level as his.

"This is about right," he said, leaning in to kiss her.

She put her hands on his shoulders to cross the space. Their lips met, sweetly, in a kiss.

Crystal pulled away, smiling. "I should just say good night. It was a wonderful evening."

"I enjoyed it, too. May I call you?"

"I'd like that." Crystal keyed in her number on his cell phone.

She slipped the phone back in his hand and said, "Call me after six. Before that I'll be at the university most days."

"Oh, damn." Jim scowled. "I forgot. I have a meeting tomorrow night."

"Call me when you can." She pressed a kiss on her fingers and brought them to his lips. "Good night."

Jim watched until she disappeared into her apartment. Crystal was a lovely woman and good company. He didn't feel much of a spark, but that was okay. He wasn't doing this to find his true love. As far as he was concerned, true love was something that would, and should, always be denied to him.

"YOU KNOW I don't like this." Jim's face was grim as he sat across the table from Daniel the next evening. The pack meeting would begin soon.

"You're not supposed to like it. But you can't ignore this. Adam is pushing you to see what you'll do. If you don't put him in his place now, you'll end up facing him in a challenge later, and one of you is gonna wind up dead."

"You don't know that it'll go that far. I just hate perpetuating this kind of medieval judgment. The pack, all of our kind, need to move past using this kind of torturous corporal punishment."

"What do you want to do instead? Fine him? Send him to his room? Goddamn, Jim, we're Werewolves. A slap on the hand isn't going to do the job."

"I know. That's how it's always been done, and that's how we'll do it, but I don't have to like it." Jim shook his head.

"They're gonna be waiting on us. Let's get this done."

The flickering torchlight created a primitive backdrop for the meeting. Most packs held their meetings before the full moon run, but Jim called the Laramie pack to meet in the dark of the new moon. At the beginning of the moon cycle, emotions ran cooler. Only adults came to meetings, and the mood was more serious. The weaker members of the pack, betas and omegas, couldn't shift without the pull of the full moon, so if fights or challenges broke out, the whole pack wouldn't be involved.

Jim really wanted his members to participate in pack decisions. He'd proposed a council made up of representatives of each ranking, but implementing that plan was proving to be an uphill battle. Werewolves were nothing if not traditional, and traditionally a wolf pack was a dictatorship, often a brutal one where leaders ruled by force and fear.

Everyone in a Werewolf pack was ranked by their standing, with the omegas the lowest-ranked members, submissive by nature. In some packs they were the whipping boys, but in the Laramie pack, Jim didn't allow stronger members to abuse them. The Laramie pack was unusual in offering protection to its lower-ranked members, but Jim insisted on treating everyone fairly.

The dominant Alpha and his mate were the top of the heap, but most packs included more alphas than just a dominant couple. Alphas were stronger and larger in both human and wolf form. All the alphas either acknowledged the leader's dominance or they left the pack to establish themselves somewhere else. Or they challenged the leader for his position. It was important to show the entire pack that their leader was strong enough to defeat all comers, which meant he was strong enough to protect every member, from the strongest to the weakest.

Jim took his position on top of the Alpha's rock. As his Second, Daniel stood just below at his feet. About thirty of the more than fifty adult members of the pack had shown up, and they filled the meeting area in a loose semicircle facing Jim.

"Any news?" Jim called out. He usually started the meetings this way. The members got a chance to announce pregnancies or new babies, their children's achievements, accidents, and illnesses. It solidified a sense of community.

A young couple stepped forward holding hands. "We'd like a mating ceremony."

Jim asked the girl, "Anna, do you accept this mating?"

"Yes. I want Zach as my mate and he wants me."

Jim smiled. At least he could enjoy this part of the meeting. "Do you have a guardian to stand with you?"

Zach's older brother stepped forward. "I will stand as guardian for Zach and Anna."

"Do you accept the responsibility to protect and support both Zach and Anna and their children if there is a need?"

"I accept my duty. I'll guard my brother's family with my life." Jim knew more than most what that responsibility meant. He'd stood as guardian for Lucas and Maggie's mating, and he hoped that these young wolves would never have to find out how hard that could be.

"Congratulations," Jim declared. "Bring your families to see me next week, and we'll set a date for the ceremony."

Jim waited for the couple to rejoin the crowd before he nodded to Daniel. He hated to disturb their joy with what he had to do next, but it was time.

chapter five

"Adam, come forward," Daniel called.

The pack parted as the alpha from the bar fight stepped into the open space. He ignored Daniel and stared up at Jim, his stance confrontational.

Jim frowned. It was not only disrespectful but also almost physically impossible for a lesser-ranked wolf to meet the gaze of a dominant alpha without dropping his eyes. Adam was showing his strength to the pack.

A palpable discomfort ran through the crowd. Some bristled with the challenge, while others dropped their heads.

Everyone looked to Daniel as he stated the issue. "Two weeks ago, in a public place, Adam challenged a human for rights to a female. This is a serious offense against pack law."

"It wasn't any challenge. I was just intimidating the punk so he'd know better than to mess with any of our females. He got the message."

"You hit the human," Daniel said.

"I tapped him. I knocked him down. He was all over Julie in front of everyone at the bar. I wouldn't let anyone disrespect one of us like that." He stared up at Jim again defiantly, clearly implying that Jim was a weak leader for not taking care of the pack female.

Smooth move, slick. I wonder if you're ready to take me on right now or if you just want to talk about it. As reasonable as Jim liked to think of himself, he couldn't control his predatory response to Adam's aggressive actions. His heart rate increased and his senses went on full alert. His whole body was poised to shift and fight.

Taking a deep breath, Jim ignored Adam's insolence and waited for Daniel to finish the charge.

"It was more than a tap," Daniel said. "You lost control, and we had to break up the fight. Even after your Alpha stepped in, you had to be restrained from going after the human." At that, Adam shot the Second a threatening look, but Daniel didn't intimidate easily. "Because of this, the Alpha decides."

All eyes turned to Jim, and he addressed the pack instead of acknowledging Adam's defiance. "Adam broke a fundamental rule of the pack designed to protect us all. Now that the public is aware of the existence of Werewolves, we have to be especially careful of how we present ourselves, whether we're known or not. The way Adam approached the human was a challenge, which is a punishable offense."

Jim turned his attention to the younger alpha. "Your punishment is to bear stripes. Do you accept?"

Adam didn't answer Jim. Instead, he stripped down and faced Daniel.

"Shift," Daniel ordered.

"No."

There was a murmur among the pack members. "Are you sure

you want to take this in human form?" Daniel asked.

"I don't want to take it at all, but you're not going to force me to shift."

Daniel signaled two strong pack members, cowboys from the ranch, to chain Adam's arms around a large oak tree at the edge of the circle. Adam held his arms out for the men, baring his broad back to the crowd.

Daniel partially shifted, a feat only a small number of Weres could manage. He became the Werewolf from the horror stories. His facial features elongated, his mouth sprouted gleaming fangs, and fur erupted on his shoulders and arms. His fingers transformed into sharp claws while his body remained human.

He stepped behind the restrained Were and sank his claws into Adam's shoulders. The younger alpha arched his back and a strangled growl escaped his lips as Daniel slowly dragged his claws down Adam's back from his shoulders to his buttocks, carving deep furrows in his flesh. Adam howled in pain as his legs buckled, and he hung from his chains. Blood gushed from the eight long cuts.

The smell of blood washed over the pack, and instinctive howls cut through the night. The cowboys released Adam and supported him until two of his buddies came up to help him away. His back would heal, but he'd carry the scars and the memory of the pain and humiliation. Before he left the circle, Adam shot one more hateful glare at Jim.

It wasn't over, not by a long shot, Jim knew.

AFTER THE MEETING, Jim left a message on Crystal's phone. It was late before she returned his call.

"I'm sorry I didn't get back to you sooner. I'm still getting the project set up, and I have a few long days ahead of me. Can I make it up to you?" She sounded truly apologetic.

"How about we start with dinner? Then we can discuss fair compensation for my loss."

SISSY HAD TAKEN a lot of time getting ready for her date. Her fair hair, usually pulled back in a ponytail, was draped softly around her shoulders, and her full lips blushed with the seldom-used rose lip gloss that she'd dug out from the back of her dresser drawer. Her clingy saffron-colored dress brought out the flecks of gold in her eyes. She sat across the candlelit table from her date, knowing she looked pretty, but she was uncomfortable, both with the way she was dressed and with what she was doing. She played with her wine glass and listened half-heartedly to the young alpha sitting across from her.

It wasn't Terry's fault she was bored and restless. She'd called and asked him out, and she'd heard the shock and excitement in his voice when he accepted. It had been a rash invitation made out of anger.

Sissy had overheard Jim telling Maggie about the woman he'd rescued from the side of the road. She knew his routine. Usually he'd take a woman out, sleep with her, she assumed, see her casually for a while, then let her go. Jim had had women in the past, but this one was different. She heard it in his voice.

Sissy had gotten her hopes up. Jim hadn't been interested in anyone for a while. She'd let herself believe he was tired of chasing around, but it seemed he was just going through a dry spell.

Yeah, a dry spell. She'd been going through a dry spell for twenty-four years, but she was tired of putting her life on hold. It was time to enter the dating pool. She'd change her attitude, be more accommodating, be nicer, more feminine. Terry had earned the honor of being asked to take her to dinner by being persistent.

She knew what the unmated males of the pack thought of her—they referred to her as the "Ice Princess." Some of them still sniffed around her, literally, but most had learned she was as frosty as the icy-white coat of her wolf form. The fact that she was a dominant alpha in the pack didn't help her love life. Her packmates were wary of her if not downright afraid, and growing up, she'd kicked enough of their asses to prove their fear was justified.

Her sister-in-law Maggie was alpha caste too, but she was sweet and good-natured, two terms that had never been used to describe Sissy. Tough, mean, scary, ill-tempered—those were the words she knew people used to describe her.

Only one man didn't think of her that way. He'd captured her heart when she was just a kid and had held it all this time, but he didn't know how vulnerable her heart really was.

Looking up from her thoughts, Sissy felt her fragile heart rip apart when she saw Jim walk into the restaurant with a pretty redhead on his arm.

Jim escorted his date to a cozy table across the room with his hand resting on her lower back. He held her chair, and as she sat, the woman looked up at Jim over her shoulder. He leaned in close to whisper something in her ear. They both smiled as he took his seat across from her.

Jim, who probably knew half the people in the room, hadn't acknowledged anyone, including Sissy and Terry. He should have instantly been alert to the fact that pack members were dining there. But his attention was focused on the human woman. He didn't even break eye contact when the waitress came over. He ordered for them, and as soon as she left, Jim reached over and took his date's hand in his as they talked.

Sissy was barely listening to Terry tell her about something that had happened at the shop where he worked as a mechanic when he suddenly stopped. He followed her gaze.

"Hey, look, Jim's here," he said. "Do you want to go over and say hello?"

Sissy shook her head and picked at her food.

Terry leaned in and whispered, "That's the lady he found on the highway. Her car slid into a ditch. Messed up the front end pretty bad. Jim called me to make sure I'd take care of her car. She's some kind of scientist over at the university."

"Terry, shut up," Sissy blurted. The young man looked surprised. "I don't care about Jim's new girlfriend or her car."

"I'm sorry, Sissy. I didn't mean to upset you."

"I'm not upset."

"Okay, but you look upset."

"Just drop it, Terry. Talk about something else."

He shrugged. "Okay. What do you want to talk about?"

"Oh my God, I don't know. If you're finished, why don't we just leave? We can go for a drive, maybe make out a little."

Terry's eyes opened wide. He signaled for the check, dug out his wallet, and grabbed Sissy by the wrist, all in one fluid movement.

Sissy knew she was probably the worst date ever, and now she was committed to kissing him at the very least. Terry was a great guy, and he was crazy about her, but he didn't have a chance with her heart. As they were exiting the door, one backward glance confirmed that Jim had never even noticed she was there.

JIM ENJOYED HIS date. Only one thing marred the evening. Even before they'd entered the restaurant, he scented that Sissy was there with Terry. He'd almost turned around and told Crystal he'd changed his mind about that particular restaurant, but this was part of it, part of letting Sissy go.

He was especially attentive to Crystal. Sissy had to see that he was seriously interested in the new woman. But it felt wrong. Hell, everything with Sissy felt wrong. When he was near her, he despised himself for wanting her, but he hated seeing her with someone else even more. His wolf self was possessive by nature, but she wasn't his to claim.

He almost jumped out of his seat when he overheard her offer to make out with Terry. If he'd believed for a minute that Sissy was serious, he'd have nailed the young man against the wall before Terry could even blink, but he was sure Sissy had said it for his benefit. It was hard sitting there ignoring her, but he had to do it. He was relieved when the younger couple left.

As dinner progressed, Jim relaxed. Crystal was intelligent and funny, and she was nice to look at. Afterward, they came back to Crystal's apartment, and she insisted he come in for a drink. She left him alone in her small living room while she went to change. Jim sank down on the couch, and he felt his tension fall away. There was no pack business or ranch business, no crisis that demanded his attention. Only Sissy, but he was beginning to convince himself that what he was doing was right.

He heard Crystal come back into the room and started to stand, but she came up behind the couch and put a hand on his shoulder. "Don't get up," she said. "I like you just fine where you are. Let me get your coat." She helped him out of his jacket, and then she reached around his neck to undo his tie.

As she leaned over him, Jim breathed in her scent and it went right to his gut. There was her characteristic spicy apple scent, but there was something else, something much heavier, dark, and musky. He turned and reached for her, lifting her over the back of the couch and onto his lap.

Jim held himself in check as she finished removing his tie and opened first one then two buttons on his shirt. It was then that urgency overwhelmed him, hijacking rational thought.

He laid her back on the couch, his mouth covering hers. His mind registered that she had changed out of her dress into something light and silky. As his tongue slipped past her lips, his hand slid under the silk and found her lace-covered breast. He swept into her mouth while his fingers slipped under the lace and found her nipple, working it into a stiff peak. She moaned into his mouth and arched into him, her hands tracing the muscles of his back.

He twisted to fit his body against hers, but the couch was too cramped. Wrapping his arms around Crystal, he rolled them to the floor, taking the fall on his back then continuing until he was braced on his arms above her. He pressed his hard length against her and came down on her mouth again, spearing her rhythmically with his tongue as he rocked his lower body against the junction of her legs. With one hand, he ripped away the thin fabric and lace that separated them, and his strong fingers claimed her breasts. He dipped his head to take one peak, then the other between his lips, suckling deeply then releasing. When he nipped with his teeth into her sensitive flesh, she screamed.

Jim reared back and looked down at the petite woman under his body. Her blouse and bra were shredded. The deep red marks from his fingers stood out against her pale skin. Her lips were puffy and swollen. She lay ravaged and breathless from his furious assault, his body still wedged between her legs.

He held himself above her for a few seconds as he willed his mind to clear. He'd lost control again. In a few more moments, he would have ripped apart her slacks and plunged into her. He pushed himself off of her and held out his hands to help her up.

She came to her feet on shaky legs as he eased her onto the couch. Her blouse was in tatters, so he stripped off his shirt and held it out for her before pulling away to the far side of the small room, where he paced like a caged wolf in a zoo.

"I'm so sorry, Crystal. I don't know what came over me."

"It's all right, Jim. You didn't hurt me."

"Yes, I did, and I could have hurt you worse." *Much worse.* She was just a human. Her body couldn't take the kind of punishment a Were's could. He had always held back with human women. What was *wrong* with him? "I'd better go. Are you sure you're okay?"

"I'm fine, really. We just got a little intense." Crystal intercepted Jim on his way to the door. Standing there in the ruins of her clothing, she laid her hands against Jim's bare chest. "You don't have to leave."

Jim forced himself not to move. Her touch threatened what little control he still possessed. His skin burned under her hands. He was still fully aroused, and he didn't trust himself.

He moved past her and picked up his jacket. "I'm really sorry," he said as he rushed out the door into the cool air.

chapter six

The next day Jim ordered a dozen red roses to be delivered to Crystal. The florist asked what he wanted the note to say. "I'm sorry I nearly raped you" seemed awkward, so he told them to just put his name on the card.

He hoped she'd take the flowers and not think too badly of him. With his recent lack of control, he figured he'd better stay away from human women. Maybe he'd just gone too long, like Daniel said. He knew a few friendly pack females who wouldn't mind if he called. He could burn through some of his pent-up energy. But a booty call wasn't what he wanted.

A WEEK HAD gone by and except for the flowers he'd sent, Crystal hadn't heard from Jim. She'd almost called him several times, but she really needed to talk to him in person and let him know that she wasn't upset by what happened.

She had spooked him, which was exactly what she hadn't intended to do. She wanted to gain his confidence so that when she had enough evidence to conclusively prove the existence of the Laramie pack, he would trust her and allow her access. But she'd almost blown it.

She couldn't resist using the pheromone. She didn't have unlimited time in Laramie, and it might take longer than she had to build the kind of trust she needed to break into a pack this secretive. She had thought the drug would help kick-start a more intimate relationship if Jim was deeply attracted to her. If they became lovers, even better. It wasn't ethical, but she could have Weston conduct any subsequent testing on Jim, which would eliminate any accusations of scientific bias.

She'd only used a fraction of the standard test dose, but the results had been almost instantaneous and overpowering, and unfortunately because of her unauthorized use of the drug, she couldn't include her findings in the study. They were atypical anyway. He had reacted too strongly to too small a dose, and despite his initial reaction, he was able to overcome the effects and resist the chemical attraction. She made a note to tell Weston to set up some new testing protocols in order to time the onset of the reaction and gauge the situational effects and relationship factors. This side job for Gen-Chem was proving to be scientifically interesting, after all. But first she had to repair the relationship with Jim.

It was late, almost sundown, but the ranch was still busy when Crystal pulled her rented car in front of Jim's house. There were cowboys working around pens of cattle, and others were loading a skittish horse into a trailer. She drove up to the main house, parked, and had made it up onto the long porch when an older man came out the front door. He looked her up and down and then said, "I guess you're looking for Jim."

The man was gray-haired but still powerfully built. She

suspected that he was also a Werve, a pack member or even a relative.

"That's right," she said. "Do you know where I can find him?"

"Oh, he's around here somewhere. I'll see if I can get hold of him." He pulled a two-way radio out of a holster. "Clint, is Jim out there with you?"

A voice answered. "Yeah, he's in the barn."

"Tell him a pretty lady is up here at the house to see him."

The old man grinned and turned his attention to Crystal. "I'm Daniel, the ranch foreman. I reckon Jim will be along in a minute. Do you want some lemonade or anything?"

She smiled back at him. "I'm Crystal. And no thanks, I'm fine."

"Okay," he replied and leaned back on the porch rail, obviously in no hurry to get anywhere.

Crystal filled the awkward lack of conversation by looking over the ranch activities. Her natural curiosity made her examine and assess the movements and physiques of the cowboys who were working within her view. She found that each one of them, including Daniel, had Werve characteristics. They were large and agile, but she realized that could just be coincidence and dismissed her observations as scientifically irrelevant.

She saw Jim striding across the open space to the house. He looked every inch the cowboy from his hat to his boots, and he didn't look particularly happy to see her there.

He cleared the steps two at a time and joined them on the wide porch. "I don't suppose he invited you to wait inside," he said, gesturing to Daniel.

"I offered her some lemonade," Daniel said. "You must be the one Jim pulled outta the ditch."

"Yes. He was very sweet to help me out."

"Yep, sweet," Daniel agreed. "That's him."

"I'm sure you've got something to do," Jim suggested.

"I guess I do. Nice to meet ya, young lady." Daniel headed off toward the barns.

"I'm sorry about him," Jim said, turning his attention back to Crystal. "He should have asked you in." He knocked the dust from his hat and held the door open for her.

"I'm sorry I came out here unannounced," she said. "Maybe it wasn't such a good idea."

"Look, I'm sorry I haven't called. Things have been pretty busy around here."

"I just wanted to tell you that I'm not mad about what happened. I don't blame you. I thought maybe we could talk," she said.

"Sure, but I'm pretty dusty and I stink. I've been working horses all day. Give me a few minutes to clean up."

Jim quickly headed upstairs. Left alone, Crystal took in her surroundings as she waited. The house was built on a large scale, like Jim, and it was just as masculine. It was all polished wood and leather. He'd led her into the great room, which was open to a two-story vaulted ceiling crossed with exposed heavy wooden beams. Large paintings of landscapes and wildlife filled the paneled walls. Deep brown leather couches and easy chairs surrounded heavy pine tables, and the well-kept wooden floors were spotted with beautiful Native American rugs.

At one end of the room, a fieldstone fireplace was set between cathedral windows that looked out over the hills. At the other end, a dining area was dominated by a massive wooden table that could easily seat twenty people. It could just be the house of a wealthy rancher, but the size of the ranch and the arrangement of the ranch house made her more certain that Jim was the Alpha she'd been looking for. It made her wonder how large the pack might be.

She hadn't planned on using the pheromone again. The first trial with Jim had ended badly, but waiting there in the lair of the Alpha was proving to be an irresistible temptation. She pulled out a tiny vial and measured out a fraction of the dose she'd used before, applying it to her fingertips.

Jim didn't keep Crystal waiting long. His eyes pinned her as he descended the staircase. Jeans hugged his legs, and his fitted T-shirt clung to his damp skin and molded to the contours of his chest. His dark hair was beaded with drops of water.

But he didn't stop. He bypassed Crystal and opened a door leading to what looked like a book-lined study, but he didn't invite her in nor close the door. She overheard him calling Daniel on the two-way. She heard him tell his foreman to go on without him tonight and to keep an eye out for trouble.

Trouble? The full moon wasn't for another day. What kind of trouble was he expecting?

As Crystal considered the possibilities, Jim came back to the great room and moved behind the long, well-polished mahogany bar. "What can I get you?" he asked as he poured whiskey into a crystal glass.

"Whatever you're having is fine."

Jim poured a shorter measure into another glass and handed it to Crystal, but he didn't sit. He downed his in one swallow.

"Thank you for the flowers. They were beautiful," she said. She got the impression she wasn't going to be encouraged to stay long.

"They weren't enough. I wanted to do something to make up for my behavior, but there's not really anything I can do. There's no excusing what I did."

"That's what I wanted to talk to you about."

"There's not much to say." Jim returned to the bar and poured himself another drink, obviously trying to keep distance between them.

"Will you come sit by me? You're making me nervous."

"I should make you nervous," Jim growled into his drink. "I'm not the kind of man you need, Crystal."

Crystal shot up from the couch and crossed to Jim. "What kind of man do you think I need? Some pale intellectual who'll sip white wine with me while we discuss scientific journals? Somebody who'll handle me with kid gloves?"

She moved in close enough that she could feel the heat of his body. "You don't know me, Jim. You don't know what I need. When you first stopped to help me on the highway, I felt something, a connection. I enjoy being with you, and I want to get to know you better." She ran her fingers lightly over the back of his hand.

She dropped her voice to little more than a whisper. "We got a little intense, but you didn't hurt me. I don't believe you'd harm me." She laid her palms against his chest and pressed her cheek lightly between them. She could feel him responding, his increased heart rate and respiration, and she was surprised at her own reaction. She was acting out her part to keep him interested, but this man made it hard to remain scientifically detached.

THE SCENT OF her arousal assaulted his senses. He felt himself losing it again. He went rigid with desire as scenarios flashed through his mind, images that were raw, primal. Crystal on her knees, taking him in her mouth. Crystal splayed out in his bed as he plunged into her. Jim's mouth on her neck, his fingers brushing aside her long blonde hair, his teeth sinking into her skin, marking her as his...

Blonde hair... Marking his mate... *Sissy.*

Jim pushed Crystal away and stumbled back against the bar. She didn't make any move to come near him. After a moment, she turned away and dug in her purse for a tissue.

"I'm sorry if I upset you. I'll go."

He heard her sniffle. "Wait, Crystal. Just give me a minute." He hated being the cause of tears. And it was no wonder she was upset. He'd run the full gamut with her from the white knight rushing to the rescue to the black bastard who tried to ravish her. He didn't know how to explain his mood swings. He didn't understand it himself, but he owed her something.

He poured himself a tall glass of cold water and drank it down as he fought to regain control. This was his body and he was determined to master it. He pushed down his arousal and brought his racing heart back to normal.

Crystal was still standing with her back to him, waiting. "Come sit down," he said. He led her to the couch and pulled up a chair in front of her. "I'm going through something right now, and it's making me unpredictable."

"Is it a woman? I don't want to get in the middle of anything." She looked at him with those blue eyes.

"There was someone, but it's over. I just need a little time."

Crystal frowned. "I've been rushing you, haven't I? I just feel like there's something there. Something between us that could be very good."

"I like you, Crystal, but I've got some issues to work through. I'm not myself right now, and I don't want to scare you."

"I'm not scared, and I'm not ready to give up on you. We could slow down and just get to know each other, like friends. Do you think we could give it a try?"

"I do. How about I follow you back to town? I could go for a burger and a shake, and I know a great little joint."

"With extra onions. No kissing." She was smiling now.

Jim was relieved that Crystal was taking everything so well. He held his hand out to her. "Extra onions it is."

IT WAS ALMOST midnight when Jim walked into the bar. He'd dropped off Crystal and headed out to the Roadhouse. The place was crowded, not unusual.

"I didn't expect to see you here tonight," Daniel said, surprised. He was at his usual spot at the bar.

"Yeah, well, I wasn't in the mood to go home yet. You have any trouble?"

"No, it's been mostly quiet. Just a little scramble out in the parking lot, but I broke 'em up and they left with a pair of pretty gals, so I don't expect to be hearing from them again tonight."

"Hey, Nancy, could you get me a beer?" Jim called to the passing waitress. He'd known her a long time. She was a pack member, and she'd been waitressing at the bar for years.

When she brought the beer, Jim eyed her up and down. Nancy was older, but her body looked just fine in her tight jeans. She'd lost her lifetime mate when they were young, and she'd never taken another, but that hadn't stopped her from marrying three or four times. "Are you between husbands right now, darling?" Jim asked.

She grinned. "Yeah, I can't seem to keep 'em around very long. I guess I just wear 'em out."

"I bet you do. What time do you get off tonight?"

"I'm getting off just looking at you, sugar, but if you give me a minute, I'll clock out, get my purse, and meet you out by your truck."

Jim drained his beer. This was what he needed—one of his kind, no questions, just taking care of needs. "I'll see you out there."

Nancy blew him a kiss and moved off to talk to the bartender. Daniel raised an eyebrow, but Jim ignored him.

"I'll see you tomorrow morning." Jim headed for the parking lot.

THE AIR WAS hot and heavy. Heat lightning streaked across the sky. Native Americans referred to the July full moon as the "thunder moon" because of the frequent midsummer thunderstorms. The name matched Jim's mood.

He'd gone home with Nancy, but instead of hitting the sheets, they'd ended up sitting at her kitchen table talking until dawn. Nancy had cooked them some eggs and made a pot of coffee, and Jim told her about what had been happening.

"Well, sugar," Nancy said, handing him a steaming mug, "I'd normally say you just need a good fuck, and I'd be more than happy to oblige, but I don't think that's gonna help you any. You've got mate troubles, and it's got your system all outta whack."

"I don't have a mate."

"Your wolf says you do."

"I don't know. Daniel says I've gone too long…"

"Oh, I know, but honey, your wolf wants what it wants, and it sounds like your wolf wants his mate. What you're describing is the mating heat. It possesses you, takes over, you lose control."

"I know about that, but it's the females that go into heat."

"True, but males react to their mates. It can be just as strong for you boys."

"But this wasn't a mating thing. It happened with human women. One I didn't even know, and the other is someone I've just started dating."

"Then I don't know, honey. It must be coming from you."

"So what are you saying? I'm the one going into heat?"

"No, I think you're all man." Nancy gave him a peck on the cheek as she sent him out the door. "Listen to your wolf, Jim. Your wolf knows."

RATHER THAN RELIEVING his tension, the full moon run that night put Jim on edge. He'd been preoccupied to begin with, trying to sort out his reactions to Crystal and the things Nancy had told him. He'd always been in sync with his wolf; he was the master of his beast. But now he didn't know who was in control.

And he was second-guessing his plan to force Sissy to forget about him. He hated hurting her. He'd treated her badly. After abandoning her at the dance, he'd basically ignored her. She'd been on his mind ever since, but he thought the best course of action was to let her alone. He owed her an explanation, but what could he say? *I love you, but I can't have you.* It was better to say nothing.

She was evidently moving on, too. She'd come out alone tonight, but then she'd run with Terry and some of the other young wolves. He hadn't even talked to her.

After the run and as soon as he could excuse himself, he headed to the sanctuary of his pool. His senses were heightened the way they normally were during the full moon, and he felt feverish and irritated. He stripped and plunged into the cool water.

Just as his head breached the surface, he saw Sissy come out of the shadows, tall and lean—and naked. Jim sucked in a breath as she dove in.

She came up about five feet away from him and rose like Venus until the water came to just below her breasts. Her wet skin glowed like polished ivory in the bright moonlight.

Jim stood mesmerized as a small rivulet of water ran from under her hair down her breast to form a drop that hung for a moment like a pearl from her nipple. It was perfect. When the drop fell, he raised his eyes to hers, only to be shocked by the desire he saw there.

Her sweet clover scent was overlaid with the essence of her arousal, a primal scent that shot straight to his groin. Even the chilly water couldn't hold down his body's reaction.

He wouldn't allow himself to have those kinds of feelings for Sissy. It was a loss of self-control, but it was also a betrayal of the debt he owed his best friend. "No, Sissy," he said, trying to back away. "This isn't right."

She advanced on him like the powerful predator she was, and he backed away.

"We don't want to do something we'd regret."

"Do you really think I'd regret this?" Sissy said. "Are you that clueless?"

"Honey, right now you think you want me..."

"You have no idea what I want," she snapped. "I waited and waited for you to finally see me, but that didn't work, so I thought I'd just come lay it all out for you. Don't you like what you see?"

"Of course I do. You're so beautiful you take my breath away."

Sissy's voice dropped to a whisper. "Then why don't you want me?"

Jim felt like he'd been punched in the chest. He couldn't answer. He wanted her more than he wanted his next breath, but she was the one woman he could never have. She stood in front of him, waiting for an answer.

Jim watched silently as a tear trailed down her cheek. When she was growing up, whenever she'd been hurt, she'd run to him, and he'd fold her in his arms and comfort her, but not this time. He couldn't touch her. This time he was the one who had hurt her, and it broke his heart. He didn't make one move to stop her as she climbed out of the pool, and out of his life.

chapter seven

Jim disappeared to the wilderness where he felt most comfortable, and when he returned to the ranch days later, he went straight into the house and shut himself up in his study.

"Not now," he growled when Daniel walked into the darkened room.

"Then when?" the ranch foreman challenged. "When this whole place falls apart around you?"

"You can handle things. I'm leaving. I'm going to be gone for a while."

"That's the most chicken shit thing you've ever said. So you're just gonna run out on everybody who needs you?"

"I guess that's about it."

"Well, I'm not gonna handle your mess. Maggie's been calling. If you're leaving, you need to tell her yourself." Daniel started out the door but paused. "You know that Adam's going to challenge if you leave the pack with me. I'm too old to deal with him. Should I just turn it over? Maybe I should give him the ranch, too?"

Jim refused to look at him. Daniel turned and headed for the door. Just before the door shut, he called out, "Oh, and your new girl, that Crystal, she's been calling, too."

The door closed, and Jim picked up the phone.

Maggie answered the phone immediately. "I've been going crazy," she said. "Something happened to Sissy the night of the run. She won't tell me about it, and you were gone. I don't know what to do." Her voice sounded strained. "Sissy says she's going to leave. She'd be gone already if I hadn't stalled her. Jim, you've got to come talk to her."

Jim closed his eyes for a moment. "She's not going to want to talk to me."

"I need you with me on this. We'll make her talk to us." Maggie hung up.

Jim had pledged to Lucas that he'd always be there for Maggie and Sissy, and as much as he wanted to avoid this, he had no choice but to go.

Two hours later, Jim arrived at Maggie's door. She flew into his arms, sobbing. Maggie had been part mother, part big sister to Sissy for most of the younger woman's life.

When Lucas had left for the Army, Sissy had just been a kid. Their mom, Anita, had died the year before. Their horse barn caught fire, and she was trying to help Daniel get the horses out when the roof collapsed. Daniel had been in no shape to take care of a child alone. He was battling his grief and the crippling loss of the mating bond that had linked him to his mate for life, so Lucas had suggested that Sissy move in with Maggie, his future mate. The two women had lived together ever since. Naturally, Maggie was devastated at the thought of Sissy going off on her own.

Feeling guilty and helpless, Jim smoothed Maggie's back. "I'm sorry I left you to deal with this. I'll make sure she's okay. I promise."

When her tears subsided, Jim sat with Maggie at the kitchen table. "Now, tell me what she said."

"She didn't say much of anything. When she came in from the run, I could tell she'd been crying. She brushed by me and locked herself in her room. I was worried that one of the guys in the pack had hurt her, but she wouldn't talk to me. She just said she needed some time."

Maggie took a deep breath. "The next day she came out and announced she'd decided to go to graduate school. Just like that, out of the blue. She said she wanted to go to the University of Hawaii, for God's sake. I think she picked it just because it's far away. She'd already started packing and boxing up her things."

"I'll talk to her." Jim started to rise then sensed Sissy standing behind him in the doorway.

"You're not going to change my mind."

Jim sat back down and motioned for her to join them.

Sissy sat across from him and met his eyes. "I've made my decision. Actually, I've been thinking about this for a while. Months ago I did some research and even applied to several graduate programs. I've just been spinning my wheels since I graduated from college. I stayed here and went to the university, and I got my degree in zoology, something I love, but I've never even used it. I just went back to work at the gallery."

Sissy reached across the table and gave her sister-in-law's hand a squeeze. "Maggie, I love the gallery. I practically grew up there. But having an art gallery was your dream, not mine. I want to work with wildlife, especially wolves, to study them and help them survive. Maybe I can even discover solutions that will help us survive among humans. This is something I need to do."

Maggie, still teary-eyed, looked numb.

Jim was shocked that she'd been planning this for months and hadn't told anyone, even Maggie, but he tried to appear more reasonable than he felt. "That's fine, Sis, and no one is stopping you, but you don't have to move. You can go to graduate school here in Laramie. I'm sure they'd be glad to have you. And later maybe, if you wanted to get a doctorate, we could talk about..."

"No." Her staccato answer hung in the air between them. "There's nothing for me here."

Jim felt her refusal like a slap in the face. For a pack member to defy her Alpha was a challenge, and his instinctive reaction was to tower over her and assert his dominance, but his mind, and his heart, knew this was Sissy. He forced himself to look down to avoid her angry eyes, swallowed his growl, and took a deep breath. She was right. There was nothing for her in Laramie. If he wasn't going to claim her, he had to let her go.

It wasn't unheard of. Young, unmated males often left their home pack to find a mate. It reduced interbreeding and kept the packs healthy, but wolves were territorial. Pack wolves had certain protocols to follow to join another pack. One pack leader would approach another and make a request and then they'd negotiate. Usually, packs traded one for one.

Healthy, unmated females were almost always welcomed into a new pack. Even a temporary trade was accepted by most packs because if the female mated and became pregnant, she and her children would be claimed by the new pack permanently.

He had to tread softly. Sissy was ready to run, and if he was going to do this, he had to guide her toward the best, and safest, situation.

"Okay, Sissy, I'll agree to this, but you have to let me work out some details. You're an adult Werewolf. A young, unmated, female Werewolf. It's not that easy to just pick up and move."

"I've already thought about that. That's why I picked Hawaii. The university has a good program for endangered species studies, and there are no packs there, so I wouldn't be intruding in anybody's territory. I can go solitary."

"It's too dangerous. You'd be completely vulnerable, baby doll." He saw her flinch at the endearment he had always used for her. "What do you think would happen if someone saw you running as a wolf in Hawaii? If they didn't shoot you, they'd put you in a zoo. There are no wolves in Hawaii. You'd end up on the news."

"I'd be careful. I can take care of myself. And I'd just as soon be somewhere there are no wolves right now."

"If you want to go away, I'll support you. Just give me some time to work this out." Jim hated the words as they left his mouth. "It might be good if you got out on your own for a while, but you need to be with a pack. Let me talk to your dad. He knows more about the other packs than I do. We'll work something out. Any pack would be glad to have you."

Without looking, Jim could sense Maggie's outrage. He knew she'd expected him to talk Sissy out of leaving, not help her along. He'd deal with Maggie later. But he couldn't read Sissy's emotions. She seemed shocked that he'd agreed with her, but she was keeping cool. He didn't want this to seem as though he was sending her away for behaving badly.

"Are you okay with that?" he asked. "Will you wait until I can work out a deal with another pack?"

"I'll wait for a while, but I want to get this done soon. School will be starting in September. Go ahead and check it out, but ultimately, it's going to be my decision, not yours." Sissy rose from the table and left Jim alone with Maggie.

"What the hell was that?" Maggie was shooting daggers at

Jim, and he knew he deserved them.

"It's for the best, Maggie," he said. "She needs to get away for a while. She's already refused every single male in the pack. If she goes, maybe she'll meet somebody new and start a life of her own." He couldn't keep the sadness out of his voice as he said the words that broke his heart. "Or maybe she'll want to come back to us."

"You know what happened the night of the run, don't you?"

"Yeah, I do." Jim dropped a kiss to the top of Maggie's head and left.

Jim dreaded telling Daniel about Sissy's decision, but he needed Daniel's help, not as her father but as the pack Second. Most of the Alphas he knew of were older, and Daniel had a closer relationship with them than he did. Jim had to find a pack leader he could trust to look out for her.

Jim knew he'd sheltered Sissy from some of the realities of Werewolf culture. Many packs were rougher than his. Since becoming Alpha, he'd made it his duty to take care of all of his people, but he was especially protective of the unmated females during the full moon runs, and the males in his pack knew not to cross him on that issue. Males were naturally aggressive during the full moon, and for some, the run and the hunt meant sex, and females could easily become prey. If the females were willing, that was fine, but Jim wouldn't stand for males using dominance or force. He hoped they could find a pack with similar standards.

Jim explained Sissy's plans, and her father immediately read the situation for what it was.

"What'd you do to her?"

"I hurt her." Jim didn't even try to block the punch that dropped him to his knees. "I didn't touch her, but I hurt her anyway." He looked up at Sissy's father from the floor. "I'm trying to make this right."

"You fool. You can't see what's in front of you." Daniel stalked out.

I've seen what's in front of me, and I can't get her out of my mind.

Since their initial conversation went about as smoothly as he'd expected, Jim let Daniel cool off before he called him up to the house.

"My best advice is for you to work this out with Sissy," Daniel said as soon as he walked in Jim's office.

"That's not an option right now," Jim said grimly. He set out an old map his father had made showing the territories of all the wolf packs in North America. "I'm not sure how up-to-date this is. Tell me what you know."

He and Daniel went through the packs one by one. Daniel dismissed some of the packs as too violent or primitive for Sissy.

"I wouldn't send my worst enemy to this one," he said, pointing. "They'll fight to the death about who's picking up the bar tab." He pointed to another pack marked on the map. "This bunch is practically a cult. They've been inbred for years, and they don't trust outsiders."

Jim texted Sissy for a list of the graduate schools she'd applied to and checked them against the pack map. Werewolves traditionally lived as far apart from humans as they could, so some packs were too remote to consider.

Daniel made some calls to people he'd met over the years and gathered as much information as he could. He shook his head in frustration. "Damn, I don't want to let her out in all this. Judging from what we already knew to what I've found out, most Werewolves aren't like us. I guess I didn't realize how good we have it here. The last one I talked to said their Alpha kept a harem of the unmated females."

"So that's a 'no.' I guess that leaves us three to choose from."

And I hope we're right about this.

The next day Jim sat down at his desk and studied the list. One was up in Alaska, another was in Montana, and there was one in Florida. They met the criteria, and now he needed to start the trading process. He didn't want to do this. He didn't, but he was Alpha. He took a deep breath and started to make the calls.

All three packs responded quickly. As Daniel had surmised, all three jumped at the chance of hosting a high-ranking alpha female and maybe getting the chance to add her to their pack.

With that done, Jim let Daniel do most of the talking when they went to see Sissy. As pack leader, Jim technically had final say, but Daniel was her father, and Jim knew Sissy would listen to him.

"It's down to these three," Daniel explained. "Personally, I like the Denali pack. They're small, but I've known their Alpha for a long time, and they're close to the university at Fairbanks. The Ocala pack is close to the main campus of University of Florida in Gainesville. But they don't have much running space, and they don't hunt since they got kicked out of the national forest for scaring the tourists. They're out to the public down there. I think they're kind of a tourist attraction, but you could probably avoid that kind of attention if you wanted."

And with the third one, Daniel paused. "I'm not as sure about the Missoula pack. They've got the university right there, but I don't know their leader. I had dealings with the old Alpha and he was fair enough, but he passed away a while back and they have a new Alpha now. I haven't heard much about him yet, but I'll ask around. What do you think?"

Sissy sat and listened to Daniel. Jim might as well have not been there for all the attention she paid him. "I want to check out the programs at the universities and scope out the areas," she said.

"Alaska sounds pretty good. I'll let you know."

A FEW DAYS later, Sissy called them together. "I've decided. I want to go to Missoula. Florida is too touristy. I don't think I could handle having paparazzi take my picture before a run. Alaska looks great, but I'm not sure I'd fit in with them. They're such a small pack, and they're all Native Americans and mostly family, and I'd stick out like a blonde sore thumb. I don't want to feel like an outsider, so I think Montana is my best bet. It's closer than I wanted, but the university has the program I want, and I already have an application in with them."

She took a deep breath. "I would appreciate it if you could set it up with the pack." She shot a challenging look at Jim. "I need to get my records to the registrar, and I'll want to get up there as soon as I can so I can get settled in before school starts."

"Are you sure, sweetheart?" Daniel asked. "I haven't been able to find out much on their new leader. He and his family joined the pack just before the previous Alpha died, then he challenged for the top spot and won. Some of the older members weren't too happy about him coming in like that."

Sissy waved off her father's misgivings. "The older generation probably would have objected to any change. I'm sure he's fine. I'm not going to get into pack politics anyway," she said dismissively. "Jim, if you could make the arrangements, I'd like to get going."

THE NEGOTIATIONS WITH the Missoula pack leader, Milton Simmons, didn't go as smoothly as Jim had hoped. He should've been in the power position, offering a female, but Milton proved to be a shrewd player. He must have figured out they'd selected his pack as their first choice, and he pressed his advantage.

"Did you say the young woman was your daughter?" Milton

asked.

"No, I didn't say that." The Missoula leader was fishing for more information he could use as leverage, so Jim decided to play his cards closer to his vest.

"Well, it doesn't matter. We'll treat her like our daughter while she's here. We have several young folks in the pack who go to the university. If it's okay with you, I'll arrange for Sissy to share an apartment with one of them, a sweet girl named Shari. She's a senior, and she has a nice place right near campus. She can show Sissy around."

"Thank you. I'm sure Sissy would appreciate that."

"I'll set it up. When is she coming?"

"I'll be bringing her myself. I thought we'd go up in a few weeks." Jim had timed the move for right after the full moon, so she'd have almost a full month to get to know the Missoula pack before she ran with them. "Does that give you enough time?"

"That'll be fine. Will you be staying long?"

"No. Just long enough to get a sense of the place and get her settled."

"You'll have to come to dinner so I can welcome you proper. And there is one other matter."

Here it comes. Jim had expected Milton would push for more.

"I have a couple of boys who've been wanting to make the move into your area. I'm sure you'll agree that a trade would be fair."

"A couple of boys? What exactly are you asking for?"

"You realize my pack is at a disadvantage here. We'll be taking care of your female for several years, even though she won't be contributing to the pack in the long run unless she decides to stay with us. Meanwhile, I have two young men who want to make a change, maybe find their mates. They're hard workers.

They'd be an asset to any pack. I've been waiting to place them in a good spot, so this seems like great timing for both of us."

Great timing for you. "I think I could manage to take one of your boys, if he seems like a good match for us," Jim said.

"I have to consider the interests of my pack. I couldn't ask them to take on this burden unless I can show your willingness to reciprocate." Milton made it sound like having Sissy in the pack would be a terrible imposition.

Jim didn't want to get in a pissing contest with the other Alpha. Milton could easily hold up the deal, and as the start of the fall semester got closer, he could press for even more concessions. "I'll consider your offer. Send me some information on your boys— names, ages, pack ranking, what skills they bring. I'll take a look and get back to you."

"Good." Milton sounded like it was a done deal. "I'll get that off to you right away. I know you won't have any objection to them, so I'm going to start making arrangements to welcome Sissy."

Confident bastard. Jim could practically feel Milton's hand around his balls. In any other case, he would have told the other guy to fuck off, but this was for Sissy. He owed her this.

chapter eight

Jim let Daniel update Sissy on the negotiations and assure her and Maggie that everything would be settled soon. Milton sent the information Jim had requested, and Jim called Daniel in to help him evaluate the prospects.

"This one looks fine," Daniel said, pointing to one of the folders. "I know of his family. They've been in the area for a long time. This says he's twenty-four, a wrangler, and an alpha. Did a couple of tours in Iraq. Sounds like a dream date," he added, a tone of skepticism in his voice.

"Why would they want to trade him?"

"This Milton fella must have a beef with him. Maybe the boy's a potential challenger. The file says he's an alpha, but it doesn't give his pack ranking. The last thing we need is another cocky young alpha like Adam stirring up trouble."

"I know, but that's not the vibe I'm getting." Jim stared at the photograph in the folder, wishing he could read paper the way he could read people. "He looks like an upright kid. There must be something else going on."

"Maybe all the Missoula females are ugly."

"This one," Jim said, looking at the other profile, "looks like a straight-on loser. He's thirty-three, a beta."

"That's a little old to be trading packs."

"File says he can work as an administrative assistant or a cook," Jim pointed out. "That sounds like Milton wants to put eyes on us. He wants his guy in my house or my business. Don't think so."

Daniel nodded. "We'd have to watch him, but that could work out for us. We might find out what Milton's trying to pull."

"How can I go back to Milton and accept this without looking like a wimp?"

"You can't, but that's okay too," Daniel said. "Let him think you're weaker than you really are. That'll be our advantage."

"I don't feel good about this. I can't let Sissy go into this if I can't trust him."

"Don't ever trust anybody but your own, Jim. That's just the way it is. She'll be our eyes on their pack."

THE AUGUST FULL moon run had been rough. Sissy ran with her friends, and Jim had tried to stay out of her way. Maggie ran by his side, but she was still upset with him for supporting Sissy's plan. He went through the motions of leading the run, but he was distracted. He kept thinking about Sissy running with a new pack without him to watch out for her.

As a result, he didn't pay attention when a group of young males split off to run down an elk. He wasn't even concerned when he heard a fight over the carcass. That was fairly common. A kill was one place where the younger wolves could assert dominance. Usually, a couple of contenders would square off and scuffle until one pinned the other. The behaviors were pretty traditional. The stronger wolf would bite the weaker by the ear or muzzle until the weaker rolled over and showed his belly. Fight over.

This time, however, the commotion escalated until it sounded as though the whole pack had joined in on the fight. Jim raced over and jumped into the middle of a brawl. He grabbed the nearest wolf by the scruff of his neck and threw him over his back and waded into the melee, snapping and growling. The wolves around him backed off, some of them already bloody and torn, most with tails tucked and heads hanging.

At the center of it all, Jim found Adam, his muzzle dripping with blood. He was standing on the elk carcass, claiming it as his prize. A smaller beta wolf named Billy lay on the ground near the kill. He was bleeding from his head and muzzle and one of his forelegs had been broken.

Adam's position atop the elk placed him taller than Jim, and rather than lowering his head in deference to his pack leader, Adam stretched his face toward the moon and howled.

That was a mistake. His proud posture left his neck exposed, and Jim went for it. He sank his teeth into Adam's throat and felt hot blood fill his mouth. Jim dragged the large young male down to the ground, forcing him into a roll until he ended belly up. Without releasing his grip on Adam's neck, Jim mounted the younger alpha's prone body, boxing in his downed opponent with all four legs. Adam thrashed, snapping at the air and trying to break loose, but Jim clamped down harder on Adam's windpipe until the young wolf lost consciousness.

Daniel and some of the ranch security force moved up and took defensive positions in the center of the circle of wolves. Jim stepped away from Adam's body and shifted to human form while his Second and the wranglers stood guard as wolves. The others around the circle began to shift back amid a chorus of howls.

"Somebody tell me what the fuck happened here," Jim bellowed. Maggie, Sissy, and Clint ran up to stand by his side. "See to the injured, and get any of the pack who weren't involved in this back to the house."

Jim kept his eyes on the group who'd been in the center of the fight. He recognized two young men he'd seen hanging out with Adam. "Get over here by your buddy." Jim motioned to the unconscious wolf.

"Who started this?" Jim called out to Jonah, one of his ranch hands. He was marked with streaks of blood, and he had an angry bite mark on his shoulder.

"A few of us," Jonah gestured to some of the others in the circle, "had just run down this elk, and we were tearing into it when we got jumped by those three and maybe a couple of others. So much fur was flying, it was hard to tell what was going on, but they weren't after the elk. They attacked *us*. We backed off to give them the kill, but they kept coming at us, fighting hard. I think they meant to hurt us, even kill us. I don't know why."

"Is that what the rest of you saw?"

Mumbles and nods indicated that they agreed with Jonah's account.

"I want all of you who were attacked to wait for Clint and Daniel at the house. They'll take your statements. Go get cleaned up and take care of your injuries." Jim turned to Adam's friends. "You two pick up your friend and carry him back to the cell behind the men's changing house." Clint and the wolf guards formed a tight pack to escort the prisoners back.

Daniel shifted and came over to Jim. "I told you we were gonna have to take care of Adam."

Jim shook his head. "This is the last damn thing I need."

When Jim got back to the ranch compound, he discovered that a lot of the pack was still hanging around, gathered in small groups. Generally, the Laramie pack was peaceful; there were occasional scuffles and the usual jostling for position, but deadly fights were forbidden. Jim walked among them, reassuring them. The Alpha questioned a few more of the fellows who'd been in the fight, and they corroborated the first story of what happened. Some thought there was a fourth wolf with the attackers, but they weren't sure.

Jim saw that Maggie was also moving around the groups, calming frayed emotions and urging them over to the picnic area where some of the women had laid out food and coffee. He caught Daniel's and Maggie's attention and met them up on the porch. "How's Billy?"

"He'll be okay. Clint splinted his leg. Sissy and Terry have taken him to the doctor," Maggie replied.

Jim turned to Daniel. "How about Adam's little pack?"

"They're stashed in the cell for now." Most packs had a reinforced room where they could isolate unruly members. "Adam woke up and wasn't too happy. How're you gonna deal with them?"

"I think I'd better take care of this right away. Go and tell everybody who's still here that I'm calling a pack meeting right now."

The moon had set, and flickering torches gave the only light in the meeting circle. From the look of it, most of the pack had hung around to see what was going to happen. Jim stood alone on the leader's rock. The pack members' nervousness and anticipation charged the atmosphere. Clint and his guards brought Adam and his two followers, wearing heavy chains and manacles, into the circle. The restraints would hold them in human form but not for long if they shifted.

Jim's voice carried over the crowd. "As I've heard from several of you, Adam, Gary, and Rick, and maybe one other, challenged a group over a kill, which is acceptable. What's not acceptable is that when the defenders of the kill backed down, Adam's group continued to attack, inflicting serious injuries on smaller and weaker members. When I entered the scene, Adam continued to challenge until he was subdued. Does anyone have anything to add?"

A man and a woman about Jim's age came into the circle, a tall, skinny teenage boy between them. The man spoke. "Jim, our son Kenny was the fourth member of Adam's group. We warned him to stay away from Adam. I suspected there'd be trouble. I should have told you. Adam's been coming around, talking to some of the kids, buying them beer, talking trash about you and how he was going to be the Alpha pretty soon. I'm sorry I didn't come to you."

The boy's mother stepped forward. "Whatever you have to do, Jim, my boy's just a stupid kid. He's only shifted three times. Please don't kill him." The woman fell onto hands and knees with her head down, submitting to Jim. Her husband pushed the boy to the ground and joined his wife, waiting for Jim's judgment.

Jim hoped he wouldn't have to execute anybody. He hated this part of his society—the fear and abasement generated by the strict hierarchy. It was that structure that had caused the incident in the first place, but Jim hadn't found any way to overcome centuries of social custom and genetic programming.

He turned to the young males in manacles. "What about you three? What were your intentions? Do you have anything to say?"

Gary, one of the followers, stepped forward, but a sharp look from Adam shut him up, and he stepped back in line with his head down. Adam raised his head defiantly. Jim's bite marks had left deep red gashes on his neck. He stared coldly at Jim, but he said nothing.

Jim leaped down and faced Adam. "Uncuff them," he ordered. When the men were unshackled, he continued. "Adam, tonight you challenged me over the kill. Do you want to demand a challenge now?"

If Adam did, Jim would have to fight him for the pack leadership, maybe to the death. The younger man held Jim's gaze for as long as he could before he dropped his eyes. "No."

There would be no dominance challenge tonight. "This is not your first offense, and it's not likely to be your last. You violated pack law by attacking humans and those who were weaker than you. You've begun to gather your own followers. You defy my leadership. It's time for you to leave this pack. You have until moonrise tomorrow to be off pack lands, and if you ever return, your life is forfeit."

Next, Jim addressed the other two. "You can follow Adam into exile, but if you leave, you can never return, even to see your families. If you stay, you'll remain locked up until you face punishment at the next pack meeting. What do you choose?"

Adam's buddies were large and strong but not dominant enough to stand up to either Adam or Jim. They shuffled their feet and looked down at the ground as they considered their choices. Gary asked, "What would the punishment be if we stayed?"

"You'd be flayed. That means you'd be whipped until there was no skin left on your backs." The sentence was harsh. It would be excruciatingly painful, but they would heal. And Jim really hoped he wouldn't have to do it.

They shot sidelong glances at each other, and Gary spoke for both, "I reckon then we'll go with Adam."

"Then your choice is made. Say good-bye to your families and get out of my sight."

That still left the teenager to deal with. "Get up," Jim ordered. Kenny struggled to his feet on quaking legs. "You heard the others' choices. Which do you choose?"

"I'll have to take the whipping, sir. I don't want to go with Adam. I knew he was no good, but I was just stupid. I want to stay here with you and my folks, even if it means losing my skin."

Jim was impressed by the boy's courage. He hadn't intended to inflict such a harsh punishment on the teenager, but he needed to hear what he would choose. "I think you chose right, son. Because of your age, I'm not going to have you whipped. For the next three moons, you won't be allowed to run with the pack. You'll be chained in the cell so you can shift but you won't be able to move."

It was a tougher sentence than it sounded. Being restrained during a full moon was almost unbearable, especially for young wolves, who would fight against their bonds until they were bloody and exhausted. "You'll also have to come to work for me at the ranch, and your pay will go to Billy and his family until he heals up from the beating he took. You can report to Daniel. Now help your mama up."

The boy's parents hugged him. His mother was sobbing, and the father thanked Jim. In some packs, the whole family could have been driven out or killed for their son's part in Adam's attempted insurrection.

Jim intended to keep an eye on the boy and on all of the younger pack members from now on. He'd been letting too much slide.

A FEW DAYS later, Jim and Daniel finished loading all of Sissy's stuff into Jim's truck. She hadn't wanted Jim to take her to

Missoula, but that had been a deal breaker with both men. They vetoed her going alone.

Sissy kept her independent face on until it was time to say good-bye to Maggie. As Maggie's lips trembled and the first tears slid down her cheeks, Sissy ran into her arms. "Oh, Mag," she cried, "I'm just going away to school. Lots of girls younger than me do it all the time."

"I know, but none of them is like my baby sister."

"I'll call. I will, I promise." When Sissy pulled away, her face was wet with tears. "Dad, you take care of her," she said as she stepped up into the truck.

Jim closed her door and gave Maggie and Daniel a nod. He just wished he felt more confident about letting her go.

The trip to Missoula was long and strained. Sissy said nothing, her earphones cutting off any attempts at communication. They stopped a few times to stretch and get drinks, but Sissy kept to herself, refusing Jim's suggestion for food.

Their relationship was broken. The easy friendship, the joking, Sissy's teasing sarcasm—those were all gone, and Jim ached for the loss.

It was late by the time they reached Missoula, and Sissy had dozed off. Jim checked them into a motel and pulled up to their rooms. He gently urged Sissy out of the truck. Still half asleep, she slid out of the seat into his arms, her head falling against his chest.

Jim was afraid to move and break the moment. He lowered his head to her silky hair and breathed in her sweet scent as he held her sleepy body to his. If she had let him, he would have stood like that for hours.

Sissy slowly came back to wakefulness. She lifted her head to meet his. Her lips parted as her eyes slowly opened. Instantly, her body stiffened and she jerked away.

Jim let her go and got their luggage. He opened the door to her room and handed over her bag and the key. As she turned to slip into the darkened room, he reached for her arm. Sissy glared at his hand on her arm and then met his eyes.

"The last thing I wanted was to drive you away." Jim released her arm and headed to his room for the night.

chapter nine

The thin wall between their rooms couldn't contain her thoughts. Sissy could hear Jim pacing. She had seen the hurt in his face, and she had never witnessed his shoulders slump in defeat. All her life, he had been strong and confident, and his face had always lit up whenever he saw her.

Maybe she was wrong in running. *If I'd stayed a little longer. If I'd only talked to him.* But no, she needed to get away.

THE NEXT MORNING, they had breakfast at a café by the motel. Jim called Milton to let him know they'd arrived, and Milton insisted that they come to his house for dinner. That left the whole day free.

Sissy finally became more animated as they planned their day. They began at the university. She loved the campus, and Jim enjoyed seeing her happy again, even if it meant leaving her there. They met with the chairman of the department to make sure he had received all of Sissy's paperwork for the graduate program. Later they went for lunch at the Oxford Saloon, a local landmark, and walked around for a while.

In the afternoon they went back to the motel to get ready for dinner. Jim could hear Sissy tapping away on her laptop in her room. She seemed confident and sure of herself, but Jim was already missing her.

When it was time to leave for Milton's house, Jim knocked on her door. She opened it, and for a moment he was speechless.

Sissy had pulled her hair up and caught it with a clip. Doing so had left her long neck bare. Her dress, light pink with thin straps, was the same shade as her sandals.

She was a beautiful woman.

She tilted her head, waiting for him to speak.

He shook his head. "Nothing."

She stepped out of the room, and as Jim started to shut the door behind her, he spotted her sweater draped over a chair. He picked it up and held it for her.

"Thanks," she said. Sissy turned her back to him, and he wrapped the sweater around her shoulders, her sweet clover scent flooding his senses.

How could he let her go?

His instincts told him to sink his teeth into her shoulder at the base of her neck and claim her as his mate right then and there, but he knew better than to trust his instincts. He wasn't about to lose control with her.

Sissy straightened. He knew she wasn't immune to his heat, but he also knew she wasn't going to take the chance of being rejected again. She pulled the sweater around her and walked away without looking back.

The ride to Milton's house was quiet. Jim had no trouble finding the place, a nice two-story brick home on a cul-de-sac in a newish subdivision. Before they got out of the truck, Jim turned to

Sissy. "I don't have a good feeling about this."

She opened her door. "You agreed to this. I'm going in to meet my new Alpha. You can come along or stay in the truck."

Sissy's words struck Jim like a slap. He growled and caught her arm before she could slip out. "I will always be your Alpha, and you are not staying in Missoula or anyplace else unless I give my okay. That's how it works, whether you like it or not."

Her eyes flashed in defiance. She pulled her arm from his grasp, but she didn't say anything.

"I'm serious, Sissy. You follow my lead in there. We could be walking into a very dangerous situation. At the very least, there's going to be a lot of political maneuvering, and I have to know you're not going to try to undermine my authority before these people."

Her nostrils flaring, Sissy said, "I'd never go against you. You know that."

He sighed. "I'm sorry, baby doll. I do know that. Let's go face the big bad wolf."

As soon as Milton answered the door, the battle for dominance began.

"Welcome. Come on in," Milton said.

Jim faced the Missoula Alpha. It was rare for two pack leaders to ever meet face to face. If packs had business to conduct, they usually sent high-level betas as representatives, as they were less likely to react aggressively.

Milton eagerly reached out to take Sissy's arm, and Jim instantly growled and stepped between them. The Missoula Alpha was only slightly shorter than Jim, but he was powerfully built, and the two men's large bodies crowded the entryway. The scent of aggression was thick in the tight space.

Milton stepped back. "I'm sorry," he apologized smoothly. "I shouldn't have come between you. Let's see if we can't take this down a notch." He smiled and gestured them toward the living room.

Jim didn't like turning his back on Milton, especially when the other man positioned himself between them and the door. But he stepped into the living room, his hand on Sissy's back.

"Go ahead and take a seat. Dinner's not quite ready." Milton hollered down the hall. "Betty, are you going to get us some drinks, or what?"

A petite brunette hurried in carrying a tray of drinks. She didn't meet any of their eyes, a mark of a beta.

Milton didn't bother to introduce her, leading Jim to surmise that the brunette was Betty, and she was his wife. He thought it was interesting that Milton had married a beta. Werewolves usually chose mates from their same ranking.

After the drinks were served, Milton took a seat in a large leather wingback chair, leaving the couch for Jim and Sissy. The Missoula Alpha was dark with black eyes and straight black hair combed back from his face. Sitting enthroned before them, Milton established they were visitors in his castle, although his demeanor was carefully casual.

Milton addressed Jim first. "How was your trip?"

"It was fine. We made good time." Jim was having a harder time making polite conversation than Milton. He was in foreign territory, and his instincts were aroused.

"May I address Sissy?" It was proper for Milton to ask permission before approaching a female of another pack.

Jim nodded, never taking his eyes off the other Alpha.

"Sissy, I want to welcome you to the Missoula pack and to my home. We're very happy to have you here, and I want you to feel at home. I'm gonna be your surrogate Alpha for the time you're here, so I want you to come to me if you need anything or you have any problems. Is that a deal?"

SISSY LOOKED AT Jim before she answered. He moved his arm along the back of the couch and laid his fingers on the back of her neck, a less than subtle claiming gesture. Sissy wanted to tell them both to bugger off, but Werewolf politics didn't work that way.

She wished that she'd talked more to Jim about how they were going to play this. She accepted that she was a pawn between the two dominant males, but she needed to show Milton that she was a strong alpha in her own right.

Sidestepping his "deal," Sissy said, "Thank you for hosting me, Milton. I'm sure I won't have any problems."

"Well, a pretty young thing like you is gonna want to socialize. We have lots of young folks in the pack. You'll fit in just fine."

"I'll only be here for two years, and I'll be spending most of my time concentrating on my studies. I doubt I'll have much time for a social life."

Jim smiled as Milton's eyes narrowed slightly. *Score one for me.* Just then, the doorbell rang.

"Speaking of school, I invited your new roommate Shari to dinner. I'm sure you two will get along." Milton made no move to get the door. "Betty!" he bellowed. Sissy glimpsed the brunette female hustle to the door and heard her greeting the new guest.

Milton stood, so Sissy and Jim followed suit. "Let's get on to dinner."

The new arrival waited in the hall with Betty. Shari was tall like Sissy, but her figure was lush and curvy. She could have been a *Sports Illustrated* swimsuit model. She had wavy dark blonde hair and vibrant blue eyes. Milton put his arm around her waist and pulled her tightly to his side. Shari smiled brightly, seemingly proud of her Alpha's attention. He introduced her as though she were a prized possession. "Sissy, Jim, this is Shari, the prettiest female in our pack. Isn't she a beauty?"

"Hi Shari. It's nice to meet you. I appreciate you sharing your place with me." Sissy smiled at her new housemate, and then turned her smile on the dark haired woman standing behind Milton and Shari. "We haven't been introduced. You must be Milton's wife, Betty. Thank you for having us over."

Betty smiled shyly and nodded, keeping her eyes to the floor. Milton seemed more amused than irritated at Sissy's blatant correction of his etiquette, but he continued on without apologizing to either his guests or his wife. "Shari has a nice garage apartment behind a house that's owned by the pack. It's got two bedrooms, it's close to the campus, and it's real quiet. It'll be a good place to study," Milton said pointedly to Sissy.

He ushered them into the large dining room. He took the head of the table and gestured for Jim to take the seat at the other end. Shari sat to Jim's left and Sissy took the seat to his right.

That left two empty place settings on either side of Milton. "Jax, get down here," he yelled.

A young man who looked to be in his mid-twenties entered and took a seat on Milton's right. He was tall and broad, almost as big as his father. His straight black hair hung across his face, covering one eye. He flipped it back and looked out from under the sheaf of hair. He nodded to Shari, but he didn't acknowledge the new guests.

"This is my son, Jackson. He went to the university for a while, but he quit. Not smart enough, I guess." Jackson didn't react. He was clearly used to being insulted by his father. "He works with me now."

"WHAT DO YOU do, Milton?" Jim knew the answer. He'd checked out Milton's finances and background before they had come, but he was just making small talk while he observed the relationship between the father and son. He scented that Jackson was an alpha, but there wasn't much assertiveness there.

"I have one of the biggest car dealerships in town. Cars and trucks, new and used. If you need anything, just let me know. I can give you the family deal. I hear you have a big spread down near Laramie."

"That's right. I keep some cattle and buffalo, and it gives the pack a safe place to run."

"That's a good deal. It must make for an easy hunt, like a smorgasbord."

"We don't hunt the livestock. There's lots of game, and it gives us a better run." Jim thought Milton was the type to take the easy route, just set out a half-dead cow and get right to the eating without the chase. "Where does your pack run?"

"The pack has a lodge and some land out to the west of town. Lots of forest. It's a real pretty place. Not a lot of game left, but we make do. Where's that food?" he called.

The door to the kitchen swung open and Betty came in, carrying a huge roast that she set down in front of Milton before she scurried back into the kitchen. She made several trips with platters of steaming vegetables and a big basket of biscuits.

Sissy started to rise from the table, but Jim pushed against her thigh under the table to keep her in her seat. "Can I help you with the food, Betty?" she asked instead.

Milton answered for her. "She can get it. She's not much of a talker, but she's a real good cook. You all dig in." He speared a big slab of rare roast beef, serving himself first before pushing the platter toward Jackson. Jackson served himself before he awkwardly handed it across to Jim, reaching right across Shari. It apparently was their custom for the men to eat first, but Jim offered the plate to Sissy and then Shari before he helped himself. Milton snorted.

The food all delivered, Betty finally took a seat at Milton's left, but she barely picked at her food. She constantly bobbed up and down, refilling everyone's glasses and bringing more food. At no time did she make eye contact or speak. Jim knew she could speak, because she had spoken to Shari when she had arrived, but otherwise, not one word.

Thankfully, eating meant the end of conversation for a while. Jim noticed that Jackson was watching Sissy while they ate. Whenever she looked up, the young man held her gaze, but if Jim looked at him, Jackson averted his eyes.

Jim thought Sissy was remaining remarkably calm. She usually wouldn't tolerate being stared at or sitting still while a man was so rude to his wife, but he was glad she was leaving the talking to him. It wouldn't help his position for Milton to see how much he let Sissy have her way.

When Milton had finished eating, he stood and said, "Come on outside with me, Jim, so we can talk. We'll leave the cleanup to the ladies."

Evidently Jackson was included with the ladies, as he was not invited to join the men. Red-faced, he rose from his seat, ignoring the men. "I'm going out, Mama. I'll be back late." He dropped a kiss on his mother's cheek. "Shari, I'll see you around." He gave Sissy a look somewhere between a leer and a smile. "Sissy, it was nice to meet you. I'm sure I'll see you soon."

Jim followed Milton out onto a long, dark porch with a wooden railing. The moon was just past full, so it was bright outside.

Being out in the open air relieved a lot of the tension Jim had felt inside the house. Milton leaned against a post and offered a cigar, but Jim shook his head.

"Okay, man to man, what do you want to ask me?" Milton asked.

Milton's openness caught Jim off guard. He didn't know whether he should go with the political answer, but opted for the blunt truth. "I don't much like the way you treat your females. I'm not inclined to leave Sissy here with you."

"I don't really care what you like. That's the way it is here. I don't pussy around with females or with lesser wolves. If you treat her so well, it makes me wonder why she's in such an all-fired rush to leave Laramie."

Jim bristled. "Sissy has the right to make her own choices, and she's chosen to follow a career. I don't bully my people, and she won't take kindly to anyone else telling her what to do. She respects the pack, and she'll respect you if you deserve it."

He squared off with Milton. "But know this. Sissy is family. If anything happens to her, I'll hold you responsible."

Milton nodded, puffing on his cigar. "I accept that. Just like I expect you to take care of the young men I'll be sending to your pack. Sissy will be under my protection. She'll do just fine with us. You'll see."

Jim thought again about their bargain. Milton might have thought he got the better end of the deal because he was sending two men in return for one female, but the numbers didn't matter. He was sending off two males he didn't care about, and in return, Jim was trusting Milton with the most precious thing in his life.

When they went back in the house, Jim was ready to leave. Sissy had made plans with Shari to move her things into the apartment the next morning. She thanked Milton for his hospitality and pointedly asked him to give her thanks to Betty, who had disappeared into the kitchen once again.

ONCE THE DOOR closed behind them, Sissy breathed easier. They rode silently back to the motel.

She was really doing this. In one day, Jim would leave her and go back home and she would be on her own, alone.

Back at the motel, Jim pulled her into his room. "I need to talk to you."

She sat on the edge of the bed, watching him while Jim paced. Finally, he stopped and faced her. "Are you absolutely sure this is what you want? Baby, you don't have to go through with this out of some kind of pride. We can go home right now if you want to forget about this."

Sissy had been asking herself the same thing since they left home. But nothing had changed. All Jim had to say was he wanted her, and she would drop everything and run into his arms. She gave him one more chance. "What do *you* want, Jim?"

Instead of meeting her eyes, he turned away. "I want this never to have happened. I want you back home with Maggie and Daniel. I want to be able to protect you."

But you don't want to love me. His broad back said it all. "I'm going to stay here. Good night, Jim."

Safely in her room, Sissy dropped her dress and climbed into bed. She made sure her breathing was steady so on the other side of the thin walls Jim couldn't hear the tears that streamed down her face. After a little while, she heard Jim's door close. She knew he would change and run. That was his way.

chapter Ten

The next morning was strained between them. They drove to Shari's apartment and moved in the boxes that Sissy had brought. Mid-morning, Jackson showed up with a friend in a jacked-up Dodge 6x6 pickup. Probably fresh off his daddy's lot, Jim assumed.

Jackson's best friend, Wade, was Shari's boyfriend. He was a non-dominant alpha and seemed to defer to Jackson who was much more assertive without his father around. Wade was broader than Jax, but his slouched posture made him seem smaller. He was dressed like Jax in urban cowboy casual—tight graphic print tee shirts with skulls and barbed wire and ball caps.

They both seemed very comfortable in the apartment, as though they spent a lot of time there. Jim had to suppress a growl every time one of the young men came within arm's length of Sissy. He suggested that he take them out to lunch, but Sissy said she'd rather just eat a sandwich and get her things unpacked.

The boys decided they would bring burgers back. They

offered to get one for Jim, but it was clear he was making everybody uneasy. They were all alphas, but Jim's dominance created an uncomfortable situation.

Jim pulled Sissy aside. "I could take you and Shari out to dinner tonight. Do you want me to stay?"

"No, I've got it under control, I think," she said.

"Okay, baby, then I guess I'll go."

"Tell Mag I'll call. I don't want you guys to worry about me."

"I can't help but worry about you. I'm leaving you here against my instincts, but I need your assurance that you'll call if there's any problem."

"I will."

Jim knew she was lying. She'd have to be dying before she called for help. He kissed her forehead. "I love you, baby doll." He turned and left before she could see the pain on his face.

JIM'S TRIP BACK to Laramie was long and bleak. He should have checked on Maggie when he got back, but he couldn't face her. Instead, he called and told her how excited Sissy had been about the university, and he described the apartment she was sharing with Shari. He kept his misgivings about Milton to himself.

A couple of days afterward, Daniel found him in the barn. "Those boys from Missoula just showed up. What do you want me to do with them?"

"Show them where to bunk for now, then bring them to the house, one at a time."

Jim crossed to the house and waited in his study. Daniel knocked on the door and then came in with a young man.

"Jim, this is Trace Bridger."

The man was tall and slim, but well built. He was dressed in the standard cowboy gear—worn jeans, western shirt, and well-worn boots. He held his cowboy hat in work-roughened hands. His eyes met Jim's, but there was no hint of challenge or fear. Jim sensed unasserted dominance, something the young alpha probably wasn't even aware of.

Jim got right to the point. "Trace, did you want this trade?"

"I didn't ask for it, sir, but I didn't fight it, either."

"Did Milton order you to come?"

"Not exactly, sir. He talked to my dad first, and Dad told me I was gonna be traded for a female from your pack."

"Why? Did you have a problem with Milton?"

"No, sir. Nothing to speak of. I don't really know the man. I just got back from Iraq about three months ago. I've been away from the pack for a while now, and I didn't know about Milton coming in until I got back."

"Why do you think he picked you and this other fella Ray to trade?"

"I don't know. Maybe 'cause he didn't know me, or 'cause I'm a good cowboy, and he thought you'd want a cowboy, what with you being a rancher and all."

"What about Ray?"

"I don't know him real well. He worked in town."

"Okay, Trace. Just one last thing. The female we sent is only going to be in Missoula for two years while she goes to school. What about you? Do you plan on staying here and joining the pack permanently?"

"Probably not. My folks are getting older, and I should be there to help them with the ranch, but they didn't say anything about me going back. You're gonna think I'm the dumbest son of a gun ever, but they just told me to go, and I did. But I wouldn't mind seeing how you run things here. My folks have got a ranch outta Missoula, and it's gonna be mine someday. It's nothing as big as this, but I figure I could learn a few things, and if I get to go home, maybe I can make some improvements to the place."

"That's good. You go on back to the bunkhouse and get settled. Daniel will fill you in on the way we operate and give you your assignments."

"Yes, sir. Could I ask you a question, sir?"

"Shoot."

"Were you in, sir?"

"I wasn't in Iraq. That was after my time. I was in the 160th Airborne Special Ops in Africa and Central America."

"You were a Night Stalker?" Awe was written all over Trace's face.

"So was my nephew Clint. He's back from Afghanistan. You'll meet him soon. He's in charge of security for the ranch."

"Thank you, sir. If I had to get traded, I'm glad I came here. I'll try to do a good job."

After Daniel showed Trace to the front door, Jim looked to his Second. "Well?"

"He seems pretty straightforward to me."

"Yeah, to me too," Jim said. "I think he's got more strength than he knows, and that's probably what got him traded. I got the feeling Milton wouldn't welcome any potential challengers. Then again, Trace didn't tell us much about Milton or the Missoula pack. After he settles in, see if you can get him talking about the pack. I'd like to know more about how Milton runs things up there."

"I'll do what I can. The boy's not much of a talker. That other one, Ray, doesn't want to shut up. You want to see him now?"

"Yeah, send him on up." While he waited, Jim couldn't help but think about Sissy. He wondered if Milton's son was hanging around. He was getting ticked off just thinking about it, and meeting the second guy from Missoula didn't help.

Ray was small for a Werewolf, even a beta. He was dressed in jeans, an old Van Halen T-shirt, and dirty sneakers. His eyes darted around, looking everywhere except directly at Jim. He seemed nervous and fidgety, but Jim suspected that was his usual manner. If there were such things as Wererats, Ray would be one.

Ray didn't wait for Jim to address him. "This is a real nice place," he said, shifting from foot to foot. "I think I'm gonna like it here."

"Well, that's good," Jim said wryly. "We wouldn't want you to be unhappy."

"Don't you worry about me. I get along with most everybody. And you can count on me to take care of whatever you need. I'm a pretty good cook, or I can keep the place clean for you. I can also answer phones and do some office work, even work a computer, and I'm a good driver. Just tell me what ya need."

"What did you do in Missoula?"

"I did just about everything. I worked for Mr. Simmons at the car lot, cleaning up and helping out, but I've done a lot of other jobs, too."

"Have you ever done any wrangling?"

"Well, I'm not much on a horse. Maybe I could help you out around the house."

"I've got all the help I need right now in the house, but I'm sure Daniel will find something for you to do." Jim turned his attention back to a stack of papers on his desk, but Ray didn't make any move to leave. "You can go now."

After Daniel escorted Ray to the front door, he returned and said, "What are we going to do with him?"

"We're going to keep an eye on him. It's pretty obvious he's a spy."

"Either that or else Milton couldn't stand him anymore and

pawned him off on us."

"Could be, but I don't want him anywhere near the house or office. Send him out on the range in the jeep. He can run food and supplies out to the men. That should keep him out of our hair for a while. And tell Clint to watch him."

Dealing with the new men from Missoula pushed Jim's thoughts to Sissy. He called Maggie to see if she had any news.

"I just talked to her. She sounded fine," Maggie said. "Her classes start next week, and she's excited about that. In the meantime, I think she's meeting some of the young folks in the pack. She said that she went out with Shari and her boyfriend and some others and had a good time. I think she said they were going off-roading this weekend."

Jim pictured her sitting in the front seat of Jackson's truck, music blaring, gathered around a campfire later drinking beer. It was all stuff he'd done at her age, but the thought of Jackson touching her sent his blood boiling.

He said good-bye to Maggie and paced his study. *If I left now I could be up there before morning. I could try to talk some sense in her, and if she wouldn't listen, I could hog-tie her and bring her home.*

If I took the chopper, I could be there in a few hours.

His phone rang, intruding on his thoughts. "What?" he growled without looking at the caller ID.

"Jim, is this a bad time?" Crystal asked.

"Oh, sorry. No, it's just been a rough day."

"Let me make you dinner tonight. You sound like you need it."

"That's nice of you, but I wouldn't be good company. I'd hate for you to waste a meal on me." Jim didn't want to go into town. There was no reason for him to keep up his pretense of dating Crystal. That had been for Sissy's benefit.

Crystal continued, "How about I come out to the ranch? I

could make us something there, then maybe go for a swim."

Jim's mind jumped to Sissy rising naked from the pool the night he decided to send her away. He slumped into a chair.

"No, it's hot and dusty here," he told Crystal. "I'll come to your place about seven."

Sitting through a dinner date didn't appeal to Jim, but he didn't want to be alone either.

A few hours later, Crystal opened the door wearing pink shorts and a flowery sleeveless top.

Jim handed her a bottle of wine. "I should have asked if I could bring anything."

"No, I've got everything. Do you want to open the wine or have a beer? I've got some on ice."

"A beer is fine." Jim pitched his hat onto a chair and followed her to the kitchen.

"I've got some steaks and veggies," Crystal said, fanning herself. "I thought we could throw them on the grill on the balcony and not heat up the house any more than it is already."

Jim had to agree. Her second-floor apartment was like an oven. "You should have told me how hot it was. You do whatever you need to get dinner ready. I'll be back in a few minutes."

He grabbed his hat and left. He was thankful for the excuse to be doing something. It had been a bad idea to come to Crystal's apartment when he was in such a foul mood.

At the hardware store, he picked up a big box fan and a couple of smaller oscillating fans. He brought them back to Crystal's apartment and set them up while she took the food out to the grill.

When she came back into the apartment, it was already a few degrees cooler. "Oh, that's so nice," she said, twirling in front of a fan, "and you're so thoughtful. I wonder how I could repay you."

She advanced on Jim, but he caught her hands before she could wrap them around his shoulders. He let her give him a thank-you kiss on the cheek, but he kept it light.

Crystal frowned, but he didn't respond. She set the small table and brought out a bowl of salad and some fresh beers. She disappeared for a minute then came back bearing a platter with two large steaks and an assortment of grilled vegetables.

"This looks really good," Jim said as he joined her at the table, "but you shouldn't have gone to all the trouble. We could have gone out."

"I know, but I wanted to just relax with you. I haven't seen you in a while."

"I had to go out of town for a few days, and it's been busy since."

Crystal talked about the heat and told a story about something that had happened at her lab. Jim made some replies, but his mind was elsewhere. When dinner was over, he helped her clear the table. He tried to make his excuses and leave, but she trapped him in the kitchen.

"Are you going to tell me what's the matter?"

"I warned you I wasn't going to be good company tonight."

"Yes, but that doesn't tell me anything."

"There's nothing to say, Crystal. I've had a few bad days. I'll get over it."

"I'd like to help you when you have bad days. That's what friends are for. I thought we were at least friends."

Jim picked her up, sat her on the counter and stepped between her legs. "We *are* friends."

"It doesn't feel that way when you shut me out." Crystal laced her fingers between his and pulled his rough knuckles to her mouth.

"I'm a private man. I've always taken care of my own problems. I'm not much on sharing, but I don't want to hurt you. You just have to accept that's the way I am."

"Okay. I'll try not to pressure you, but isn't there something I can do to take your mind off your worries?" Crystal's tongue flicked out and brushed over his knuckles, tracing the seam between their fingers.

"Oh, I imagine there's lots of things you could do, but I'm really going to have to beg off tonight. I've got to get back." He leaned in to give her a quick kiss, but she pulled his head toward her and slipped her tongue into his mouth.

He let her have the kiss, but then he pulled away and said, "You're trying to make it hard for me to leave you."

"It was my intention to make it hard."

He laughed. "Well, you did that too, but I've still got to go."

"Okay, but next time..."

"We'll see," he said, pulling away. He lifted her off the counter and guided her toward the door. "Dinner was great. Thank you. You're great. And beautiful. But I have to go." He gave her a peck on the cheek, grabbed his hat, and left.

CRYSTAL WATCHED HIM leave. He was backing off. Something had him keeping her at arm's length, and she needed him closer. She assumed it was the woman he'd mentioned. Whatever it was, she needed to find a way to bring him around. If she could gain his confidence, or even better, force a significant Werve response from him, she'd have some leverage to use to examine the pack, but she hadn't dared use the pheromone again until they'd established a better protocol for the dosing. His first reaction had almost driven him completely away, and the second time out at the ranch had been almost as bad.

Too hot and restless to sit around the house, Crystal drove to her lab, where she found Weston hunched over his computer.

"Hey, boss," he said, looking up. "What brings you out tonight?"

"It's too hot to sleep, so I thought I'd go over my notes in air-conditioned comfort. Anything new? What did you get from the athletic subject with the high Werve markers?"

"Nothing. That was a bust. He didn't know anything about Werves around here. His parents probably know, but they've hidden it from him. As far as I can tell they've raised him as completely human. I tried to talk to them, but they refused to come in."

"We shouldn't get our hopes up too high. They're closed-mouthed around here," Crystal mused. "I'm positive Jim Winter is our Alpha. The artificial pheromones worked enough to prove he's a Werve, but he's very strong. He was able to resist the biological response."

"Have you thought about just flat-out confronting him?"

"He'd never admit to anything unless I had something to hold over his head. I'll keep working on him, but maybe there's a back door into the pack. This project is too important to throw away because of one stubborn Werewolf."

"Maybe there is something," Weston offered. "I have a friend who's at the University of Montana. He's not into Werve research, but he knows I am, and he told me they'd had a Werve contact them. He'd walked right into the biology building and asked to talk to the researchers. He offered to be a test subject. They didn't have anything for him, but my friend thought I'd be interested. I didn't think to bring it up because it's out of our territory."

Crystal nodded. "You could be on to something," she said. "A member of the local pack in Montana would be likely to know something about other packs. Call your friend. I want you to go up there and interview him. Find out all he knows. Make some promises if you need to, but that's all. I don't want to get another pack involved in our testing."

DR. WESTON CALLED his colleague at the University of Montana and arranged to meet with the volunteer test subject. He flew up as soon as he could. None of his leads had proven to be productive, and Dr. Chandler certainly wasn't impressed with his perform-ance in Laramie. On top of that, she'd managed to land the biggest prize so far when she accidentally met the Alpha. Stuff like that never happened to him. If she got her Werve to open up, there wouldn't be reason to keep an assistant around except to take samples and analyze results, tasks that could be done by any graduate student.

When Dr. Chandler had asked him to come to Laramie and assist in the project, he'd jumped at the chance. She was becoming known in the Werve research community, which meant more opportunities and larger grants, and there was a lot of money in Werve research. She was most interested in the government grants. They gave her more freedom to pursue what she called "pure research," but the big money came from pharmaceuticals. If this Missoula subject panned out, it could be a big break. He'd share in the credit for their findings and ride her coattails to a lucrative commercial grant of his own.

The cab dropped him off at the Skaggs Building, the center of the UM biochemical complex. He waited under the scrutiny of the security guard until his friend came to greet him.

"Weston. Good to see you." The Montana researcher wore a white lab coat, with an honest-to-god pocket protector, over slacks and loafers. He shook Weston's hand vigorously.

"Prescott. Nice building you have here."

"I'll show you around later if you want. We have some interesting research going on right now, but your subject already arrived. I got him settled in an interview room. May I ask what testing you plan to do?"

"Not much today. I just want to talk to him. I might take some DNA samples. I brought consent forms, of course."

"Of course. Well, follow me. Here's your ID badge." Prescott handed Weston a laminated ID that read *Biomedical and Pharmaceutical Sciences*. "Keep it on you while you're in the building. Would you like to borrow a lab coat?"

"Thank you. That would be a good idea. I came straight from the airport."

Prescott swiped a card through a scanner and ducked into a lab, emerging with a starched lab coat, which he handed to Weston. "Here's the interview room. Will you need anything more?"

"No, I've got a lab kit with me if I need it."

"Well then, I'll let you to it. You have my number. Give me a buzz when you're finished, and we'll grab a bite."

Weston nodded. He slipped on the lab coat, thinking he should have worn a tie, but as soon as he opened the door of the interview room, it was apparent it didn't matter what he was wearing.

The man seated in the room appeared to be homeless and reeked of alcohol, unwashed clothes, and other less pleasant odors. Weston doubted if anything would come of this interview, and he'd have to go back to Laramie empty-handed. But he was there, so he gave it a shot.

Despite the stench, he closed the door behind him and took a seat opposite the subject and pulled a folder, a digital tablet, and a portable lab kit out of his briefcase. "I'm Dr. Weston. And you are...?"

"Otis."

"Fine, Mr. Otis."

"No, Otis is my name. Otis Meyers."

"Okay, Mr. Meyers." Weston began typing on his tablet. "So you contacted the school here and volunteered for some tests? Is that right?"

"I sure did. I heard people like you were paying good money to test on Werves like me, so I thought I'd come on down."

"So you are a Werve?"

"I sure am. I turn on every full moon, regular as clockwork."

"Would you mind me taking some DNA samples to verify that you are a Werewolf?"

"No problem. I'm not scared of needles. When do I get my money?"

"We'll work that out as soon as I decide what tests you'd be suitable for. Here, sign this release form." Weston handed the foul-smelling man a consent form and a pen. He took back the paper signed with big print letters, pulled on latex gloves and holding his breath, took several swab samples from the man's mouth. "Roll up your sleeve, please." He scrubbed the man's dirty arm with several alcohol wipes until a clean spot appeared and collected a blood sample. After he had labeled and put away the samples, he started his questioning.

"Mr. Meyer, are you a member of the Missoula pack?"

"I'm not really supposed to talk about pack."

"Do you want your money? Because the tests I do require you to answer my questions."

"Well, okay. Yeah, I'm pack, but I don't have much to do with them, and they don't have much to do with me."

"You don't spend time with the pack?"

"No, not since the old Alpha died. Lawson was a good man. Always took care of me, gave me jobs to do to earn a little money, not like that Milton."

"And is Milton the Alpha of the pack now?" Weston asked, typing in all that the man said.

"Yeah. He's a rock-hard bastard, that Milton. Came in and took over, and he don't much want me around. I guess I ain't good enough for 'em."

This was going nowhere. At least Weston's nose had become accustomed to the smell. "Tell me, Otis, do you know anything about the pack down in Laramie, like any of its members?"

"No, I don't know nothing about them 'cept I hear they've got it pretty good. Got a big ranch to run on, and the Alpha treats 'em good, gives them jobs and all. Matter of fact, I heard a couple of our boys are down on that ranch right now. I still got a few friends in the pack. They tell me stuff. They said a pretty female from Laramie came up here, and Milton sent a couple of boys down there."

"A Laramie female is here in Missoula now?"

"That's what I hear. I ain't seen her or nothing."

"Do you think you could find out about her? I'd be very interested," said Weston. "I could pay more."

"Milton wouldn't like me snooping around." Otis shook his head over and over like he was trying to talk himself out of something.

"Mr. Meyers...Mr. Meyers." Weston paused in his typing. "If you could get me information about this female who's here in Missoula or the Laramie pack, I could ask for some extra payment for you." He pulled out his wallet and took out a twenty-dollar bill and flashed it at Otis. "I'm only going to be in town for two days, so this has to be soon. Do you understand?"

"Yeah. You want me to find out about the girl," Otis said, his eyes glued to the money Weston was holding.

"Okay. Here's twenty for today, and here's my card with my phone number. I want you to call me tomorrow morning and let me know what you found out. There'll be more money if you have something useful to tell me." Weston knew that as soon as Otis left, he'd head for the nearest bar and drink up the twenty, but, hopefully, he'd remember there was more money where that came from.

chapter eleven

Weston woke to his phone buzzing. He fumbled for it and found his glasses. The number read *Unknown.* "Hello."

"Is this Dr. Weston?"

"It is. Who is this?"

"I heard you were interested in a certain young woman from Laramie." The voice was smooth and deep, not Otis's scratchy voice.

"I'm not sure what you're referring to," Weston said, half excited and half frightened by the tone of the voice on the phone.

"I think you know exactly what I'm referring to. Otis told me you were asking. I have some information you would be interested in."

Weston just waited.

"I'd like to meet."

"I can meet you at the Skaggs Building on campus. Do you know where that is?"

"No. I'm not going to the campus. I'd rather meet somewhere

public. There's a deli and market just across the river from campus. Be there at 10:30." He gave Weston the name of the deli and the address.

"Who is this?" Weston demanded.

"It's Milton Simmons." The call ended.

Holy shit. Milton, the Missoula Alpha. Weston didn't know whether to jump up and down or be terrified. He considered that it could be some kind of trap, but it could be much, much more. He showered and dressed quickly and called a cab.

The market looked safe enough. Weston had been picturing someplace out of *The Godfather*, a dark restaurant filled with Milton and his Werve muscle, but it was light and open and fairly busy. He noticed there was a meat market featuring local beef. Appropriate for a Werve meeting, he thought.

It was easy to spot Milton. He and the two goons flanking him were the largest men in the store. Weston approached with more than a little trepidation. "Mr. Simmons," he said and held out his hand.

The older man made no motion to shake Weston's hand. He just pointed to the small bistro chair opposite him, so Weston quickly sat.

"I'll get right to it," Milton said, producing the card Weston had given Otis, now crumpled and stained with something dark that looked like blood. "I heard you were asking about the Laramie pack. That's something we don't generally talk about with strangers, but I have an interest in your research, and I don't have any love for the Laramie bunch, so we might be able to come to a deal.

"I had you checked out. You were on the research team in Seattle that developed the artificial mating hormone. Now that interests me. I have an unfortunate couple in my pack who are having trouble establishing their mating bond. If I could get hold of some of that hormone, I'm sure it would help them out."

Weston paused. "I don't have access to that particular formula."

"Then we have nothing to talk about." Milton pushed away from the table.

"Wait. Please. I could maybe request a sample."

Milton settled back in his chair. "That's good. If you can have it overnighted, we could talk tomorrow."

"I'll need some indication of what you can give me." Weston was sweating now. Dealing out a restricted test drug could ruin him, but Milton was dangling a pretty big carrot in front of him.

"I can give you whatever you want to know about the Laramie pack. I have someone inside the pack."

"What about the Laramie female who's here in Missoula? I'd like to talk to her before I leave."

"I don't know what Otis told you, but there aren't any Laramie pack members here." Milton rose from the table. "I'll call you tomorrow morning. If you have the hormone for me, we'll talk."

Weston paced his motel room. He'd called Dr. Chandler's old lab at the University of Washington in Seattle and ordered a sample of the mating hormone they'd developed, explaining that she wanted to do some further analysis. He'd had to justify his motel address, but he bluffed it by saying he was doing some fieldwork.

He knew he had stepped over the line, but it could pay off big. His phone rang minutes after the courier left. "I'm assuming you have it," said Milton.

"I do. And now I need my information," said Weston. "Where do you want to meet?"

"Come outside. I'm in the parking lot."

Weston didn't know the protocol for making an illegal deal. Did he take the stuff with him or stash it? He decided to take it in his briefcase. He really didn't want Milton or one of his Werves coming back to his room with him.

When he exited the motel, the rear door of a black Escalade swung open. Weston peered into the dark interior. The middle row of seats had been removed, leaving only Milton sitting in the back seat. Weston climbed in, and even in the relative openness of the huge SUV, he felt uncomfortably close to the Werve Alpha.

Milton made no move to start the conversation, so Weston began. "Okay, I got what you asked, but first you've got to give me the information I need."

"That's not a problem. Here's a phone number. My man in Laramie is named Ray. He lives out at the Winter ranch. You know Jim Winter, right?"

"Yes, the Alpha. I haven't met him, but my colleague has. I believe she's been out to the ranch."

"Well, you call Ray. I told him to tell you anything you wanted to know."

"That's all you have for me? A phone number of someone I've never met. I'm risking my whole career for this. How do I even know he'll talk to me?"

"He'll talk to you. I'm his Alpha, and I told him to cooperate fully, and so he will. He has full access to the ranch and has met a lot of the pack members. What do you want to know?"

"I want to interview some pack members, get medical and family histories, and take DNA samples."

"Perfect. Ray can point you to folks who'd be willing to talk. Not everybody in the pack is in love with Jim Winter. Now, the hormone?"

Weston pulled out the vial. "This stuff is very powerful. You administer it orally, to the female only. Just one dose. You can mix it with water or food if you want. It will take effect almost immediately. In our clinical trials, it performed very well. The female went into a strong mating heat, and in the resulting mating process, it facilitated a very strong mating bond between the partners. You know, of course, that the bond is irreversible?"

Milton raised an eyebrow at the flustered scientist.

"Of course you know that." Weston was dripping in sweat. His hands trembled as he handed over the vial. "That's it then. I'm free to go?"

Amused, Milton said, "Yes, you're free to go." As Weston fumbled with the door handle, he added, "Dr. Weston, do I even need to say that this never happened?"

The threat was clear. "No," Weston said. "It never happened."

OVER THE NEXT few weeks, Jim and Crystal fell into an easy relationship. Crystal felt like things were going well between them, but they'd definitely entered "the friend zone." They got together once or twice a week for coffee if he had to come into town. Sometimes she'd call and invite him for dinner and a movie on DVD, but he didn't initiate any kind of intimacy beyond a kiss on the cheek or a peck on the lips. When she tried for more, he stopped her. He had introduced her to Maggie, and she and Maggie had gotten together once. Maggie had mentioned that her sister-in-law, Sissy, and Jim were very close, but that Sissy was away for a while. Maggie kept it light and conversational, but there was a hint of warning in the woman's voice.

Crystal considered bringing up Sissy to Jim, but so far he had shied away from any conversations that went much beyond the weather or what had happened the previous day. It seemed like her plan to get Jim to trust her and let her close to the pack was doomed to failure.

On the other hand, she was busier than ever in the lab. Weston had worked a miracle in Missoula. That Werve he'd gone to interview had given him all kinds of information about the Laramie pack. Apparently in the pack, not all Werves were created equal. Weston's contact had pointed him toward a small group of pack members who lived in campers and trailers outside of town and who apparently kept to the fringes of the pack. Some of them were more open to talking, especially when the talk was accompanied by money.

They now had a small pool of subjects to interview and test, and they were getting some usable data, but much to her disappointment, the Laramie subjects absolutely refused to talk about their Alpha.

AS THE FULL moon approached, Jim became more and more preoccupied with Sissy. He checked in with Maggie often for news about the younger woman, who called at least once a week and emailed frequently.

Maggie worried that she was being too clingy, but Jim was glad she was keeping in close contact. Not seeing Sissy regularly and not knowing what was going on in Missoula was killing him, but Maggie seemed satisfied.

Jim was concerned about Sissy's first full moon run with the new pack and knew that Maggie was as well, but neither of them wanted to worry the other.

The day of the run, Maggie came out early, as usual. She seemed fine, keeping busy with the preparations, but Jim sensed that something was wrong, and when he came to take her to the pack circle, she broke down.

"Oh, Jim, I'm so afraid for her," Maggie whispered. "I just

can't imagine it. I've never been away from the pack during the full moon, but I'd be terrified."

Jim pulled her close. He was terrified for Sissy, too, but he didn't want to make Maggie feel worse. "It'll be all right. Lucas and I both had to face that when we went off to the Army. It's weird running with a new pack, but she'll do great. She hasn't said anything to make you worry, has she?"

"No." Maggie sniffled. "She sounds happy. I just feel this— ominous weight."

"Do you want me to call her?"

"No, I'm sure she's getting ready for the run. I don't want to upset her. She'd tell me if there was a problem."

Jim wasn't so sure about that, but he hoped Sissy wouldn't let her pride get in the way of her safety. He led Maggie to their places, and they began the run as usual. Everything went smoothly, certainly better than the last few moons, but it was lonely for both of them.

SISSY WAS ON edge the day of the full moon. Shari had been babbling on about the joys of finding her mate. She and Wade were going to ask Milton to allow their mating. If he agreed, they'd begin arrangements for their mating ceremony. Wade and Jackson were coming by later to take them to the pack lodge.

Jackson—Jax—had been coming around a lot. The first week he'd dropped by almost every night. It was logical as he and Wade were good friends, but he'd made it clear he wanted to get closer to Sissy. When they were all together, he wasn't bad, but whenever he got her alone, he got pushy. She was getting tired of it.

The first weekend after she arrived, they'd taken their trucks out to the hills and met up with a bunch of young folks from the pack. Some of the guys had brought heavy-duty jeeps for some extreme hill-climbing. It was exciting to watch the jeeps creep up the boulder-strewn crevices, and Sissy enjoyed meeting everybody. When the sun went down, they built a bonfire and broke out hot dogs and beer.

Jax had stayed close to her all day, but once night fell, it became clear he was staking a claim. He'd drape his arm around her. She'd just as quickly shake it off. When it got chilly, she went back to the truck to get her jacket, and he followed her. He backed her against the truck and boxed her in to nuzzle her neck.

"You smell great," he said. "I bet you taste great, too. Let's go somewhere I can check that out."

Sissy had to admit his body felt good against hers. He was broad and muscular, only slightly taller than her. They fit together well.

She'd been thinking a lot about how she was going to establish herself with the new pack. At home, she'd asserted her dominance since childhood, and over time she'd scared off every male her age in the pack. And where had that left her? Alone and a virgin at the age of twenty-four. Now she had a chance at a new start. She'd never be a doormat, but maybe she could bend a little.

Jax pressed his hips against her, and she felt his erection between them. He held her chin and slid his lips over hers. At his insistence, she opened her mouth, warming to his kiss. Jax nudged his knee between hers to open her stance, and he pulled her hips forward so she rode his hard thigh.

Sissy moaned a little as the seam of her tight jeans caught her in just the right place, and she rocked against him. That was all the encouragement Jax needed. He shoved up her shirt and yanked open the button of her jeans.

His actions snapped her out of her sensual reverie. "Stop it,

Jax," she said, pushing at his chest.

"Oh, baby, come on," he urged, trying to slip his hand inside her jeans.

"I said stop."

In response, Jax pinned her to the truck as he dove in for a rough kiss.

"Get off of me." Sissy grabbed him by the shoulders and brought her knee up as hard as she could.

"Oow!" he howled. "What the hell?"

"If I tell you to stop, you stop. And don't call me 'baby.'" Sissy grabbed her jacket and headed back to the bonfire. She heard his truck peel out of the parking area behind her.

When she got back to the group, Shari looked puzzled. "Where's Jax?"

"He took off. I guess you're stuck with me."

Once classes started, Sissy didn't have much free time. If Jax stopped by after work, she'd excuse herself to her bedroom to do homework. She only went out when there was a group, and she didn't let herself get caught alone with Jax.

Now that the full moon had arrived, she felt nervous. At home she knew the routine, but she didn't know what to expect from the new pack. Shari had told her there'd be a pack meeting before the run.

The guys arrived in late afternoon and they all headed out. The others were high-spirited, obviously feeling the pull of the rising moon, but Sissy was quiet as they drove out of town and into the forest.

The lodge was a large, two-story log cabin style building set back into the mountainside. There was a covered porch across the front of the lodge with thick fieldstone columns. Broad steps ran between fieldstone abutments that led down to a clearing where the pack was gathering for the meeting.

Just as the sun set, Milton walked out of the lodge and stood on the end of one of the stone piers. Everyone gathered around in a wide semi-circle. He motioned for Sissy to join him. He put his arm around her, and Jax came up behind her, making her feel trapped.

Milton smiled and addressed the pack. "Some of you have already met our newest member. This is Sissy from the Laramie pack in Wyoming. She's under my protection. I want you to make her feel welcome."

There was applause. She greeted people she'd met before and was introduced to new ones. After that, she walked down the steps, Jax beside her, while Milton asked for any other business.

Shari and Wade came forward. Wade asked for permission to claim Shari as his mate. There was a long pause while Milton considered their request. Wade and Shari exchanged looks. Finally, the pack leader asked, "Who will stand guardian for this couple?"

Jax came forward. "I will."

"Are you prepared to protect and support Shari and Wade and any children they may have?"

"I am."

"Then I agree to this mating. It is good to strengthen and increase the pack, and I think Shari and Wade will bring strong new lives to us."

Again, there was applause as Shari and Wade walked back into the circle. "Does anyone else have business for the pack?"

There was some shuffling, then a man stepped forward. He was tall and thin, in his mid-fifties, a beta. "I have some business." A woman, likely his wife, started after him, but some of the others held her back.

"What is it, Harris?" Milton asked.

"You know what the problem is. You can't just claim our property for the pack."

"I can do whatever I think is best for the pack."

"What's best for *you*."

Without a word, Milton flew off the porch, partially shifting in mid-air, and slashed his claws across the other man's face, cutting deep grooves that welled with blood. He took his unresisting opponent down to the ground and knelt on his chest as he sank his claws into Harris's neck. The man's wife screamed for help, but no one came forward. Jax, Wade, and a few others stepped up to stand at Milton's back, but no one challenged him.

Milton retracted his claws, and stood with his hands still dripping with blood. The scent of the blood provoked some of the members to change and howls filled the air. "Does anyone else have a problem?" Milton bellowed as he changed into a huge black wolf. He howled and bounded off into the woods, most of the pack following him.

Sissy stood frozen, shocked by the sudden violence. She watched the fallen man's wife and an older couple rush to help him. She started forward when Jax stepped in front of her. "No, leave it. They'll see to him."

The moon, the blood, and the violence were pulling hard at her. She looked around for Shari, but she and most of the others were already gone. She needed to shift. The others had just dropped their clothes where they stood and changed, so she stripped self-consciously, aware of Jax's very human eyes watching her.

As soon as she shifted, she took off, hoping to leave Jax behind, but he quickly caught up and ran by her side. He was a black wolf like his father, and he ran smoothly amid the thick trees.

It felt good to run after the tense scene at the lodge. The terrain was much rougher than what she was used to, and she let Jax take the lead.

The heavy forest hid the others from view. Howls came from several directions, immediately followed by the resonating sounds of a hunt. She entered a clearing and saw a group of wolves had just taken down a large deer. Moonlight bathed the meadow, as the larger wolves tore into the still-struggling buck while others circled around, snarling and snapping.

The sounds and smells stirred a primal response in Sissy. Jax nudged her roughly to join the kill, but she shook him off, resisting the pull of her instincts.

She turned and had only taken a few steps when she ran into another primal scene. In front of her, two wolves were having sex. It took a second to realize that the male was Milton. His massive black form topped a sleek golden wolf—not Betty, Sissy was pretty sure. His teeth were buried in the female's neck, and he had forced her head and shoulders to the ground.

Sissy stood transfixed, unable to turn away. She'd heard whispers of Weres who had sex while in animal form, but at least in her old pack, it was taboo. Surrendering to the moon's pull was a celebration of their dual nature, but she'd always been taught the importance of retaining your humanity and not giving over completely to the animal side. In all of her runs, she'd never seen any Weres having sex, and she assumed that if any did, they wouldn't do it right out in the open.

She became aware that Jax was standing close, shoulder to flank, and when he nuzzled her head, she took off in a flat-out sprint. She didn't want to deal with him. She dodged through the trees, trying to get her bearings, but she hadn't been paying much attention to where she was going. She'd followed Jax through the woods, and now she was alone in unfamiliar territory. Then, Jax crashed through the brush just behind her. She put on another burst of speed, not knowing whether she was headed toward the lodge or away from it.

Suddenly, the woods opened into a small clearing. She darted to cross it when out of the side of her eye, she saw Jax coming toward her. He lunged into the air and hit her side just behind the shoulders. They rolled together and Jax came up on top of her. Sissy tried to get to her feet, but he had her pinned on her back. He growled and snapped at her, but she evaded his jaws, wiggling further under him until he couldn't reach her without letting her up. From underneath, she clamped down on his foreleg. He tried to snap at her muzzle, but he couldn't reach, and she wouldn't release her grip. Finally, he twisted enough for her to break free, but not without leaving a big chunk of his skin and fur behind.

She sprung to her feet and took a defensive stance, but rather than pursuing the fight, Jax limped away.

He disappeared into the woods, and she was left standing alone, more than a little shaken by the whole night. She was reluctant to follow him, as she had no idea how to get back to the lodge. She could hear a few scattered howls in the distance, but the mountain valley muffled the direction. Scents of wolves were all around but no clear paths. She followed the only scent trail she could recognize, Jax's.

They were exhausted, but he was hurt, so she caught up to him quickly. She kept her distance, watching him warily. Jax stopped a few times to lick his wounded leg. Sissy saw that he was bleeding heavily. She must have gotten her teeth into more than skin.

They made their way back slowly. She could smell the cars parked near the lodge. When they emerged from the woods, Jax limped to the spot where they'd dropped their clothes. He shifted back to human form and flopped onto the ground, holding his arm. The shift would speed the healing, but he still had a large, bloody gash.

Sissy shifted and quickly pulled on her jeans and zipped up her hoodie. She held her T-shirt out to Jax. "Here, wrap your arm in this."

"What the hell were you doing? Did you think I was going to rape you?"

"Were you?"

"Shit, here comes my father." Jax looked down at the ground when his father walked up. Sissy stood her ground and kept her eyes on Milton.

"Did she do this to you?" Neither Jax nor Sissy answered. "I guess my son's too much of a pussy to handle a little girl like you." Milton looked her up and down then stalked off.

"Great, just fucking great," Jax muttered. Sissy tried to give him a hand up, but he waved her off, leaving her to wait next to his truck. Staggering, he grabbed his clothes and put them on with one hand. He wrenched open the passenger side door of the dual cab truck, where Shari and Wade were waiting in the back seat, and yelled at Wade, "You drive."

No one spoke on the drive home. When they arrived at the girls' apartment, Wade pulled up with the engine running while the girls got out, then peeled out on smoking tires before they were even inside. Shari went straight to her room without saying a word.

Sissy figured that everybody must be mad at her. She did feel bad for embarrassing Jax in front of his dad, but he had it coming. She had no doubt that he'd wanted to have sex with her, but he seemed surprised she'd thought he might rape her.

Sissy had to apologize to Shari. This had been an important day for Shari and Wade, and she hated that it had ended the way it did. When she approached Shari's door, Sissy heard her talking, presumably to Wade, so she went to the kitchen for ice cream. Maybe a peace offering of Ben & Jerry's might help to smooth things over.

When she came back to Shari's door, she heard the other girl crying. Sissy knocked on the door and opened it a crack. "Shari, I'm sorry about tonight. Can I come in?"

chapter twelve

Shari, who was sitting on her bed, sniffed and nodded. Sissy came in and perched on the edge of the bed. "Cherry Garcia or Chunky Monkey?" She held out the pints and two spoons. Shari shook her head.

"Look, I'm sorry if I messed up, but I didn't know what to expect," Sissy said. "Nobody told me we were going to have a big gory dominance show then go out and fuck like dogs."

Shari wailed like she'd been hit, then buried her face in her pillow and sobbed.

"Don't cry." Sissy leaned over to smooth Shari's thick blonde hair. The thought suddenly hit her. "Oh my God, the gold wolf, that was you."

Shari wailed even louder.

"Oh, honey, I'm so sorry. I didn't mean... Is that why Wade is angry? Did Milton force you?"

"It's not like that."

"I don't understand. I mean, I thought you were so happy

being with Wade."

"I am. I love him, but Milton is the Alpha. He does this sometimes, takes first rights before you're mated. Wade didn't think he'd do it with me because he likes Wade. Wade will get over it, I suppose. I mean, he knows it's not my fault."

Sissy was furious. "What does Milton think this is, the Middle Ages? It's unbelievable. I heard that other packs were rougher, you know, more traditional, but this is ridiculous. Is this always the custom here?"

"I don't know. My mom told me I should expect it. I don't think our old Alpha did stuff like this, but Milton says he was old and weak, that he let the pack get out of control. That's why Milton came here. He said he was sent by the High Council, or something like that, to take over and get our pack back in shape."

"I've never heard of any High Council."

"Well, maybe I'm getting it wrong. I don't remember exactly." Shari reached for the ice cream. "I guess Jax is pretty pissed."

"Yeah, I didn't know what was happening. I saw Milton—" Sissy winced, sorry she'd mentioned that again— "and then Jax was on me, and I freaked out. I thought he was trying to rape me, so I bit him."

"I don't think he'd do that. He's not like his father. He can be a butthead sometimes, but he's not mean. Milton's always treating him like shit, but then he expects everybody else to act like Jax is the prince of the world. Jax is just messed up."

"Yeah, I get that. Are you going to be all right?"

"I'm okay. I just want Wade to understand. They're out getting drunk right now, so they'll probably be over it tomorrow."

"I hope so. You get some sleep." Sissy tucked in the other girl and picked up the cartons of melting ice cream. She wasn't sure she could take this as matter-of-factly as Shari was. Sissy thought she should probably call Jim and let him know what was going on, but she also knew he'd come running up there and take her home. And Maggie would freak out.

She decided to keep this to herself for now. She supposed that every pack was different, and she'd just been sheltered. This was only her first run with the Missoula pack. Surely things would get better. Next time she'd be prepared.

At least she was enjoying her classes at the university. She'd made friends with some of her human classmates. She was in a study group with some of them, and she'd gone out for beer and pizza a couple of times. It was an interesting experience having non-Were friends. In Laramie, she knew a lot of humans in town and from school, but all of her close friends belonged to the pack. The pack had always been the heart of her life.

Now she was trying to keep her personal life separate from the pack. The Missoula pack had welcomed her, and most of them had been nice, but she didn't plan on getting attached to them. She'd concentrate on her classes, have fun with her new friends, and keep to herself on the moonlight runs. Neither pack, Laramie nor Missoula, was going to rule her life.

SISSY ENTERED THE student union and looked around. She was supposed to meet a classmate, a human girl named Lynn. She spotted her friend at a table with some other girls. They were all clustered around a laptop. As Sissy approached, Lynn noticed and motioned her over.

She pulled Sissy in and pointed to the screen. "You've got to look at this hunk."

Sissy glanced at the screen. Stunned, she took a closer look. Jim stared out at her from the screen. The girls were looking at a photo of *Jim*. He was naked, and looking good. It was a website called "Fur and Fangs," a shifter fan site. Sissy had seen them before, out of curiosity, but not this one.

Ever since Weres had been outed to the public, there had been a lot of curiosity, especially sexual interest. Rumors abounded about the animal instincts and sexual prowess of shifters, and some Weres had taken advantage of the publicity and become celebrities. There were Werewolf bars in some cities and even Werewolf strippers and calendar models. Sissy knew some of them appeared on these websites, but she couldn't believe Jim would do anything like that. Maggie and most of the pack were vocal about the potential dangers of trading in on the fact that you were a Werewolf.

"Yeah, he's quite a stud," Sissy said, straightening, "but we'd better go over our notes before class starts."

"You've got a lot more self-control than I do if you can look at that and still think of chemistry."

I am thinking about chemistry, Sissy thought wistfully.

As soon as Sissy got back to her apartment, she went to her computer and pulled up the site. She'd had a hard time paying attention during class. Maybe she was wrong. Perhaps it was someone who looked like Jim. But when the site came up, it was definitely him.

There were several images. In one he was fully dressed on his horse, but two others were nude shots. One showed his perfect butt, and he looked good. He could easily rival those professional calendar models. Sissy was shocked to see a photo of Jim in his wolf form.

She looked around the site some more. He was in a section called "Hot Alphas." It featured Jim and a few others she didn't recognize. Each male was laid out like a centerfold spread with photos and personal information. Under Jim's picture was a caption that read, "Jack: a real western cowboy. He likes to ride hard, and he's good with a rope and a whip. He always puts his brand on what's his, but he's not ready to be tied down to one woman."

Sissy snorted. *I can believe that.*

"Jack's" quote said, "I like a woman who can stand on her own but also knows when to submit. I'm always on top."

"What a crock," Sissy said. Visitors to the site had posted comments on the site, all begging for "Jack's" attention.

One by the screen name "wulfluvr" said, "Fur and boots—a hot combination."

Another had written, "Ooh, Jack, you can tie me up anytime." It was signed "sub4u."

How pathetic. Sissy looked at a few more of the men featured on the site, but the others were all about the same: pictures, fake information and quotes, and lots of comments. The viewers could vote for "Wolf of the Month," and this month, Jim was in the lead.

Her first instinct was to call and tell him about it. But as she continued to check out the site, she realized that the website had been posting pictures of Jim for several months.

How could he not know about this? The pictures were great. They looked almost professional, like he'd posed for them. The more Sissy looked, the madder she got. Obviously there were things he kept from her. Jim liked being top dog, and he never minded when women fell all over him. Maybe the adulation of the pack and all the women of Laramie wasn't enough for him. Maybe he had to flaunt himself on the web. Sissy slammed her laptop shut.

Sissy fumed about the website for a week, even going back to the site, thinking she must have been wrong, but no, there was Jim in all his glory. When Maggie called for their weekly chat, Sissy didn't have much to say. She let Maggie rattle on about local news and gossip, not paying much attention until she realized that most of the news had centered around Jim—Jim did this and Jim did that. He had become the center of their little world—her family, the pack, the ranch. Even hundreds of miles away, she couldn't get away from him.

Sissy interrupted Maggie. "Maybe you don't know everything he does."

There was a pause on the other end. "Sissy, what are you talking about?"

"I just get tired of you singing Jim's praises all the time. You don't know everything about him."

"And you do? What happened? Did you two have a fight? He didn't say anything about talking to you."

"No, I haven't talked to him. He doesn't call. He's probably too busy, what with..." Sissy stopped herself.

"With what?" Maggie demanded. "What aren't you telling me?"

Sissy hadn't intended to tell Maggie, but she knew her sister-in-law would pry it out of her. "I found a website."

"I'm listening."

"And there were pictures of Jim, nude pictures."

"What?"

"It's one of those Werewolf fan sites. Do you know what I mean?"

"Of course, I've heard of them. Sites where humans meet Weres for sex."

"They're not dating sites. They're more like Were porn. Kinda like *Playboy*, with nude pictures and profiles. Anyway, some of the human girls at school were looking at one of the sites, and there were pictures of Jim, nude and as a wolf. They look like they were taken on the ranch."

"And you think he put up those pictures himself?"

"I can't imagine that he doesn't know about them. He seems to be very popular on the site."

"I can't believe it."

"I don't know what to think. The pictures make him look like a male model. A very hunky male model. Maybe somebody offered to take the shots, and he went for it."

"Oh, honey, someone else must have put those pictures up. I have to tell him about it."

"Like I said, I just don't know. Sometimes I think I don't know him very well at all."

"You do know him. He's a good man, and he's been a good friend."

"I know, Mag. Maybe I'm wrong about this."

"Email me the site, and I'll tell Jim. I'll let you know what happens."

"Okay. I'd better go. I've got homework."

Maggie's voice became serious. "Is everything really all right up there? I'm afraid you wouldn't tell me if something was wrong, and I get so worried about you being all alone there."

"I'm not alone. I love my classes, and I'm making friends. Really. I promise I'll tell you if anything happens," she lied. "I love you, and give my love to Jim."

MAGGIE WAS UPSET, but she didn't want to talk about it over the phone. She told Jim she was coming to the ranch. When she arrived, he knew something was wrong.

She said, "There's something you need to see."

She led Jim to his study and sat at his desktop computer. When she pulled up the website, he saw what kind of site it was, and laughed. "Aw, Maggie, don't worry about that. There are lots of those kinds of sites out there."

"Look at this." She clicked on a picture, and it zoomed to fill the screen.

Jim's laugh died in his throat. There he was, standing naked on the Alpha's rock.

chapter thirteen

"Let me see that," he said, taking the mouse from Maggie. He scanned over the other pictures. They'd all been taken either before or at the start of a run, and judging from the backgrounds, they'd been taken in the spring and summer over the last few months. "How did you find this?"

"Sissy found it. Some of the girls at school were looking at the site, and she recognized you."

He navigated through the site, but he didn't find pictures of anyone else from the pack. There was a contact page, but it only gave an email address.

Infuriated, he unlocked a drawer of his desk and took out a small leather-bound address book that contained all the contact information for his pack members. He flipped through until he found who he was looking for.

"Riley, this is Jim. I want you to check out a website for me." Riley was a grad student in software engineering at the university, the pack's computer whiz. Jim gave him the URL of the website, and he could hear Riley clicking the keyboard as he spoke. "I need to know who controls the site, how they get their pictures, and anything else you can find out. And I want those photos off the site. Now."

"Wow, Jim. Is that you? You usually aren't this—"

"Naked? Public? How about angry, because I am angry. I want to know how photos of me got onto this site."

"Anybody could have sent them in. That'll be hard to find, but I'll snoop around and get back to you."

A few days later Riley came out to the ranch. Jim called in Daniel and Clint to also hear what Riley had to say.

"This site is one of several owned by the same company, an outfit out of Nevada that markets all things furry," Riley observed. "They have the sites and also sell calendars and T-shirts and even arrange public appearances. You were set to be Mr. August on the next calendar, by the way, but I let them know a lawsuit would be the least of their worries if they didn't rethink that. They were real disappointed, but I don't think you'll see any more of your pictures on their merchandise. But 'Jack' does have several amateur fan sites that aren't connected with the main site. I can't really do anything about those without legal actions that would probably involve your name. But I did get the company to take down your, uh, Jack's, Facebook page."

"Fuck. How could all this happen without me knowing about it?"

"It's pretty easy. Anybody can put anything up on the Internet, at least until they get caught, and once it's out there, well, it's out there. Fortunately, they didn't have your real name. The fan sites are pretty harmless, and when they see that you're not on the main site any more, they'll probably lose interest.

"But I did find something more serious. There was a linked

ad to an exclusive, fee-based fan site. Let me show you." Riley pulled up a new site and logged in. "The company denies any connection to this other site, but they're probably lying, and I'll keep snooping. Anyway, you have to pay to join that site, so I made up a fake membership and paid with a prepaid credit card. You owe me thirty bucks, by the way. There are more photos, and there are offers to sell more personal information. I tried to buy your information, but they'd already taken it down."

Riley walked them through the site. Some of it was pretty silly stuff. There were sections with tips for attracting Werves and full-moon charts. But there were maps that showed pack areas, including Laramie. There were also member chatrooms, and Riley showed Jim where illegal wolf pheromones were offered for sale. The computer whiz pulled up a chat, and Daniel let out a whistle. "Lookee there, Jim, isn't that your stalker gal?"

Jim recognized a picture of Debby from the bar.

Riley gestured to the screen. "Yeah, I wanted you to see this one. She was bragging about a new experimental pheromone that she got her hands on. It's released through tactile contact so you can target the specific Were you want, or you can touch a bunch of people and see who reacts. It'd make it easier to pick the Werewolves out of the general population."

"That explains a lot of things," Jim said. "I didn't react to Debby until she touched me. This stuff could get a lot of people in trouble, including girls who come looking for big, bad wolves. That could be exactly what they find. I still can't figure how or why she came after me."

"She was probably a fan of 'Jack,' but if she was able to buy information that got her to Laramie, then other people might know and come looking too," said Riley.

Jim clicked through the new site. Some of the photos were

blatantly pornographic, and there were even some sex videos being offered. "Shit, I wasn't in any of these, was I?"

"No, your pictures were just more of the same that was on the other site. I think all they had access to were photos from our runs."

"Which means somebody out here on the ranch took those pictures," Clint said. "It has to be one of the pack, maybe one of the family members who doesn't shift. It's pretty easy to hide a small digital camera, or a cell phone."

"We've got to find out who's taking the pictures and put a stop to it. We should also alert the other packs. Riley, can you get the word out? We should have someone monitoring these sites. We need to know about things like that new pheromone before it bites us in the butt."

"Yeah, most of the packs are linked into a secure wolf information network. There's also our political action committee. They should be looking into the illegal stuff. I'll get on it."

THE FULL MOON night was beautiful, the October air crisp and cold. Moonlight cut sharp shadows and glistened off the frost on the fallen leaves. Sissy was on Jim's mind. This was her favorite time of year to run. Her silver coat would shimmer in the moonlight, just like the frost. He felt her absence like a hole in his heart, and he knew Maggie felt it as well. She ran by his side, and he sensed her sadness pulling at them both.

After the run, Jim took Maggie in his arms and let her cry. She sniffled and wiped her nose. "I'm sorry. I was just missing her so much."

"I know. I felt it. I miss her too, but she'll be back next month for Thanksgiving."

Jim gave Maggie a hug, and she went to help set up the food for those who were staying after the run. Daniel told him they'd caught the photographer, and Jim was anxious to question the culprit.

He met Clint and Daniel by the changing sheds. "Who've we got?"

"Teenage kid, name of Andy Moffett," Clint said. "It wasn't hard to catch him. I placed some of my men around the family area and the pack circle and told them to watch for anyone taking pictures. One of the guys spotted a kid sneaking up on the pack circle just before moonrise. He radioed it in, and I caught him snapping a shot just as you stripped to shift. I took the camera, a pretty nice one, and we kept him in the cell room during the run. I've located his parents too, and they're waiting with him now. The kid hasn't even had his first change yet."

Clint led Jim back to the cell, where the boy's parents were huddled on a bench, their son sitting across from them in a barred cell looking terrified.

In the other cell, Jim noticed that Kenny, the young man who'd gotten in trouble with Adam last month, had shifted back to human form. He was still chained where he'd been held during the run as part of his punishment. His ankles and wrists were bloody from straining against his shackles, specially made to hold a Were. Otherwise, he looked like he'd come through his ordeal in one piece, probably better than the scared kid who had to spend the entire run in a cell with just bars and chains separating him from a raging out-of-control Werewolf.

Jim turned his attention back to the boy and his parents. "What'd you think you were doing, son?"

"I didn't mean to hurt you. I didn't think anybody'd see them." The boy was close to tears. Jim motioned for Clint to release the boy from the cell, and the kid fled to his parents who hugged him but made him stand and face his Alpha.

"This is serious and very dangerous. You've opened me up to a lot of attention. Other than violating my privacy, it doesn't much matter that some girls are ogling my naked body, but there are stalkers out there and crazies—hunters who'd love to bag a big Werewolf and religious fanatics who think we're evil. You could bring down trouble on all of us. Do you understand?"

"I didn't think about that. I was just online in a wolf chat, and I was talking about how I couldn't wait until I could change, and how I'd sneak out of the kids' compound and watch you shift, and some guy offered me good money if I'd take some pictures and send them to him. I didn't give him your real name or anything."

"But you did give him your name, and your address."

"Yeah. He sent me this cool camera. He said my camera wasn't good enough."

"Did you ever think he could find the pack if he knew where you lived?"

"Oh, man. No, I didn't think of that. I wouldn't do anything against you, Jim. I think you're awesome. So do all of my friends. I can't wait until I'm old enough and can shift and be like you."

Jim wished he could smile, but this was the second kid in as many months who'd gotten in trouble because he hadn't been paying attention to what was going on in the pack. He didn't even know this kid, and he barely recognized the parents.

He addressed Andy's parents. "Did you know about any of this?"

"No, sir," the father answered, standing with his eyes lowered. "We didn't have any idea, but you can be sure I'll give back all the money he made, and I'll take any he's spent out of his hide."

"You can give the money to the pack fund. We'll keep the camera," Jim said. "How long until his first shift?"

"Not long. His body's changing. He's been packing on muscle

and sprouting hair. We figure six months, tops."

"Andy, I want you and your friends to come out here to the ranch Saturday. I'm going to start a corps of you young guys. You know what that means?"

"No, sir."

"Well, it's a special unit, like in the Army. You'll have some training, learn what it means to be part of the pack." Jim shot a look to Kenny as he hung in his chains, listening to every word.

They locked gazes. "I have a young man in mind to lead it," Jim said, nodding toward the prisoner. Kenny grinned back, looking as happy as anyone who was naked and chained to the floor could be.

Jim nodded, sure that he'd made a good choice. Kenny was young, but he'd shown courage and respect, two qualities Jim wanted to impart to the young members of his pack. "Somebody let Kenny loose and treat his wounds," he said, and turned to Andy's family. "I'll leave Andy's punishment up to you."

SISSY DREADED THE full moon, but this time she'd be on her guard. She rode out to the lodge with Shari and Wade. She hadn't seen Jax except for a few times when he'd come over with Wade to pick up Shari. Hopefully, he'd lost interest in her.

She kept to herself as they waited for moonrise when Milton appeared on the lodge steps like a demigod. He greeted them and asked if anyone had any business to bring before the pack. This time no one stepped forward. Milton led with a howl, and they shifted and began the run.

She had already decided that she'd keep some distance from the pack and not stray too far from the lodge. Her wolf wanted to run, but she kept to a slow pace, keeping tabs on her location so she didn't get lost again.

She scented the crisp air, the rotting mulch on the forest floor, and the mixed smells of the wolves who'd run ahead of her. She heard a soft scuffling in the underbrush, probably a ground squirrel or vole, and stopped to investigate. A snack might be good, even though the odds of catching a little critter weren't good. Then she heard another sound behind her, and caught a familiar scent. Jackson. She turned to face him and widened her stance, ready to fight if necessary. He approached her slowly, head and tail relaxed, not showing any signs of aggression, and stopped about twenty feet away.

He didn't make any motion to come closer, but he whimpered, a vocal question. It wasn't threatening, but she didn't feel like dealing with him. He'd ignored her for the past weeks in human form, but now he wanted to be friendly in wolf form. She tensed to spring and growled her answer. Jax tossed his head and ran away, off into the trees.

That was easy. Sissy trotted along, allowing herself to enjoy her wolf. It was a beautiful night with an absolutely clear sky, probably the last one before the snows. She could hear most of the pack far in the distance now. She turned to head back toward the lodge. Some of the pack had already returned. She'd heard a small group pass her by. The older folks usually didn't run far, just enough to shake off the pull of the moon, and she didn't mind getting back early and joining them.

She heard more coming up behind her off to one side, and she stopped to let them pass, but they stopped, too. A little spooked, she started up again, and so did they, getting closer. The fur on the back of her neck prickled, but they pulled away to the side and ran past. She caught a glimpse of two large gray wolves through the trees.

It was probably nothing, just more of the pack returning, but she was ready to be finished with this run. Nervous, she jumped at shadows and sounds. She missed having Jim and Maggie beside her and knowing her dad and friends were close by. She just wanted to get back to the lodge, so she broke into a run—and then suddenly they were directly in front of her.

Sissy skidded to a stop. She could see them clearly now, and she didn't recognize either of them, but then she didn't know most of this pack in their wolf form yet. Warily, she watched them, readying herself to attack or run. One of them took off to her right and circled behind her. He closed in, forcing her toward the wolf in front.

She tried to cut off to the side, but then they were on her. One tried to throw himself on her back, but she twisted and knocked him off. The other clamped down on her neck with his powerful jaws. He forced her head to the ground while the other one came over her from behind. She tried to gain her footing and throw him off, but he was too heavy.

Then something hit them from the side and bowled them all over. Sissy came up to see Milton's huge black form standing between her and her attackers. His teeth bared, he snarled and snapped at the gray wolves, and they backed away, then took off running.

Milton changed back to human and faced her. "Shift," he ordered.

Frightened and naked with the large man, Sissy obeyed.

"You really are more trouble than you're worth. Where's Jackson?"

"I don't know. I didn't want him riding shotgun on me, so I shooed him off."

Milton moved closer to her, but she stood her ground. "I told him to stay near you. I'd hoped you two would hit it off. You'd be a good mate for him. He needs someone strong, and he needs the dominant genes for his children. I made a mistake by marrying a weak woman who bore me a weak son, but you could make up for that, turn him into what he needs to be."

"I don't have any intention of mating with Jackson, or anyone else. I'm just here to go to school, and then I'll be out of your hair."

"It's not going to be that easy. You need somebody to protect you. If you were with Jackson, you'd be under my protection. No one would dare touch you."

"I can take care of myself," she said, not feeling as confident as she hoped she sounded.

"Like you were taking care of yourself a few minutes ago?"

She lifted her chin high. "I would have hurt them."

"Yeah," he snorted, "you would have hurt them, then they would have had you, both of them. Think about that. Jackson's not so bad, and I think you could use a friend." Milton shifted back into wolf form and trotted off, leaving her shivering in human form and alone.

Sissy shifted back and cautiously made her way back to the lodge. She had to wait on Shari and Wade. Jax came in from the run, but he ignored her and left in his truck.

She knew she was in over her head and should call and tell Jim, but she couldn't bring herself to do it. He'd order her home. She loved the graduate program, and she liked being on her own. It was good to finally feel like an adult. Next month was Thanksgiving, and she'd be home for the run. After that, she'd have almost another month to the end of the semester to figure out what she was going to do.

Sissy didn't give the incident much thought for the next few weeks. She had some big projects that she wanted to finish up before she left to go home. But a few days before the Thanksgiving break, she was surprised when Milton and Wade showed up at her apartment. Milton greeted Shari with a kiss on the cheek and said, "I need to talk to Sissy." The pretty blonde took the hint and left with Wade.

Milton took off his hat and coat and motioned for Sissy to sit across from him. "How's school going? Shari tells me you spend a lot of time studying."

"School's fine," Sissy answered tersely. She didn't see the point of going into detail, because that was clearly not why they were there.

"Are you planning to come back to Missoula after Thanksgiving?"

"Of course," Sissy said, wondering what this was leading up to. "The semester doesn't end until almost Christmas, and then I have a year and a half before I finish the coursework for my master's."

"Have you given any thought to what we talked about?"

Ah. She should have guessed. "Not much. Seriously, I'm not interested in taking a mate and settling down."

"Well, I wanted to talk to you before you go back to Laramie. I think you've been a little shocked by some of the things you've seen since you've been here." He waited for her to comment, but she didn't.

Milton continued. "You know that every pack is different. This pack is different from the one I was raised in. It takes a while to adjust to new surroundings and new ways, but underneath it all, Werewolves are pretty much the same wherever you go. We run, we hunt, we fight, and we fuck. You've grown up in the Laramie pack under Jim's wing. He and your dad sheltered you, maybe too much."

Milton was right. They had sheltered her and treated her like a child.

"Do you think none of this stuff goes on with your pack? We're not humans. We play rough. It's in our nature. We live by our senses. Blood and sex. It's a part of us. If you haven't seen it before, it's because Jim hid it from you.

"Jim and I talked about this that night at my house when we went outside. He wanted me to promise to shield you. He said you weren't ready for the darker side of pack life. I told him I wouldn't do it. I could see you were plenty old enough to know what was going on."

Sissy took a deep breath. She wished Jim could have given her a heads-up. "He didn't mention it to me."

"I bet he didn't. Now, if you don't like being treated like the adult you are, you'd better stay in Laramie. And that's exactly what's going to happen if you go telling tales to him. He'll see to it that you don't come back. He loves you, darlin', but he isn't ready for you to grow up, and by letting you go, he said pretty clearly that he wasn't going to claim you himself. I think you know that, and that's why you're here."

Milton leaned forward and took Sissy's hands between his. "The other night I said I wouldn't protect you, but I was just angry. I won't let any harm come to you. I'll step in if need be, but I know you can look after yourself."

And with that, Milton rose, pulling Sissy to her feet with him. She walked him to the door. "You have a good holiday, visit with your friends, and then come on back here to us." Milton gave her a peck on the cheek. "You don't want to miss Shari's mating ceremony, do you?"

chapter fourteen

Sissy flew back to Laramie after her last class on Wednesday. Daniel and Maggie picked her up. It was great to see them, and she and Maggie stayed up late talking. Maggie gave Sissy all the pack news, and Sissy told her all about school and Missoula, and a little about the pack there. She brought photos of her apartment and her new friends.

Maggie didn't mention Jim, so Sissy finally asked.

"Oh, he's doing fine, keeping busy," Maggie said. "I don't see a lot of him."

"Is he seeing anyone?" Sissy had to ask.

"He's become friends with that scientist from the university. I've met her. She's very nice, and they enjoy each other's company, but he's not serious. You know Jim."

Yeah, I know Jim.

On Thanksgiving morning, Sissy woke up to the mixed smells of bacon and pumpkin pie. She shuffled into the kitchen, and Maggie motioned her to sit at the kitchen table and served her a big breakfast. "Eat up," the older woman said. "We're going out to the ranch in a little while, and I'll finish cooking out there."

That was the way, every year. "What's on the menu?" Sissy asked. "Anything different?"

"The guys are taking care of the meat. They're going to barbecue some elk and venison, and I think they're going to try to fry the turkey this year. I'm in charge of the rest. I just hope they don't burn the ranch down."

Sissy helped her load all the food into the truck. "I don't know why you have to do this every year," Sissy said. "Jim has a cook."

"A ranch house cook. They live on eggs and chili. Anyway, I like doing this. We're all family, but we don't get to sit around a table very often. Everybody's always so busy before the runs. I look forward to this." Maggie took Sissy's face between her hands. "And I'm thankful this year to have you back with us, if only for a few days."

Sissy kissed the shorter woman on the forehead. "I've missed you too, Mag."

When they arrived at the ranch, some of the wranglers helped Maggie carry all the food into the house, giving Sissy a chance to walk around. It had only been a few months, but so much had happened. It felt good to be home, but she felt different.

The ranch was a hive of activity. Jim always hosted a big spread for the hands and their families and any of the pack who wanted to come. The barbecue pits were fired up, and mouth-watering smells carried through the cold air. One of the big outbuildings, a meeting hall, had been cleaned and the kids decorated the long tables with paper turkeys colored with crayons. Not that long ago, Sissy had been one of those kids.

But she wasn't a kid anymore.

She wandered into the main house through the kitchen. The family would eat in the house. Maggie stood in the kitchen, cooking with Sissy's grandmother and her aunt. She greeted them and gave them a hug and a kiss, but she escaped apron duty by saying she wanted to go find her dad and grandpa.

As she entered the great room, the first person she saw was Jim. He was surrounded by men, but he stood apart from them by his physical presence.

Her breath caught in her chest. She hadn't expected seeing him to hit her as hard as it did. She wanted to be mad at him. She *was* mad at him for still trying to shelter her even when he was letting her go. Milton's revelations had stung. He was able to be straight with her. Why couldn't Jim? But it didn't matter how angry she got. She'd loved Jim for so long, she didn't know how to stop.

Jim became aware that she was in the room. He turned toward her and everything else dropped away except the two of them. They'd always had that connection.

The moment was broken when the other men spotted her. Daniel and her granddad surrounded her with big hugs. Jim hung back. She fielded lots of questions about school and Missoula. Daniel wanted to know details about Milton and the pack, but she put him off.

Jim waited until all the others had greeted her. He folded her in his arms. "I've missed you so much, baby doll."

"Have you?" She pulled herself from his arms, not ready to forgive him. "I haven't heard from you since you dropped me off in Missoula." Even as she said it, she wondered why she always had to fight him. She couldn't ever just let it be easy between them.

Her grandmother came in from the kitchen and told Daniel that everything was ready, and he should bring in the meat. Suddenly, everyone was in motion. Sissy and Maggie carried steaming bowls of vegetables—mashed potatoes, sweet potatoes, corn, squash, and green beans. Others brought out dressing, cranberry sauce, hot rolls and butter. The long table began to fill up, and the sideboard was jammed with dishes.

Maggie and her sister rolled out a cart with their beautifully roasted turkey just as Daniel arrived with a glistening deep-fried bird. The men followed him bearing roasts and sausages like trophies of their prowess. Everyone laughed at the procession, but you could never have too much meat at a table full of Werewolves.

Finally, everybody found their seats. As usual, Sissy and Maggie were on either side of Jim, and Daniel sat at the other end. In between were Sissy's grandparents, her aunt and uncle, Jim's nephew Clint, and Maggie's family—her parents and her sister and brother-in-law—a few cousins, and a face Sissy didn't recognize. He was a handsome cowboy, about her age, and he looked as though he felt a little out of place.

Jim stood to address them as he usually did. Sissy couldn't help but compare him to Milton, even though there was really no comparison. Other than the fact they were both big commanding men, they were like light and dark, and her heart would always pick Jim over any other.

"We have a lot to be thankful for this year," he began. "The weather was mild, and most folks had a good harvest. We had a good breeding season, and we got a strong bunch of calves. We've had more births than deaths, and we can look forward to at least one mating ceremony this spring.

"Today, we welcome a new member to our table. Trace came to us from Missoula, and he's been working out just fine. Since he doesn't have any family around here, I thought he should share this holiday with us."

Several people around the table said "Welcome" to the young

man, and he blushed a bright red. Sissy watched him with interest, wondering why she hadn't heard of him.

"Most important," Jim continued, "we welcome Sissy back home, if only for a few days." He speared her with his eyes, making her breathing stop for a moment, before he smiled and said, "Let's eat."

Everybody dug in, and the noise level escalated as people visited up and down the table. After seconds and pie and coffee, well-fed folks moved into the great room. Sissy overheard Jim asking Maggie, "Could you pack up a plate for Crystal? She's all alone, and I told her I'd be over later." The human over at the university, Sissy mused.

Jim visited with everyone for a few more minutes, but then he snagged Maggie away from kitchen detail. "Maggie and I are going to go out and say hello to the hands and their families," he announced. "Sissy, do you want to come with us?"

Sissy shook her head. "No. I went out and visited before dinner. I think I'll just stay here."

Maggie came back about an hour later, alone. By then, half of the family was napping in the comfortable leather chairs around the fireplace while the other half was watching football on the big-screen TV.

"Where's Jim?" Daniel asked. He had been dozing off his meal.

"He had to go out," Maggie replied.

"Yeah, I heard. He's taking food to those less fortunate," Sissy said sarcastically, the words tripping over her tongue almost against her will. She decided to clear her head. She grabbed her jacket and stepped out on the long porch. Some of the wranglers had a football game of their own going in the yard, and there were already some scrapes and bloody noses amid the good-natured scuffling.

She felt Trace come up beside her. "I guess I should be out there," he said, nodding to the disorganized fracas, "but they'd probably kick my butt."

"You're definitely safer up here."

"I was wanting to meet you. I mean, we're kind of linked. You went to Missoula, and I came here."

"Do you like it here?" Sissy asked.

"Yeah, Jim and Daniel and all the guys are great. I'm learning a lot, but I miss my folks. How about you? Do you like Missoula?"

"I love the university, and I've made some friends."

"What about the pack?" he asked.

Sissy paused. She wasn't sure how much she should say, considering she hadn't said anything of note to Maggie or Jim. "I don't know. They're different. I haven't met a lot of them, just Shari, Wade and Jax and some of their friends."

Trace nodded. "Yeah, the 'little pack.'"

"Why do you call them that?"

"They're kinda their own group. They don't mix much with the rest of the pack. I guess we aren't as rich as them, or something. That's just what I heard. I don't really know Jax."

"Oh," Sissy said. Interesting. She wondered how many others felt that way. "I don't think I've met your folks."

"Probably not. They live a ways out, and they don't usually come to the runs any more. They run with a few friends out on our ranch. I don't think Milton likes that. Maybe that's why he traded me."

"You didn't ask to be traded?"

"No, they just told me I had to go."

"Oh, I'm so sorry," Sissy said, feeling a bit of guilt. "I never would have agreed to the trade if I thought someone would be forced to leave against their will."

"It's all right. I like it here. Like I said, the people here are real nice, and everything's more..." He struggled for the word. "It's more peaceful here."

It seemed to Sissy that nothing had been very peaceful lately. Maybe Milton was right about what Weres were really like. Jim and his pack put up a good show of civilization, but they could be brutal, too. "You know, we had a terrible fight here right before you came," she said.

"Yeah, I heard, but I also heard that Jim took care of the fellows who started it. He protects his own. I like that about him. You might be better off here where Jim can take care of you than over in Missoula."

"Thanks for the advice, but I can take care of myself."

Trace had given her a lot of things to think about. He hadn't said anything outright, but reading between the lines, it sounded like there was a lot of strife in the Missoula pack and not everybody was happy with Milton's heavy-handed treatment. She wished she'd found out more about the incident with the older man Milton had attacked so she could ask Trace about it, but he'd probably tell his parents and it'd get back to Milton that she was asking questions. She decided to just let it lie.

"We'd better get inside," Sissy said.

She turned to go, and Trace caught her arm. "Just be careful up there, especially around Milton. If you need anybody to talk to, you can always call me. You can trust me, I promise."

"Okay, Trace. Thanks." Sissy slipped out of his grasp and went to find Maggie. She was ready to go home.

IT WAS THE day before the full moon, and Sissy felt the pull in her bones. When Maggie said she had to go out to the ranch to check on some preparations, Sissy jumped at the chance to go with her and get out of the house.

On the ride out to the ranch, Sissy debated telling Maggie some of her concerns about the Missoula pack, including the warning Trace had given her. She and Maggie had always had a good relationship. She'd never kept much back from Maggie until her feelings about Jim had begun to blossom into something more than a childhood crush on her big brother's friend, and even though they didn't talk about it, Sissy knew Maggie was aware of how she felt.

Ever since Sissy had decided to leave Laramie for graduate school, Maggie had become so overprotective. Sissy was hesitant to give her anything more to worry about. And Jim was worse. He would likely charge in and start a war if she even mentioned anything negative about Missoula. At the very least, he'd put her under house arrest so she couldn't go back.

Sissy wondered what she'd do if Jim ordered her to stay in Laramie. As her Alpha, he had the right to do that, but she wasn't sure if she'd obey. She'd defied him before, but there were limits to what he'd put up with, even from her.

Meanwhile, the country music playing on the radio was enough to keep the silence between Maggie and Sissy from becoming uncomfortable.

When they arrived at the ranch, Sissy knew Maggie had errands to attend to, but that didn't matter. She wandered over to the corrals and watched as wranglers cut out cows and herded them into a smaller holding pen.

A couple of cowboys were sitting on the top rail of the smaller pen watching as each cow was loaded into a squeeze chute, a tight chute that pinned the cow's head and held her in place. Sissy stepped up on the bottom rail near them, and the cowboys turned to look at her. One of them gave a low whistle. "Sissy, you sure are looking pretty."

"Thanks, boys. What's going on?" She'd spent a lot of time at the ranch, but she'd been raised in town. She knew more about art than cows.

"Well, you see, the vet there is gonna stick his arm all the way up..." Daniel came up behind the cowboy just then and pushed him off his perch. He landed in the dirt to the laughter of his buddies.

"The vet's checking to see if the cows are pregnant," Daniel said, giving Sissy a kiss on the cheek. "You boys get back to work." He put his arm around her, and they walked toward the barns. "We sure have missed you. You broke a lotta hearts when you left."

"Then it's a good thing Jim had Crystal to ease the blow of my leaving," she said, uncomfortably aware of the acid in her tone.

Daniel laughed. "You've got a mean tongue on you, girl. Don't give her too much credit. She doesn't hold his heart." They entered the horse barn, where Jim was examining a palomino mare. He looked up and grinned when he saw Sissy.

"Come here and look at this lady," he called to them.

"She's beautiful." The golden mare had a white blaze on her face and four white stockings. Sissy ran her hand over the honey-colored coat. The horse's skin rippled under Sissy's touch, and the mare turned her head slowly, her round, dark eyes meeting Sissy's hazel gaze.

In most Werewolf tales, animals were terrified when they scented Werewolves. Dogs would go crazy barking and growling and horses would bolt away. But unlike the stories, most Weres handled animals well, communicating with them on subtler levels than most human handlers could.

Watching Sissy over the horse's back, Jim smoothed the thick blonde mane. "I bought her because she reminded me of you. Her name is Scheherazade, but I've been calling her Sarah."

Sissy smiled. "That's nice. I've never had a horse named after me before. What if she turns out to be ornery or unmanageable?"

"Then the name would be perfect," Daniel said, and the men laughed.

"Well, I think she's gorgeous," Sissy snapped.

"That's another reason her name is perfect," Jim said, smiling. "Do you want to ride her? She's well-trained and has a good temperament, but I haven't taken her out on the range yet."

"I'd love to, but it's been a while since I've ridden."

"We can take it slow."

"Okay. Dad, will you tell Maggie?"

"Sure, honey. Let's get you saddled up."

Jim went to get his horse and came back on the large, dark bay he'd favored for several years. Marshall had a shiny black mane and tail and was big enough to carry a man Jim's size. Sissy greeted Jim's horse with an affectionate rub between his black eyes. Daniel gave Sissy a hand up, and Jim and Sissy rode out of the compound.

When they reached an open stretch, Jim asked, "Do you want to try going a little faster?"

"Sure, I think I can handle that." Sissy urged Sarah into a trot and quickly fell into the horse's rhythm. She'd almost forgotten how good it felt to be out riding under a cold blue sky. She'd ridden a lot as a teen, but she hadn't had much time for it in the last few years.

Jim came up beside her, and Sissy took off at a lope. They ran the horses across the field until the trail ducked into the trees and they had to slow down.

Sissy's cheeks felt cold. "That was so much fun."

"Let's walk them for a little while," Jim suggested. They dismounted and led the horses along, breathing in the cool air.

After a while, Sissy asked, "Did you ever want Maggie?"

chapter fifteen

Jim looked startled at the question. Sissy didn't blame him. She was surprised at herself for asking.

"No. I love Maggie, but she was always the one for your brother. Do you want to hear about the first time she got under Lucas's skin?"

"Of course." She'd heard this story, but it had been years.

"It was a summer evening before a run, and all the kids were playing around," Jim began. "We must have been about six, and she was just a little thing, always following us around, so I told her to get lost. She stopped and we kept going, but then Lucas looked back. Three bigger kids, a lot bigger than us, were picking on her. I guess she'd started crying when I shooed her away, and they were calling her a crybaby. Before I even thought about it, Lucas had turned around and plowed into all three of the boys. He was punching them and yelling to leave her alone. I was just standing there like a big dope when my dad and Daniel waded in. They had to pull Lucas off of the boys. They all had black eyes and bloody noses. It was quite a scrap. Daniel was yelling at all of them, and Maggie came over and stood by Lucas and put her little hand in his. And that was it. We could hardly shake her after that." Jim stopped and looked at Sissy. "I think she knew he was her mate even then."

Sissy gazed at Jim. She knew neither would say what was on both of their minds. Finally, she broke the awkward silence. "Tell me some more about them."

"Well, there was another time when Lucas and I were about ten. It was another full moon run. It must have been fall because I remember it was chilly, and we had jackets on. Back then we didn't have the changing sheds or the kids' area. We just had the big hall, and when the adults went on the runs, they left us with some of the human wives and older girls. We thought we were too big to get left with babysitters, and I could usually convince Lucas to sneak away so we could creep up on the pack circle and watch as everybody shifted. Then we'd go on our own run, pretending we were wolves, too. We'd gotten in trouble for sneaking out before, but I didn't care.

"That night, Maggie wasn't with us. We'd given her the slip or she wasn't interested. I don't remember. Anyway, we watched the pack shift and take off, then we went running. You know night vision isn't as good for kids as it is for full-grown wolves, so we were running flat out in pitch dark, like fools, and Lucas ran straight off a little cliff and landed on some rocks. I scrambled after him, and he was lying there at the bottom. I was scared to death. I could tell his arm was broken. He was whimpering, and the only thing I could think to do was to try to find my dad or Daniel, but Lucas said no. He told me to go get Maggie and tell her. She'd know what to do, even though she was so little.

"I put my jacket over him and ran back to the hall as fast as I could, but I had to find her without attracting attention, then sneak back out. Anyhow, I found her and told her what'd happened, and she went right into action. We got out of the hall and crept into the big house and got supplies—some antiseptic and a big wooden spoon for a splint and an elastic bandage. Then we ran back to where I'd left Lucas.

"Maggie fixed him up like she'd been nursing all her life. Lucas wouldn't let her put his arm in a sling. We were more scared of getting in trouble than we were about his broken arm. She splinted his arm, and we managed to get it back inside his shirt and jacket. That must have hurt like a bitch, but he didn't cry. We were so stupid, we thought nobody'd notice he had a broken arm."

Sissy smiled. "Did you get away with it?"

"Of course not. We had to go slow getting back to the compound because Lucas couldn't run, and by the time we got back, all the adults had returned and everybody knew we were missing. My dad and Daniel and your mom and Maggie's parents were all waiting for us, and Lucas and I knew what we had coming. Justice was pretty swift back then. Maggie's folks were going to take her home, but Lucas and I got marched behind the barn. My dad said, 'You know you're going to get a whipping for this.' We knew. So we had to drop our pants and reach for the wall with both hands."

Sissy smiled.

"Daniel was about to take a swing with his belt when all hell broke loose. Maggie came running around the side of the barn just as Lucas's broken arm gave out. He yowled, and Maggie threw herself between Daniel and Lucas. She was yelling, 'Don't you touch him. His arm's broke.' And both of us boys were standing there, bare assed and waiting for our whipping. And Daniel was swearing, and my dad was laughing, and Maggie's parents came chasing after her and just stood there. I wish I had pictures."

Jim laughed at the memory. "I think we were all grounded for about two months, and Maggie's folks didn't want her to have anything to do with us after that. Of course, that didn't last. Nothing could keep those two apart."

Except death. The thought hung unspoken.

"Sissy, baby, I have one more story I need to tell you," Jim said. "Did your dad tell you how Lucas died?"

Sissy took a deep breath. "Dad told me that Lucas was on a mission in El Salvador when his helicopter was hit. He said you went in alone and killed the people who shot him down, and the Army offered you a medal for valor and you refused it."

"That's not the whole story."

Sissy watched Jim as he leaned against his horse. She guessed he had been putting off telling her this.

"The only reason your brother was there in the first place was because of me. He should have been home with Maggie."

Sissy frowned. "Maggie said he'd always planned to go into the Army."

"*We* had always planned to go into the Army, but by the time we were old enough, Maggie and Lucas were in love. He was torn up about what to do. She left the choice with him, but I think she knew that it was my dream for us to join up together. I should have just left and joined without him, but I didn't. Maggie was still too young for them to mate, so I kept after him to go while we still could.

"Looking back, I'm sure he thought he'd let me down if he decided not to go. This was something we'd been talking about all of our lives, and I was selfish enough that I would've been let down. So we joined up like we'd planned."

Sissy watched as his face faded from reflective to regretful.

Jim paused. "It was exciting. We were in an all-Were Special Ops unit. The military had found out about Weres long before the rest of the world. We were the elite — Rangers, Night Stalkers, even SEALs. I thought I'd stay in for a good long time, but for Lucas, it was definitely a short-term deal. He'd go in, do his time with me, then he'd go back to Maggie. As soon as we finished flight school, they were mated, and it's hard for mates to be apart. I know he wanted to be with her."

"I thought he loved flying."

"He did. We both did, but he was a better pilot than I was. He was smarter, always in control. I was reckless, always writing checks my ass, or my friends, had to cash. It was always that way with us. I'd jump in blind, and Lucas would make sure I got out of whatever scrape I'd got myself in. I know you think I'm a control freak, but that side of me came late.

"Lucas would have made a much better pack leader than me. I know my dad was afraid of what would happen to the pack when I took over. When we were growing up, he'd always talk to Lucas about pack business, but I never paid attention, and he'd say, 'Lucas, you're going to have to be the responsible one.'"

"That's terrible."

"Honey, I was spoiled rotten. I was young, rich, and privileged. I knew I'd inherit all this someday, but I thought my old man would live forever. I was happy for Lucas to be the responsible one. That meant I could stay the wild one. In fact, when we were in flight school I was given the call sign 'Barker.' At first I thought it was an insult, like they were calling me a dog because of my wolf, but then they told me it was because I was so wild, so they named me after Clive Barker, who wrote *Hellraiser.* That fit me just right."

"What was my brother's call sign?"

"He was called 'Lunar.' If somebody started losing it, the guys would say that he was 'going lunar' because the full moon was the only time that Lucas ever lost control. Evidently, I was 'lunar' all the time. Anyway, we were in Africa for a while, and it was pretty rough, so when we first got posted to El Salvador, I thought I was in heaven. It was a tropical paradise. But I got bored. There wasn't as much action as I was used to, so I started creating my own action off post. I drank a lot and started fights, and there was always a girl or four waiting for a little attention. Things were pretty loose there, so I started staying out until the last minute before going back to base."

Jim took another deep breath. Sissy saw the pain in his face.

"The day your brother died, I came rolling into base half lit. I'd been drinking and whoring around for two days, fighting or fucking everybody who came near me. I'd just hit the bunk when I got called. I was struggling to get my eyes uncrossed and my boots tied when Lucas came in and saw the shape I was in. He offered to take the run for me, and I let him." Jim turned away from her.

When Sissy didn't say anything, he said, "Did you hear me? I let him take my run, and he died. It should have been me, not him."

Sissy came up behind him. "You couldn't have known."

Jim spun around to face her. "Don't defend me."

"What do you want me to say? That I hate you? Maybe I should, but I was so young when he died. I've known you all my life, and I've never known you to be anything other than a good man. I'm sorry he died, but I can't wish that you'd died instead.

"Does Maggie know what happened?" she asked.

Jim nodded.

"And Dad?"

"Yes, I told them."

"Did they blame you?"

"Daniel did. I straightened up, but I didn't plan on coming back to the ranch, maybe ever. But then, out of the blue, my dad died. He'd been out on the range in a jeep. It flipped and damn near cut him in half. Daniel called and when I came home, he had to help me take over the pack. And Maggie, she always knew what I was like, and she loved me anyway. I never deserved the kind of loyalty they gave me."

"But you do now." Sissy wrapped her arms around him and laid her head against his chest.

Jim expelled a jagged breath, like he was letting go of a ghost that he'd held on to for a long time. "Come on, baby. It looks like snow. We'd better head back." He kissed the top of her head and held her for a long moment before he let her go.

They were quiet on the ride back, Jim lost in his thoughts, every so often looking over at Sissy to reassure himself. He'd told her everything, and she was still there, riding by his side.

Maggie was waiting by her truck when they rode in. Sissy dismounted and handed the reins off to Jim. "Thank you for the ride," she said. Her words were polite, but her eyes, looking deep into his, told him how much his confession meant to her.

Sissy gave the horse a final rub on the nose. "Sarah is a wonderful horse."

"I bought her for you. She'll be here any time you want to ride."

THE DAY OF the full moon, Jim walked around the compound greeting everyone who'd come out for the run. His mood was considerably brighter than it had been for a long time. He smiled and joked with the older folks and even chased after some of the kids.

The last few days had been perfect. With Sissy home for

Thanksgiving, Jim felt right for the first time in a long time. He'd taken a chance when he bought the horse for her. At the time, he didn't know if she'd ever want to ride it, but riding with her and saying the things he had to say had loosened the barbed wire he'd wrapped around his heart.

It had been so long since they'd just been natural around each other. After the last couple of years, he'd been afraid that they'd never get along again. Every time he was around Sissy he'd say the wrong thing or do something to set her off. He'd never been that clueless around a woman before, but he'd never been able to see Sissy as a woman. He could now.

Pushing her away had hurt them both. They'd take their time and get to know each other again. She'd probably want to finish school, although he'd try to convince her to transfer back to the university in Laramie. He could wait for her. He'd give her the chance to experience everything she wanted, as long as he could be a part of her life in the end.

When they arrived, Sissy was immediately surrounded by friends she hadn't seen since her move to Missoula. He was disappointed that he didn't have her to himself, but watching her was almost as good.

She stood out in her circle. Even with the overcast skies, her blonde hair caught the light and lit up her face like a halo. Her cheeks were pink with the cold. She laughed with her friends, but he knew she was aware of his eyes on her. She'd dart a look at him from time to time and smile.

Jim assumed she'd run with her friends like she did before she left, but he planned to snag a little time alone with her when the run was over. He wanted to make sure they were okay with each other. There were still things he needed to say. He'd suppressed his feelings for so long that it was hard to accept that there truly could be something between them.

He needed to talk to Maggie and make sure she felt comfortable with him pursuing this relationship, and he'd have to clear it with Daniel, even though he'd probably get punched again. But mostly, he had to hear from Sissy that she wanted him. With their history of miscommunication, it was easy to believe that he could be reading her all wrong.

"It's starting to snow," Daniel observed as they walked out to the clearing where the pack awaited.

"It's late this year. Maybe it was waiting for Sissy to get back," Jim said with a smile. He took a deep breath and felt the cold enter his lungs.

They entered the pack circle and Jim, naked in his human form, took his place on the Alpha's rock. He scanned the crowd until he spotted Sissy. She was looking up at him. All his doubts about leadership vanished. He wanted to be the best, for her.

He greeted the pack and then gave the howl that started the shift. His cry was met by a chorus of howls. This was his pack. He shifted and leaped off the rock to lead the run. The pack followed and he ran among them for a while, but he wasn't in the mood for a crowd that night. He'd kept track of Sissy's group with their howls, so he headed over to intercept them.

The moon was a bright spot obscured by low clouds. About fifty yards ahead of him, Sissy stood outlined by the dim light, waiting for him, her platinum fur dusted with snow. As he watched, she stretched out her front legs and lowered her head onto her paws. With her head almost on the ground, she looked up at him with golden eyes, inviting him. He'd never felt the call to mate as a wolf this strongly.

She bounded off at a run, and he went after her. For a while, they ran together side by side. She kept up with him easily. When they would slow, one would nip the other, and they'd be off again.

SISSY WAS ECSTATIC, but she was also torn. She wanted to stay with Jim like this forever, but she couldn't face being let down again. Their wolves understood each other perfectly. Their bodies ran in perfect sync. Running, turning, slowing, they matched each other step for step. His scent filled her with longing. He was her mate. They were meant to be together, but she couldn't help but wonder if the feeling would hold true when they shifted back. As humans, everything was so complicated between them.

Their talk had opened up a door for them to pass through together. Sissy understood Jim's reticence toward her. He carried a burden of guilt for her brother's death, and he'd taken on all the responsibilities of taking care of her family and the pack when he wasn't much older than she was now. In his mind, wanting her, being with her, meant betraying her brother's trust.

She could never fully comprehend his tangle of feelings. She'd never thought of him as her brother; to her he was just Jim, always there and always special.

They ran long after the moon had gone down and the others had gone back to the ranch. As they neared the compound, she stopped and lay down, her heavy breathing creating puffs of frost in the cold night air. Jim lay beside her, and she rested her head on his paws. He licked her muzzle and snuggled his head on the soft fur of her shoulders. They stayed together until the sun appeared over the horizon.

JIM WAS AFRAID to move. He wanted to talk to her, to kiss her and tell her not to leave, but he was afraid to shift and be alone with her naked. He didn't think they were ready for that.

He didn't want this time between them to end, but the rising sun was pulling at him to shift. He rose and together they padded toward the house, shoulder to shoulder, lost in the perfect moment. As they entered the yard, Jim nuzzled his head under hers, licked her nose, and then he bounded away behind the house, leaving her alone.

chapter sixteen

Jim was in the great room when Daniel found him and poured them both a drink.

"How was your run?" Daniel asked.

"It was good." Jim sighed. He had a feeling that the older man and Maggie had been watching them come into the compound.

"You sound like a lovesick pup."

I am a lovesick pup, Jim mused. "When I was a kid, I had it bad for Sally King. You remember her?"

"Sure do. All you boys had it bad for her, and she finally ran off with a rodeo cowboy."

"I asked my dad how you know when you've found the one. He just said, 'You'll know it when you feel it.' I didn't know what he meant."

"And you do now?" Daniel raised an eyebrow.

"Yeah, I do now."

"What are you gonna do about it?"

"Nothing yet. I have things I need to take care of, and so does she."

"You're a damn fool," Daniel said, shaking his head and walking away.

Jim offered to take Sissy back to Missoula in his helicopter, but she'd bought round-trip tickets. Instead, he took her to the small Laramie airport. Maggie came along, so they didn't have time alone. He insisted on parking and coming in with her and carrying her bag.

As they waited in the check-in line, Maggie and Sissy chatted about school and the upcoming Christmas break while Jim stood there holding Sissy's bag. After checking in at the counter, Maggie reluctantly gave Sissy a final hug. It was Jim's turn.

"I hate for you to go back so soon," he said.

"I know, but I'll be back at Christmas."

"Can I call you?" Jim felt like a teenager asking for a first date. Actually, his first date had been easier. He'd been more confident of the outcome.

"Of course." Sissy smiled and held out both of her hands.

His fingers interlaced with hers, linking them palm to palm. "I want us to talk some more." He felt her heart beating in his hand.

"I've got to go now or I'll miss my flight," she said softly, her gaze never leaving his.

Jim squeezed her hands and drew in a deep breath filled with her sweet scent. He hefted her carry-on bag onto her shoulder and helped her adjust the strap. Before she turned away, he cupped her chin and brought his lips down on hers. Just a soft kiss, but he held it as long as he could. "I love you, Sissy," he said, breathing the words into her hair.

WITH A LAYOVER in Denver, the flight was a surprisingly long. There were so many things to figure out, and Sissy had a lot of time

171

to think.

I love you, Sissy. Jim had said those words to her so many times before, but this time they'd sounded different. This time, the words were more like *I want you, Sissy. I want you to be mine.*

Isn't that what she had always wanted? She loved him. There was no doubt about that. But was she ready? Would he want to claim her as his mate? Would she be overwhelmed by him, the way so many others were? When she was close to him, her body took over. All she wanted was to be with him, to have him take her and claim her.

Some of her longtime friends had taken mates, and she hardly saw them anymore, and when she did, they only talked about their men and their babies. It was like they'd lost their individual personalities when they mated.

And there were risks. Mating went beyond sex and marriage. Mates formed a metaphysical bond. They became a part of each other. And when they lost their mates, they lost a piece of themselves. She'd watched her dad almost go crazy when her mother died. And when Lucas died, Maggie had almost died, too. Maggie managed to pull through, but something had been missing in her ever since.

Sissy wasn't sure she could ever surrender herself that much. It would never be enough for her to just be Jim's mate. She'd begun something on her own, and she wanted to see it through.

She'd always wanted to be a wildlife biologist, and she loved the graduate program at UM, and if Jim's pushing her away had driven her to follow her dream, maybe it was a good thing. She wasn't ready to give it up.

Shari picked up Sissy at the Missoula airport and immediately started questioning her about her stay in Laramie.

"Did you meet Trace and Ray?" the other young woman asked.

"I met Trace. Who's Ray?"

"He's the other one who got traded for you."

"Milton sent two guys to Laramie?"

"Yeah, didn't you know?"

Evidently Jim hadn't given her all the details of the trade and never introduced her to the other guy. Maybe he'd been protecting her again, or maybe he just didn't want to discuss pack business with her, even when it concerned her.

Sissy shrugged. "Trace seemed very nice."

"He's nice enough, but he's just a dumb cowboy."

"Not like the 'little pack,'" Sissy said, recalling the phrase that Trace had used.

"Oh, you heard about that. Some of the rednecks think we're snobs because we don't spend all of our time at rodeos and stock auctions."

This was a different side of Shari. The other woman had never been interested in Sissy's life before, and Sissy was sure Milton had put her up to it.

Sissy decided she'd have to keep her eyes and ears open to see what was really going on in the Missoula pack.

JIM SAT ON the couch at Crystal's apartment. He was not looking forward to what he'd come to do. He was going to tell Crystal that he couldn't see her anymore. The last few days had proven how wrong he'd been to deny his feelings for Sissy. He'd never want anyone else, and while he hadn't really pursued a romantic relationship with Crystal, they had become friends, and he felt he owed her an explanation. He'd tell her as easily as he could. Afterward, he'd call Sissy, or maybe drive up there to see her. Either way, he wanted to let Sissy know how much their time together had meant to him. They'd have plenty of time to talk, and then when she came home at Christmas...

Crystal handed him a drink and curled up next to him. "Do you want to watch a movie or something?" she asked.

"No, I need to talk to you."

Crystal smiled. "I've been wanting to talk to you too, really talk. We've gotten to be great friends over the last few months, but I want us to be closer. We've spent all this time together, but I hardly know anything about you. It's time we opened up."

"I'm sorry." He pulled away and took her hands between his. "I've enjoyed spending time with you. You're a beautiful, intelligent woman. In the beginning I thought maybe we could be more, but my heart was always someplace else. I gave it away a long time ago."

"To Sissy," Crystal said flatly. "Maggie told me."

Jim didn't answer.

"And so that's it? We can't even be friends?"

"I don't feel right about seeing you now when Sissy and I finally have a chance. I can't explain it. I don't expect you to understand."

"I do understand," Crystal said quietly. "I know what you are."

Jim sucked in a breath and waited for her to go on.

"You've found your mate, and I know what that means."

"I don't think I know what you mean." Jim had to be sure this wasn't just semantics.

"Jim, I know you're a Werewolf. I've known it all along. I didn't intend to deceive you, but I was afraid if I told you, you'd shut me out, and I didn't want that. I was hoping that we would get to a point where we could be honest with each other."

Jim stood to give himself some distance. "Where did you get that idea? Because I'm big and strong? I'm sorry, but there are a lot of large men, human men."

"I'm a genetic scientist. I've studied Werewolf genetics for several years. I came to Laramie specifically to gather genetic data on the Werewolves in this area."

"And all those nights you called me over for pizza and a movie, you never thought to mention this theory of yours? Or even what you do? That's absurd. Were you studying me?"

"No. I was trying to get to know you. You can't imagine how excited I was when you stopped for me on the highway and I realized who you were. I've met lots of Werves—I'm sorry; you probably don't like that term—Werewolves, and I know what to look for, and there, on my first day in town, a Werewolf comes to my rescue. I couldn't believe it, and I certainly wasn't going to say anything until I was sure."

"Oh, and you're sure now?"

"I am, but I was hoping that you'd trust me enough to tell me the truth."

All Jim wanted to do was get far away from Crystal, but he had to learn what she knew. "So has your research been going well or is it all as speculative as this fantasy?"

"Stop it, Jim. We both know that truth. It's not fantasy. I have hard data. We have a small pool of test subjects, but it'd be easier if they weren't so afraid to come forward. I hoped you'd give me access to the pack."

Jim dropped the pretense. "And if I put a stop to it, what then?"

"Don't do that. We're very discreet. I'm not surprised you haven't heard about it. All of our information is held in the highest confidence. This is important research. The medical implications alone are huge—disease control, longevity studies, regenerative healing—and the pheromone research..."

Jim's blood went from simmer to boil. "The pheromones. You

used the mating pheromones on me. I was beating myself up for losing control. I was afraid I'd hurt you, and you were doping me up and studying my reactions. And I guess the girl at the bar was yours, too. Did you know she's chatting about her 'experiment' on the Internet? Very discreet. Is that all I am to you, a lab rat?"

"It wasn't like that," Crystal protested. "The pheromones have a new release mechanism I was working on, and we had to test it, but I should never have used you as a test subject without your consent. I'm sorry. It was an emotional decision. I just had to know."

He'd heard enough. Jim grabbed his jacket and headed for the door.

Crystal dashed in front of him. "I was wrong to do what I did to you, but my research is important. Together we can help a lot of people, yours and mine."

"You haven't done anything but help yourself and put my people in jeopardy. Your research here is done. You're going to leave and go back to Seattle, and if any of this comes out, any names, any mention of Laramie or the pack, I'll see that your reputation as a scientist is ruined."

LATE THAT NIGHT, Sissy was surprised when Jim's name showed up on her phone. He'd said he'd call, but she hadn't expected to hear from him so soon.

This was exactly what she had been worried about. She wanted to hear his voice, but she didn't want Jim taking over her life, and she wasn't going to check in with him every fifteen minutes. It was bad enough having Maggie worry over her.

"Hey, baby doll. It's Jim."

She smiled. "I know." His voice, even over the phone, made her flush. She wanted to give in to the warmth spreading though her body and just lie in bed and listen to him talk. But she wouldn't allow herself to fall under his spell.

"I just wanted to hear your voice. I wish we'd had more time to talk before you left. I feel like there are a lot of things left unsaid."

"I know. There are, and we do have to talk, honestly. We tried for so long not to hurt each other, and that's all we did. I don't know if we know how to be together." Sissy wanted to say more, like how she didn't know if he could ever treat her as an equal, but she didn't say anything. That conversation wasn't for the phone.

"We can work that out, baby."

"I hope so, but not tonight. I've got a ton of work to catch up on."

"Okay, I'll let you go. Can I call tomorrow night?"

"No, I won't be home until late. My roommate and her mate-to-be are having a party, and I promised I'd be there."

"When would be a good time?"

Sissy sighed. "I don't know, Jim. I've got so much to finish up before the semester is over. Give me some time. I'm trying to figure out some stuff for myself."

"Would it be better if I came up there, so we could talk in person?"

God, no. "I'll be home in a few weeks. We can talk then."

"Okay. If that's what you need. But I miss you. I've missed you since the moment I left you in Montana."

The silence stretched out between them like it could only do on the phone. Too far away to see. Too far away to hold. After a while he said, "I love you, baby."

"I love you too, Jim." It was true. She just didn't know what it meant.

JIM'S CALL THE night before had left Sissy confused and irritated, and right now a relationship that would change her life forever was the last thing she wanted to deal with. She had classes all morning, a big final project that she needed to work on, and later there was going to be a party out at the pack lodge to celebrate Shari and Wade's upcoming mating ceremony.

She was trying to get some work done, but Shari kept popping into her room all afternoon for advice about which dress to wear and whether to wear her hair up or down. Sissy tried to beg off on the whole thing saying she had too much schoolwork, but when her roommate started to cry, Sissy had given in.

When they arrived, only a few cars were in the lot. Sissy had never been inside the lodge before, but when they went in, it didn't look like it was set up for a party. It had standard western lodge décor, big rooms with dark wood and heavy leather furniture, but most of the rooms were dark and empty of furniture.

Wade showed up and pulled Shari off somewhere in the lodge, leaving Sissy standing in the hallway.

Jax came out of a side room. "You look really pretty tonight."

Sissy hadn't gone to a lot of effort. Since she didn't know how formal the pack was about such occasions, she'd picked out a simple pale green, silk dress and slicked on some lip gloss. She hoped the party didn't go on too late. "Thank you. Where is everybody?"

"They'll be along later. My father wants to talk to you." Jax ushered Sissy to an office off the main hallway, where Milton sat behind a huge desk.

"Sissy, come on in and sit down." He gestured to a heavy wooden chair in front of the desk. She sat, feeling as though she was on the witness stand.

"So, your trip home was good, I hear."

"I guess you heard all about it from Shari." When he didn't react, she answered. "Yes, it was good to see my family again."

"You know I'd like you to think of us as your family."

What was he getting at? "Well, you guys can be my second family while I'm here."

Milton came out from behind the desk and leaned back in front of Sissy, forcing her to look upward if she didn't want to be staring at his crotch. He stood too close, towering over her, attempting to intimidate her. He might be the Alpha, but he wasn't *her* Alpha, and she could hold her own around dominant men.

"I've been hoping that you'd want to stay with us," he continued, "but it sounds like you got cozy with Jim. I heard all about your romantic trail ride and moonlight run, and Shari said he called you as soon as you got home."

"How'd you hear about that?" Sissy hadn't mentioned anything about the run to Shari. "Was Trace watching us? Does he report back to you about our pack?"

"Trace, no. He's just a big farmboy. I sent him away to put some pressure on his folks. They have a nice stretch of land that the pack could use. No, Ray's my man down there. He wasn't invited to your cozy family dinner, but he was keeping an eye on you. He told me you had a nice long talk with Trace. I imagine Trace tried to warn you about me. Ray also told me how you stayed out all night with Jim. Did he propose to mate with you? I don't smell his mark on you." Milton sniffed at her rudely.

"That's enough." Sissy rose from her chair, but strong hands came around from behind and held her in place. She turned her head and saw two men she didn't know holding her down. Jax and Wade stood between her and the door.

"We're not done here yet," Milton said, a glint in his eye. "You know what I want. I'm going to ask you one last time. Will you take Jackson as your mate?"

"No. How many times do I have to tell you I won't mate with Jax?" Sissy struggled against her captors.

Milton ignored her. "If you agree to go through with it right now and mate with him tonight, then we can all get on with our lives. I'll buy you a house, of course, and you can have a fancy mating ceremony later. You can even keep going to school if you want."

"And if I won't?"

"That isn't an option. You'll either mate with him tonight or you'll mate with him at the next full moon."

Milton wasn't going to let her go without a fight. Sissy shifted, but Milton was quicker. He had her down on the floor with his teeth sunk into her neck. She felt a sting in her flank, and then she was out.

chapter seventeen

When she woke, her head hurt and she was naked and cold. Locked in a barred cell with no windows, she realized someone must have injected her with a tranquilizer. In the dim light, she saw Shari wrapped up in a blanket, asleep in a chair across from the cell.

"Hsst! Shari," Sissy whispered. "You've got to get me out of here."

Shari stirred and opened her eyes. "Oh, honey," she said. "You're awake. They made me stay down here to tell them when you woke up. It's so awful."

Sissy noticed Shari was still in her crumpled party dress, and her eye makeup streaked down her face. "You used your party to get me out here alone."

"I didn't know. I thought it was going to be a party. They didn't tell me until after we got here."

"You've got to help me," Sissy said. "You're the only one who can. Call Jim and tell him what's happened. He won't hurt you if you tell him you're helping me."

"I can't. Milton would kill me, and Wade, too. You've got to cooperate." Shari moved closer and whispered, "Look, Jax isn't so bad. He's got a lot of money, and he'll probably be Alpha here someday. Just let him take you," she said with a shrug.

"It's not that big a deal. It's not like you're... Oh, God, you're a virgin, aren't you? I don't think anybody thought of that." Shari considered the new information. "Don't tell Milton you're a virgin. He'd probably want you for himself. I'll tell Jax, and he'll be gentle with you. When you mate and he marks you, it's supposed to feel really hot, hotter than regular sex, and it happens every time you have sex. Come on. Let me tell them you'll do it."

"How can you be so stupid? I'd never mate with anyone under force, and I wouldn't mate with anyone I didn't love."

"You're the one who's stupid," Shari shot back. "Mating's not about love. It's about security for life. It's a partnership. Wade's going to be good for me and our children. He's already higher in the pack than his parents, and he's going even higher."

"That's only because he kisses Milton's ass," Sissy said. Shari huffed and started up the stairs.

"How secure did you feel when Milton was raping you?" Sissy called after her. She heard Shari suck in air as though she'd been gut-punched as she continued up the stairs.

Sissy heard Shari yell, "She's awake. Can I get out of here now?"

She should have at least thought to ask Shari for a blanket. Hugging herself, she looked around her prison. Two walls were solid rock. This was probably the basement of the lodge, buried into the mountainside. The other two walls of the cell were open with heavy steel bars. The door had a slit to pass food through and a heavy lock. There was a metal drain in the center of the floor that appeared to have been welded in place. A nasty-looking mattress occupied one corner and a bucket in the other, presumably her latrine. Clearly, this kind of cell had been built to hold an out-of-control Werewolf.

The cell was positioned in the corner of a larger room. An open staircase led down from the main floor above to the solid rock floor. There were no windows. A bare light bulb hung from the ceiling outside of the cell. The only furnishings she could see were a couple of straight chairs and a small table, probably for her guards.

Sissy sat on a corner of the mattress. She tried to figure out how long it would be before someone realized she was missing and came looking for her. She emailed Maggie almost every day, and they talked on the phone a couple of times a week. She would tell Jim if Sissy didn't answer her phone, and he'd come for her.

I just need to hold out for four or five days. That's no problem. Jim will get me out of here. He'll probably want to kill Milton, but not before I kick Milton's ass and Shari's, too.

Jax came down the steps. He brought Sissy a blanket and a bottle of water. When she came up to the bars to get them, he had a hard time meeting her eyes.

"I'm sorry about this, Sissy. It wasn't my idea. Dad got fixated on the idea of us mating the first night he saw you at the house."

Sissy wrapped the blanket around her shoulders. "How long do they plan on keeping me down here?"

"As long as it takes. They're going to starve you. You'll only get water and maybe some fruit or bread, enough to keep you alive, but no meat. You know what'll happen. If you don't get any protein, your metabolism is going to go wild. You'll start shifting involuntarily, which will use up even more of your energy. And then when it's close to the full moon, they'll give you some meat that's laced with mating hormones. You'll eat the meat whether you want to or not. In fact, you probably won't even remember I told you all this by then. The hormones will make you go into heat, and you won't be able to resist mating."

Sissy huddled in the corner, unable to believe what she was hearing.

"Let me come to you, Sissy," Jax coaxed, his lanky hair covering half his face. "I'll make it all right. I really do like you, and I think you could like me. I promise I'll be good to you. I'd never treat you the way my father treats my mother."

Sissy closed her eyes. *This was a nightmare scenario.*

"Please, Sissy. I'll be gentle with you. Shari told me you're a virgin, so I'll go real easy. I'd hoped you'd like me. I didn't want it like this, but I really don't want to mate with you when you're out of your head with drugs. Do you understand what I'm saying? You're gonna be begging for somebody to take you by the time the pheromones take effect, and I'll have to or my dad will have you instead."

Sissy wanted to kill someone. She didn't care if it was Jackson or Milton. She opened her eyes and hissed between clenched teeth, "Just get out of my sight, Jax."

"WHAT'S UP, MAGGIE?" Jim hugged Maggie and followed her to the kitchen where they usually talked, especially when she had a problem.

"I don't know. I'm probably worrying for nothing, but I can't get hold of Sissy."

"What do you mean?" Jim's trouble radar instantly spiked.

"I haven't talked to her in over a week. Her roommate said she'd lost her phone."

Jim frowned. "And you're just now telling me. Why didn't

you call me sooner?"

"I didn't want to get you worried. Like I said, it's probably nothing."

"Well, let's call Shari and see if we can talk to her that way." Jim pulled out his phone.

"You can put that away. I already did. I talked to Shari the other day, but Sissy wasn't home. That's when Shari told me about the phone and said she and Sissy have both been swamped by final projects and papers."

Jim shoved his cell back in his pocket. "What about emails?"

"I'm getting emails almost every day. Sissy said she'd lost her cell phone somewhere on campus, and she'd reported it as missing. She wanted to check the lost and found before she canceled it and got a new one. She didn't want the hassle of setting up a new phone if she could get her old one back. I don't know if she's had time to check yet. She said if she didn't find it, she'd just get a new one when she gets home."

"Do you want me to email her and tell her to call?" Jim took out his phone to send an email.

Maggie sighed. "No, don't do that. I almost didn't call you because she hates it when we smother her."

"I know," he said. "I called her when she got back to Missoula, and she told me how much work she had to do. She also said she was trying to figure out some things for herself. She didn't really want to talk on the phone. She said she wanted to wait until she gets home. I don't think we should push her. As long as you're getting emails, let's let her finish up the semester. She'll be home soon."

"I used to be so level-headed." Maggie shook her head. "You must think I'm the worst mother hen ever."

Jim placed a comforting hand on Maggie's shoulder. "No,

darling. I just think you're missing Sissy. We all are. Even Daniel was talking about it not feeling right without her here. I don't think she has any idea how big a hole she left when she went off on her own." He gave Maggie a big hug. "You call me if you're lonely and want to talk. I'm pretty lonely, too."

SISSY SHIVERED UNDER the thin blanket. She didn't know how long she'd been in the cell. It had to have been days, maybe weeks. Surely Maggie would tell someone when she didn't hear from Sissy. They usually spoke every other day. Jim would come. He wouldn't leave her there. Meanwhile, she did have occasional company.

Milton paced in front of her cell. "Ray tells me that Jim is weak. Why do you want to stay with him? He may be big and tough, but he doesn't want to lead. He depends a lot on your old man Daniel, and there's no discipline. He even wants to start some kind of pack council with betas on it. Who gives a shit what betas think?"

Milton whirled around to face Sissy. "Wolves don't do democracy, Sissy. It's not in our nature. We respect strength, and if we aren't strong, somebody stronger will come along and take what's ours."

Sissy took a deep breath. "He'll kill you when he finds out."

"I don't think so. He'll be pissed. Maybe he'll file a petition with the pack leaders, but it'll be too late. On the next full moon, you'll be mated to Jackson. You'll be too weak to resist, and once the mating is accomplished, there's nothing he can do about it."

Sissy narrowed her eyes. "I'll *never* mate with Jackson. You know that. You're just going to start a war and get a lot of people killed."

Milton wasn't listening. "I thought about taking you myself. I still might. But Jackson needs you. I'll show him how to handle you. He can gain a lot of strength from you when you form a mating bond, and once you're settled together, well, if Jim has an accident and gets himself killed, then you and Jackson can go to Laramie and challenge for leadership. Then I'll have both packs under my control."

JIM CALLED TO wish Maggie a happy birthday and find out what time she wanted to go to dinner. Usually Sissy would go out with them to a nice restaurant, and then they'd come back home for cake and ice cream. It was going to be hard for Maggie this year, but if he had anything to do with it, Sissy would never be away from home for Maggie's birthday again.

"Oh, Jim, I don't feel like going out, but I do want you to come over."

He'd expected Maggie to be a little blue, but he didn't like the way she sounded. "What's the matter, darling?"

"I'll talk to you when you get here."

Jim showed up at Maggie's house with a chocolate fudge cake, her favorite, and a bouquet of yellow roses, but she barely noticed them.

He followed her into the kitchen. She put the flowers in a vase on the counter, fussing with the arrangement. He came up behind her and put his hands on her shoulders. "I know you're missing Sissy, but she'll be home in a few days for Christmas break. We can all go out then."

Maggie turned to him and crumpled in tears. "She forgot my birthday."

Jim held Maggie in his arms. "Oh, honey. I'm sure she just got caught up in school and lost track of the time. Does she have a new phone yet?"

"Not yet."

"And she didn't send you an email?"

"She's been emailing, and I got one today but she didn't even mention my birthday. I know she's busy, but her emails are so impersonal. It's like talking to a stranger."

"May I see them?"

Jim checked Maggie's log of emails. She was right. Anybody could have written them. They were brief and only mentioned school and a few things she was doing with her friends. They all ended with "Give my love to everybody," but no one was mentioned by name. He didn't want to worry Maggie further, so he kept his voice calm, but everything inside of him was screaming that something was seriously wrong. "Have you talked to Shari?"

"Not since I called that one time. I tried again earlier this week but Shari didn't answer."

"Well, let's give Shari a call right now." He punched in the number, and she answered after a few rings.

"Shari, it's Jim Winter. Is Sissy there?"

"No, she's not home. She finished her finals, and she and Jax and some others went camping out at the lodge reserve. I think they were having one last bash before everybody goes home for Christmas break."

"Do you have Jax's number? I'd like to get in touch with her."

"I can give you his number, but it won't do you any good. They're out of cell phone range out there. There's no signal. I can get her to call as soon as I hear from her. That's the best I can do."

"That would be good. You have a good Christmas if I don't hear from you before that." *You lying bitch.*

Something was definitely wrong.

Jim turned to Maggie. "I don't want to worry you, but I think we need to check on Sissy. Shari said she was on a campout, but that sounds like an excuse. I want you to call the registrar at the university tomorrow morning and get the names of her professors. Call them and find out if Sissy's been attending classes, then you call me as soon as you hear anything. I'm going to send Daniel over here to stay with you tonight."

Maggie gnawed on her bottom lip. "You're scaring me, Jim."

He took Maggie in his arms. "I don't mean to worry you. It could be just some college-age stupidity. God knows we were stupid when we were that age. I'd stay with you myself, but there's something I've got to do." He gave her a kiss and wiped at her eyes. "I'm sorry your birthday is ruined, but we'll make it up to you over Christmas when Sissy is home."

Jim was on the phone to Daniel as soon as he was out the door. He explained the situation and told his Second to round up Trace and Ray and have Clint keep them at the house. "Use some armed guards, chain them up if you have to, then get over to Maggie's house. She shouldn't be alone."

chapter eighteen

When Jim arrived back at the ranch, Clint was waiting in the study with Trace. "Where's Ray?" Jim asked.

"He tried to run, so I've got him locked up. He hasn't said much so far, just denies he knows anything about Missoula pack business."

"What about you?" Jim turned his steely gaze on Trace. "What can you tell me about what's going on?"

"I don't know, sir. Clint just came and got me. I heard him talking to Daniel, and it sounds like you're worried about Sissy, but I don't know anything about her. I could call my folks. They might know something, but I doubt it. They haven't been close to the pack for a while. I'm sure Milton wouldn't trust them with any information, and I don't want to put them in danger." Trace hesitated. "I tried to talk to Sissy at Thanksgiving."

"What about?"

"I just wanted to know if she was fitting in. She got real defensive, said she could take care of herself. I think I offended her.

I guess I shoulda told you about that. She looked thoughtful, you know, like something was on her mind, but she didn't tell me and I didn't sense she was scared."

"Why would you be concerned about Sissy?"

"The pack up there is rougher than this one. They settle things by fighting, including disputes about females. The females don't get much say in the matter."

Jim charged up into Trace's face. "And you didn't think to tell us about that?"

"At first I didn't know how it was here. I thought maybe all packs were like that, but after I met Sissy at Thanksgiving, I was worried about her safety."

"Well, I'm worried about her safety too, real worried. We haven't heard from her in a while, and I talked to Shari and I think she was lying to me."

"That Shari'd do anything Milton or Jax told her to do. You can't trust her."

"You could have told us that earlier, too. If Milton or Jackson wanted to hold her, where would they have her?"

"Milton has a house in town, but if they were keeping her locked up, they'd have her at the pack lodge. Especially if they thought you might try to come get her. The place is like a fortress. It's built right into the side of the mountain. There's only one road going in, and it'd be hard to approach it without being seen, and there's only one entrance to the lodge."

Trace thought for a moment. "If they have her, she'd be in the basement. They have a locked cell down there with bars, and there aren't any windows. It's carved out of solid rock. I saw it once when I was a kid, and I hoped I never ended up in there." Trace looked at their distraught faces. "I'm sorry. I guess I'm not helping much."

Jim tried to remain calm. "It'd help if you could draw a map of the area and the layout of the lodge. Show the spots where Milton would likely post guards."

Trace winced. "Okay, I can do that. I'm sorry I didn't tell you before, but you've been real good to me since I've been here, and I do want to help you."

"Good, because you're going to Missoula with me at first light. I'll go over the map you come up with in a bit." Jim turned to Clint. "I want to talk to Ray and see what we can get out of him. Have him brought to the kitchen."

It didn't take long for two armed wranglers to bring Ray into the kitchen in handcuffs. He looked a little scuffed up.

"I don't know why you're treating me like this," Ray whined, testing the cuffs. "I ain't done nothing wrong."

Jim looked him squarely in the eyes. "Why'd you try to run and resist Clint and his men?"

"I was scared. They came in calling for me, and you ain't exactly trusted me."

"Show me I can trust you. Why did Milton send you here?"

"Just to work. He needed to trade somebody, so I volunteered. I thought it'd be good to work down here. I've just been trying to mind my own business and do a good job for you."

Jim appraised the man standing before him. "Why do I think you're lying?"

"I don't know, God's truth."

Jim held out the cell phone that Clint had taken off of Ray. "What do you think I'm going to find in here?" he said, flipping it open. "Looks like there's one number you've been calling at the same time several times a week. It's a Missoula number. Whose number is it?"

"It's my girlfriend. I've been missing her real bad."

"What's her name? I'd like to give her a call."

"Ahh, her name's Louanne, but she's probably not at home right now."

"Clint, go get one of the disposable cell phones in my office. They're with the emergency supplies. I need to make a call."

While Clint left, Jim let Ray squirm in silence. When Clint returned, Jim told him to put the phone on speaker and dial the number and ask for Louanne.

When someone picked up, Clint slurred his speech and asked, "Lulu, sweetheart, you there?"

Milton's voice could be heard clearly. "Who is this? How'd you get this number?"

"Oh, sorry, mister," Clint answered. "I been drinking a little. I musta dialed wrong."

The call clicked off at the other end, and Clint closed the phone. Everybody looked at Ray.

Jim cocked his head. "So, do you want to start over with your story, or is Milton your girlfriend?"

"Well, you know how it is," Ray said, averting Jim's eyes. "Milton told me to keep him informed of what you were doing, but I didn't ever have anything much to say. I never saw much, and nobody talked around me."

In one fluid move, Jim picked up the scrawny man by the front of his shirt. The cuffs clanked. "What about Sissy?"

"I don't know nothing about her, I swear," Ray said, shaking. "Milton doesn't tell me what he's doing."

"How many men does he keep around him?"

"Maybe ten or twelve, maybe more. He don't trust nobody, not even Jax."

While Clint took Ray back to the holding cell, Jim went to the study to check on Trace. He'd drawn a clear diagram of the lodge and the road approaching it, and he'd marked likely spots to post guards.

Jim studied the maps. Without looking up he said, "What about Milton's guards? Do they have any training?"

"Not that I ever saw. They're more like a bunch of bullies. They come out and stand around Milton like they're his posse."

Jim looked at Trace. "One last thing. Can you shift at will?"

Trace nodded. "Yeah, but I never let Milton know that."

"Good." Jim nodded. "Now, how many of Milton's men do you think can make the shift without the full moon?"

"Milton and Jax," the young man answered promptly. "Jax is Milton's Second, but our old Alpha's Second is still there, the last I heard, and I think he's working with Milton, so that'd make three. Maybe one other. I doubt there's any more than that."

"You did a good job, Trace. Go get some sleep and be back here at six."

Clint was waiting outside Jim's office. When Trace was out of earshot he asked, "So what's the plan?"

"I'll fly Trace up with me in the morning. Maggie's going to call Sissy's professors. That might give us some information about how long this has been going on. I'll rent a car at the airport, and we'll go see what we can get out of Sissy's roommate. I want you to get me some satellite images that show the terrain around the lodge, see if you can work up a line of approach. You can send it to me when we get there. I also want you to have your men standing by. I'll call for backup as soon as I know what we're up against. We'll need a force that's comparable to whatever they can put in the field, both men and weapons. We don't want to go into this battle with our dicks in our hands. And have someone keep an eye on Trace tonight."

"Do you trust him?" Clint asked.

Jim thought about the question for a moment. "Yeah, I do. I think he's being straight with us. You could smell the fear rolling off of Ray. I haven't gotten any of that with Trace."

Clint nodded. "I'll take care of everything here. Get some sleep. I have a feeling the next few days are going to be rough."

Jim forced himself to rest for a few hours, but he was up at four. He and Clint went over the helicopter preflight checklist carefully. They were loading the necessary gear when Trace came by, looking up at the vehicle, eyes wide. "I've never ridden in one of these."

"Now you get your chance," Jim said as he finished. "Don't get airsick."

The flight was uneventful and mostly quiet before Trace finally said, "I'm worried about my folks. I've been thinking I've been behind the curve in all of this. I left them when I was eighteen, joined the Army. I was gone for a while. I'd probably still be gone but my dad broke his leg, so I came home to help.

"When I got back, things had changed, but I didn't ask many questions. My parents seemed a lot older, but looking back now, I think they were real worried. They were staying away from the pack, and they warned me not to get in with Jax."

Jim glanced at him. "I take it you didn't need that warning."

Trace shook his head. "No. I didn't like the man, but Milton tried to feel me out to see if I wanted to work for him. I told him I had plenty of work on the ranch, and he let it go, but I guess that's what got me traded. I think he threatened my folks, maybe threatened a lot of folks. I just thought he was an asshole, but I didn't think he was dangerous. If I had, I'd have told you."

"I want to believe you would have, but you're going to be able to help me now, and if we get through this, you're going to have to help your folks and your whole pack. Think you're strong enough for that?"

"Yes, sir. I'll do what I need to do to make it right."

It was almost noon when they reached Missoula. Jim rented an SUV at the airport, and they drove to Shari's apartment. They stopped down the street when they recognized Jax's truck parked out front.

After a while, Jax and Wade came out and got in the truck and left. Jim removed a large duffel bag, and he and Trace walked up to the apartment and knocked. Shari answered the door, her mouth falling open at the sight of Jim.

He shoved the door open. She ran for her phone, but Trace grabbed it out of her hand and held her arms back.

"What are you doing here?" she asked, struggling.

"We just want to have a little talk with you," Jim said.

Trace gently pushed Shari down so she sat on the couch. He stood behind her, and Jim pulled up a chair in front of her.

Jim leaned forward. "Where's Sissy?"

"I don't know." She sniffled, avoiding his gaze. "Probably at Jax's."

"We just watched Jax leave, so I don't believe you."

Jim told Trace to check Sissy's room. The young man came out holding Sissy's cell phone. "I found this, and it looks like her clothes and makeup, toothbrush and everything are all still here."

Jim's eyes narrowed. "You told Maggie that Sissy had lost her phone."

"She . . . she must have found it." She gripped the cushions on either side of her.

Jim punched in Maggie's number, and she picked up on the first ring. "Sissy?"

"No, honey, it's Jim. I'm in Sissy's apartment. What did you find out from the school?"

"Her graduate advisor said she hadn't been to classes in three weeks. I've been going crazy. Where is she, Jim?"

"That's what I'm going to find out right now. Call your parents to stay with you until we get this sorted out. I'll call you as soon as I know anything."

Jim hung up and brought his face within inches of Shari's. "You're going to tell me the truth, *now*."

"Okay." Shari's hands shook. "She's been gone for a while. I thought she was shacking up with Jax, and I didn't want her mom to worry."

"Wrong answer." Jim gripped her face in one hand and yanked her to her feet. "Trace, tie her to the bed. I bet between the two of us, we can convince her to tell us the truth."

Trace pinned her arms behind her while Jim went to the kitchen and rifled through the drawers until he found a large butcher knife. "This ought to work." He came back out to the living room, holding it up.

Shari's eyes widened as Trace began to drag her toward the bedroom. As Jim advanced on her with the knife, she panicked. "Please. I'll tell you anything you want."

Jim nodded for Trace to stop, and he walked over to her, knife in hand. When she didn't immediately begin to speak, Jim used the big knife to flick off her top button, then the next.

"Milton has her. She's at the lodge," she blurted. "When we went out there, I didn't know they were going to do anything to her."

"What have they done to her?"

"I don't know. I haven't been out there since the night they took her. They locked her up in the holding cell."

"Why? Is Milton trying to use her to get to me?"

"No, he wants her to mate with Jax. When she refused, he

locked her up. He's got some fucked-up idea that Sissy can turn Jax into the kind of man Milton wants him to be. He thinks when she mates with Jax, he'll magically get stronger. They're holding her until the full moon when they're going to force her to mate with Jax."

Jim's roar of anger shook the apartment. He fought the urge to shift and slash her throat to stop her words.

"I don't know why she's resisting. Jax is a good catch. He'll be leader someday," she said, her eyes hot on Jim. "But she's still hung up over you. One night when she'd had too much to drink, she told me how she threw herself at you, and you didn't want her. She should have taken what they offered, and she and Jax would be mated by now."

Jim was rigid with the effort to control his wolf. Sissy was his mate. He'd failed her once and then he let her go, and now he'd failed her again, but running after her would get both of them killed.

Jim looked at Trace. "There are chains in the duffel bag. Chain her up and gag her. I don't want to hear another word out of her."

When Trace had the young woman secured, they threw Shari's jacket over her chains and pulled up her hood. Jim grabbed her purse and phone, so it would look like she'd gone out. They got her loaded on the floor of the SUV and covered her up, and Trace drove. When they were well away from Shari's neighborhood, Jim called Clint. "They have her at the pack lodge. What do you have for me?"

"I'm sending images to your phone now. Do you see that cliff to the southeast of the lodge? I think that would give us the best cover to get close, but we'd have to get everybody up the cliff before we move on the lodge. Check it out with Trace and see if he's familiar with it."

"I will. We'll go out there tonight to scout it out. I need you and Daniel both. You're the only ones besides Trace and me who can shift at will."

"And Sissy," Clint reminded Jim.

"Yeah, and Sissy, if she can. I don't know what shape she's going to be in. From what Trace's told me, we can expect three to five shifters, and probably ten to twelve others who'll be armed, so we'll need at least nine more men and weapons."

"I've already alerted everybody, and we should be loaded up and ready to go in about an hour. We'll have weapons, climbing gear, light explosives, everything we'll need. It'll take us twelve hours to get there if we go the speed limit, and I don't want to get stopped with weapons on board. I thought I'd send Daniel and one of the men in your truck ahead of us, and they can watch out for the law. The rest of us will follow in vans."

The magnitude of what they were doing struck Jim. He'd been in military operations many times before, but never with so much personally at stake.

Clint must have sensed the stress in Jim's silence. "Sissy's like my sister. We'll get her, Uncle Jim."

chapter nineteen

"I know," Jim answered. "I'll check back and let you know where we can rendezvous. And tell Daniel to talk to Maggie and make sure she stays put. We don't need her in the middle of this."

The sun was setting as Trace and Jim drove the SUV out of town. When they got within a few miles of the pack lodge, Trace pulled onto a small side road and parked. "This is as far as we can go on the road without risking being seen. We're still about five or six miles out, but Milton may have posted a lookout."

"Then we're on foot from here." Jim checked to make sure Shari was still securely chained in the back of the SUV before they set out. Since she could only shift with the full moon, she was stuck in the chains until they let her out.

The men shifted for their recon. Jim watched Trace. His shift was quick and smooth, and as a wolf, he was only slightly smaller than Jim. They crossed the road and hung back in the treeline that ran parallel to road. Within a mile they spotted a truck parked off the side of the road. Two men sat in the front seat. The two men were unaware of the wolves, so Jim got close enough to hear that they were grumbling about being bored and cold.

As they neared the lodge, they pulled deeper into the woods. The road ended in a gravel parking area next to a clearing, where a floodlight created a pool of yellow light. The lodge had floodlights on the corners and lights on the porch. Inside, Jim could see several rooms on the first floor were brightly lit. As Jim and Trace skirted the lighted areas, sniffing for anything that was amiss, they counted two guards at the edge of the parking lot, a guard to the side of the lodge at the end of the road, two more at the base of the lodge steps, and another two on the porch.

They skirted the edges of the open space, and Jim checked out all the possible approaches to the lodge. Trace had been right. The place was a fortress. When he'd seen enough, they ran deeper into the woods to shift back to human form. "I've never seen it like this," Trace said.

Jim kept his voice low. "They've got to be expecting us. How many did you count?"

"I saw nine, counting the two in the truck."

"So did I. We can probably assume there are a few more inside the lodge. Did you recognize the trucks?"

"Milton's truck was there, and so was Jax's, which means Wade is probably inside, too. I didn't recognize the others."

"I want to check out the cliff area before we leave."

Trace nodded. "I can lead you there. It's not far."

The men moved quietly through the forest until they came to a steep cliff. They looked down. Jim estimated the drop to be about two stories.

"Let's climb down and go back along the ravine," he said.

The cliff face was steep and crumbly, but some exposed roots gave them the handholds they needed to get most of the way down, and they dropped the rest of the way. Once they were on level ground, Trace said, "The cliff isn't as tall further down, and the ravine runs all the way back parallel to the road, then it turns and bisects the road about a half mile before the turnoff where we parked."

"Do you think Milton will post guards on the ravine?"

The young man shrugged. "I would, but I don't know if he would. We can watch out for them as we go back. There's a lower wash that runs along the outside of the ravine. We used to play out here as kids. If we stick to that, we shouldn't be seen."

They shifted back to wolf form and silently ran along the wash. As they neared the road, Jim bumped Trace. They spotted two shadowy forms hidden in the trees flanking the ravine where it met the road. The two wolves backtracked until they were out of sight. They crossed the road, staying hidden in the darkness, until they got back to the SUV and shifted to human form again.

"We need to get a room and check in with Clint. We could use something to eat, too."

They headed toward the highway and the airport and found a small motel. Jim paid for four rooms, telling the night clerk he was expecting some associates for a sales meeting the next day. They dropped off their gear and headed to a truck stop with a brightly lit café.

Jim parked at the edge of the parking lot in case Shari, who was still chained up in the back, tried to make a ruckus. He called to the back, "You stay real quiet back there, and we'll bring you something to eat."

Inside, the truck stop was warm and noisy. "Order something big," Jim said. "We ran off a bunch of energy back there, and we're going to need every ounce of strength we can muster tomorrow."

They each ordered a porterhouse steak, potatoes, and eggs.

Trace said, "Can I ask you something? Would you really have hurt Shari to make her talk, or were you just bluffing?"

Jim paused. "Well, we didn't have to find that out, did we? But the only good bluff is the one you're prepared to carry through if someone calls you on it."

Jim ordered a burger to go for Shari, and they went back to the motel. He pitched one of the room keys to Trace and said, "Get some sleep. The men will be here before light."

Jim determined it was dark enough. He hoisted Shari over his shoulder, carried her into his room, and plopped her down on the bed. He called Clint, who told him they were making good time. Jim gave him their location. He washed up, came out, and sat Shari up. "I got you some food, and I'll give it to you as long as you don't try to yell. Is that a deal?"

She nodded.

Jim sat on the side of the bed and pulled her over in front of him to sit between his legs. He left some of the chains on her, but he loosened the ones around her arms and hands. Then he took off her gag and handed her the takeout sack.

"Are you going to make me sit here in your lap to eat?"

The pouting expression on the young woman's face made him want to hurt her, but all he said was, "Yes. That way I can break your pretty little neck if you decide to act up, so just eat and be nice."

"I expect you want me to sleep with you, too." She looked at him, fluttering her eyelashes.

Jim smiled. She was far too confident about her attractiveness. "Oh, I'll be sleeping with you, but you're going to be wearing those chains, so I don't expect too much action out of you."

Shari sniffed, sticking her lower lip out. She ate the burger and then asked to go to the bathroom.

"Do what you're going to do, because I'm not getting up with you again tonight." He put the gag back in her mouth and carried her into the bathroom. When he stood there waiting for her to go, she looked at him with pleading eyes. "You go on," he told her. "It's not anything I haven't seen before, and I'm not leaving you alone, even for a little while."

Reluctantly, Shari worked down her pants and sat. When she was done, he carried her back to the bedroom, manacled her hands, and fixed her chains securely to the head of the bed. He covered her with a blanket and lay down beside her and turned off the lights.

Sleep didn't come for a long time. Jim ran through possible scenarios, laying down the plan in his mind. He checked off men and weapons and equipment—anything that would keep his mind from picturing Sissy. She had to have been waiting for him to come and rescue her for weeks. How could she know that Shari had been covering her absence? Did she think they didn't care? Had she given up hope?

SISSY TRIED TO clear her mind, but everything was foggy. She was lying naked on the cold stone floor, where she'd just changed back to human form. She was shifting involuntarily now, spending more and more time in wolf form. She tried to stand, but her legs were too weak, so she dragged herself across the rough stone to the filthy mattress, and pulled strips of the torn blanket around her.

She couldn't hold on to rational thought any more. Sensations and emotions beat down on her in waves—hunger, cold, pain, despair, and finally, killing rage. She had no control over the powerful shivers or the painful muscle contractions that shook her body.

The scent of raw meat filled her nostrils, and she shifted instantly. She saw men outside her cage. Snarling, she threw herself against the bars, saliva dripping from her jaws.

Dimly, she saw Milton watching her shift from a shivering, incoherent woman into a raging beast. She knew he thought she'd be more subdued by this time, but her wolf was still out of control.

"Throw the meat in there, but don't get too close," she heard him warn. "She'd rip you apart to get at that meat."

They'd been starving her, giving her only water and some bread and food scraps. Her body craved the protein he'd been withholding. At this point, she'd tear into any meat. She guessed the chunks of beef were laced with a hormone that would bring on her mating heat. After a couple of days of hormone therapy, she'd be desperate to mate with Jax when the full moon pulled at her.

Adult females went through reproductive cycles that produced periods where the females were more fertile and extremely receptive to sex, but the mating heat was different. It was a specific instinctive response designed to create both a physical and psychic bond between mated partners.

Scientists had identified and recreated the hormone, but they hadn't been able to determine how it worked. It somehow triggered a change in both the male and female that forged a link, allowing each partner to sense the other's presence and moods.

The hormone would release naturally when triggered by certain mating behaviors and scents, but more so by an instinctive recognition of the one other whom both body and mind accepted as its mate. Scientific tests had shown that by using large doses of the artificial hormone, they could override instinct and bring on the heat without the natural triggers.

Unable to control herself, Sissy gulped down the last morsel of meat.

"Hose her down," Milton ordered. "She stinks."

When the strong stream of cold water hit her, Sissy retreated to the corner of her cage and shifted back to a shivering human.

IT WAS STILL dark when Daniel, Clint, and ten others from Clint's security force arrived at the motel the next morning in Jim's truck and two vans. Jim wasn't surprised to see Randi, Sissy's best friend, with the group. Clint had been training several females for his security team.

Jim pointed the team toward their rooms. "You guys keep out of sight and get a few hours rest. We've got a hard day ahead of us. Daniel, Clint, Trace—come with me."

Jim described what he and Trace had seen the night before, and they went over the terrain map and plotted in the guard positions they'd spotted. Jim told Clint, "You're going to hang back until we're in position, then come in with the chopper, stir things up, and give us cover. Once we're in the lodge, you can set the bird down and come in right behind us. We'll need you in the lodge, and you'll be in a position to help evacuate the wounded if necessary." He pointed out a clear area of the parking lot where Clint could land the helicopter.

"The rest of us will go in from the staging area on foot," Jim said. "We can get the best cover if we stay in the ravine all the way to the lodge, but the cliff is about twenty-five feet high at that point."

"No problem. I brought ropes and hooks," Clint responded. "I'm sure you can even get this old man up there." Clint hooked a thumb toward Daniel. Daniel just grunted.

"What are we facing in terms of men and equipment?" Clint

asked.

Trace spoke up. "As far as I know, Milton hasn't given his men any special training. They all hunt, so they know how to shoot, and they can fight, but not necessarily as a unit. I didn't see any special communications equipment on them. Did you, Jim?"

"No. They probably have a few walkie-talkies for the guys out on the road. They were all armed, but it looked like they'd brought their own weapons. I saw some bolt-action deer rifles and a couple of shotguns. Some of them had sidearms. Only the two on the porch of the lodge had real assault rifles. I didn't get the feeling they actually expect an attack. It was more like Milton wanted them there as a show of force, in case we did try to come after Sissy. I'm sure they haven't gotten wind of the fact that we're here, and I want to keep it that way."

They went over the details again, and then Trace and Clint left to check on the rest of the team.

"What are you going to do with her?" Daniel asked, nodding toward Shari. Still gagged and chained to the bed, Shari squirmed and glared at Jim.

"I'll take care of her," Jim said, loosening her chains so she could sit up. He removed her gag, but she immediately flew into a list of threats that she'd evidently been running over in her mind for the last hours, so he gagged her again. He led her to the bathroom, waited for her, then chained her back on the bed.

Leaning in close, Jim said, "I should just kill you for what you did. You know that, don't you? But when this is all over, I'll let your new pack leader decide your punishment. If you'll shut up, I'll give you some water before we go."

Shari nodded, and he removed her gag and fed her from a bottle of water. "Are you just going to leave me here all chained up?" she asked after she swallowed.

"It's not nearly as bad as what you did to Sissy," he reminded her, replacing the gag. "If I remember, I'll send somebody back to let you loose. If not, I'm sure the maids will find you tomorrow. You can try to explain to them why you're chained to a bed." Jim went back to ignoring the female's muffled screeches and got ready for what he had to do. He dressed and made some calls. He arranged for the rented SUV to be picked up at the motel, and he settled up the bill for their motel rooms, keeping his room for one more night to hold Shari.

He checked in with a frantic Maggie and tried to sound confident. "I'm going to see Milton today, and I'll convince him to let us have Sissy. We should all be on the road home by tomorrow."

"I know you're lying, Jim," Maggie said, "but I trust you to bring her home."

"You know I will," he said. *Or die trying.*

He paced the small room. His body prickled with the need to shift and fight, but they couldn't go in until after dark. He pushed the impulse down and centered his thoughts on the next few hours.

As he walked out the door, he remembered to hang the "Do Not Disturb" sign on the knob.

chapter twenty

Jim and Daniel walked into the café. A large silver Christmas tree stood in the entryway, and the whole restaurant was festooned with red and green tinsel garlands. It was Christmas Eve.

Jim put on a big smile for the hostess as he scented the room. If there were any Werewolves in the café, they'd have to take care of them before they alerted Milton, but fortunately the room was wolf-free. He'd called earlier and arranged to use a private dining room for his "regional sales meeting." He needed a private room big enough to fit all of his team for the briefing, and the small rooms at the motel weren't big enough for fourteen large-sized Weres.

The hostess beamed at him as she led him back to the private room. Jim turned on the charm. He mentioned that if this worked out well for his meeting, it might be a monthly event as he had several sales teams operating in the Northwest. And he'd paid well for the spread he'd ordered.

Just as he'd requested, tables had been pushed together to

form one large conference table. A buffet had been laid out along one wall with hot chafing dishes full of scrambled eggs, bacon, ham slices, and home fries. An assortment of biscuits, rolls, muffins, and sweet rolls, and gallons of hot coffee and juice would complete the meal.

"Is this what you wanted?" she asked, eager to please.

Jim said. "This is perfect. The only other thing I need is a copy machine. I'm sure you have one around here someplace."

"There's one in the office you can use."

"That's wonderful. Now if you could show my associate the copier, I'd appreciate it. Then could you scoot on up to the front and watch out for my sales team? They should be arriving shortly."

"I'll send them back," she said, then left with Daniel.

Jim had told Clint to have the men, and Randi, dress casually and enter the café in groups of twos and threes. Pretty soon they were all assembled.

"Grab a plate and fuel up," Jim announced. "It's going to be several hours before we can go in, and I don't want anybody running on empty later tonight." He gave them time to eat, then posted a watch at the door before he started the briefing. He passed out copies of the terrain maps and the layout of the lodge that Trace had drawn.

Jim assessed the team. Daniel was on one side of the table, steadfast and experienced; Clint on the other, fierce, strong, and loyal. Trace sat next to Clint. Jim noticed that over the last few days, Trace had come into his own strength, morphing from an uncertain young man into the dominant alpha his pack would need.

Both Trace and Clint would be leaders someday, and he was glad to have them with him. The others were a mixed group: two were men from the pack he'd known most of his life, five were wranglers from the ranch, and four were Sissy's age—friends who were willing to lay down their lives for her.

"Clint tells me that each of you volunteered for this, and I want you to know I appreciate it," Jim said. "You should all be home with your families today, but we're all family here, and Sissy is a part of that family.

"What we have to do is not going to be easy. We're going into an unknown situation against an unknown number of men, on their turf. We're likely to be outnumbered, and we could be walking into a trap.

"That said, I don't think they're expecting a full-out assault. They don't know what Sissy means to each of us. That's a strength for us. They're also not well-trained or well-armed. Each of you has been training with Clint, and that's another strength for us. We have a plan, and if we execute the plan, we'll catch them by surprise."

Jim and Clint walked them through the strategy they'd laid out and answered questions until they were satisfied that everyone knew his or her part. They arranged a rendezvous spot close to the lodge but well off the road where they would assemble, change, and prepare their gear.

Then the team members left the café in casual groups, laughing and chatting. Jim brought up the rear, paid off the tab, and winked at the hostess, but when each of them got outside they put on their game faces.

Jim dropped off Clint and Sissy's friend Terry at the airport. Clint would fly Jim's helicopter to a secluded field a few miles from the lodge and wait for the signal to attack. Trace led the small convoy across town and back to the rendezvous location. They pulled the vehicles into the brush out of sight. It was about an hour to sundown, but in the woods during winter, dark would descend quickly. Those who wouldn't be shifting changed into dark clothes and helped each other apply camo face paint. Next, they all sprayed themselves with various wildlife scents to confuse the guards in the woods.

Clint had stocked the vans with everything they'd need. Jim saw that his nephew had assembled an impressive array of firepower. Daniel handed out four Bushmaster combat rifles and extra magazines to the best shots. They'd each been trained to use the assault rifle. Jim was surprised to learn one of their top shots was Randi. She caught him looking at her.

"What?" she asked. "You think I can't shoot because I'm a girl? That's precisely why I shoot. I'm not as big and tough as some of you guys, but I'm just as deadly."

Jim held his hands up in mock surrender, and moved on to inspect the others. They adjusted Sig Sauer semi-automatic pistols in holsters and checked their clips.

"At least we don't have to worry about being poisoned by silver bullets," Daniel commented. Jim grunted. That was just more of the false mythology. Lead bullets would do the job just fine, but with their Werewolf physiology, they could withstand a lot more damage than humans.

They all carried Ka-Bar military knives on their belts or in their boots. Once the shooting started, the fighting would move in close. Jim was impressed with his nephew's thoroughness. He must have ordered the equipment months ago, planning for any contingency. Jim was glad he'd put Clint in charge of security. He couldn't have asked for anyone better.

Even Jim, Daniel, and Trace, the three who would shift to wolf form, were given gear. Their clothes and opposable thumbs would go away when they shifted, but Clint had rigged up harnesses and packs that would stay with them after a shift. Jim and Trace got harnesses to carry the climbing equipment. Daniel had a special pack with the explosives that he would use to blow open Sissy's cell door.

Once everyone was geared up, they took their positions. Two of Clint's men left to go up through the trees and take out the guards in the truck. Jim had made it clear that their objective wasn't to kill everybody they met. He couldn't know if some of the Missoula pack was working for Milton against their will.

That was the problem in Werewolf society. Free will for the lower ranks could be nonexistent if the leader wanted it that way. It was nearly impossible for most of the pack to disobey the dominant Alpha. The team would try to take down their opponents with less than lethal force, but they were prepared to kill if they had to.

Jim and Trace went ahead of the main group to take care of the guards posted at the entrance to the ravine. They split up and circled silently through the trees to come up behind the sentries. Jim spotted Trace moving abreast of him on the far side of the ravine.

The untrained lookouts were watching forward for anyone approaching the ravine and never heard the two big men slip up behind them. Jim put his man in a chokehold until he passed out. Trace took his man down and ground his face in the dirt to muffle his cries. Silently, the others came forward and gagged, cuffed, and chained the men.

Jim, Trace, and Daniel shifted and ran down the ravine, keeping an eye out for other sentries. When they got to the section of cliff nearest the lodge, all three shifted back to human form and removed the harnesses that held the climbing gear. Jim and Trace threw ropes topped with grappling hooks, set the hooks, and scrambled up the twenty-five-foot cliff face. At the top, they set their ropes more securely and added a few more, so by the time the rest of the team arrived, five ropes dangled to the ground below. The strongest among them stayed on the ground and anchored the rope for the others until the last one duck-walked up the crumbling cliff.

When everyone was at the top, the shifters changed into wolf form and the others took their designated places. The timing was important in their attack. They spread out using the cover of darkness, the trees, and the trucks in the parking lot. They counted on the oil and gasoline odors from the parking area to mask the scent of the approaching wolves.

The attack began with a noisy assault by the men who had come up the road after disabling the guards in the truck. The idea was to make the Missoula wolves think they were being attacked from the road and draw them away from the lodge. The first shots and yells had most of the small force leaving their positions to defend the road just beyond the lodge area.

To create additional havoc, Clint arrived in the helicopter. He swooped, shining a bright spotlight on the scattering guards. Terry rode shotgun with Clint and sniped at the Missoula men on the ground.

The noise and light created panic. Some guards ran toward the road, while others ran toward their cars and trucks to get away. Instead, they ran right into the waiting assault team.

Jim and the other shifters bounded across the clearing for the lodge. One of the guards on the porch shifted into a large shaggy gray wolf. The Laramie snipers laid down covering fire for the Laramie wolves as the lodge guards took cover and fired back. Jim felt a burning as a bullet grazed his shoulder, but his eyes were on the lodge door, the one weak spot in the fortress.

The custom-made lodge door had a carved wood frame with

a large decorative inset of etched glass, showing a wolf howling at the moon. Jim's objective was to go straight through.

Trace launched past Jim and smashed into the gray wolf standing between them and the door, clearing the way. Jim sailed through the door in a shower of glass, and Daniel came right behind him.

According to Trace's diagram of the lodge, Milton's office was on the right side of the wide hall, and a big meeting room was to the left. Jim's mission was to locate Milton and Jax and keep them busy while Daniel freed Sissy. Jim threw himself against the door to Milton's office and splintered the door jamb while Daniel sprinted past him down the hall, toward the dungeon where Sissy was being held.

Jim skidded to a stop. The room was empty.

As he ran out to check the room across the hall, three men came flying out of the meeting room. Jim caught one man in his jaws and shook him. The other two made it outside, where the rest of his team waited.

Jim dropped the unconscious, bleeding man and strained to pick up the sound of anyone hiding in the other empty rooms. He could hear close fighting and shots from outside. By the sound of it, Trace was still battling with the Missoula wolf on the porch, but the lodge itself was strangely silent.

Then he heard a shot from the basement.

He bolted toward the back of the lodge and the narrow stairs that led down into the basement. At the bottom, he saw a man on the ground, his throat ripped out and his gun still in hand.

Daniel had already shifted to human form and was struggling to get the backpack off his back so he could set the explosive. He was talking to Sissy, but she was backed up against the wall, snarling at her father.

"When I got down here, she was human but bone-thin. She could barely stand. But then she shifted," Daniel caught his breath. "She's stronger now, but she doesn't recognize me."

SISSY HEARD THE gunshots and shouts from above, but she was weak and feverish and wasn't sure if she was hallucinating. The guard, who'd been nodding off across from her cell, jumped to his feet and pulled out his pistol. When a wolf appeared, the guard shot at him, but the wolf easily bypassed the bullet and vaulted off the stairs, taking out the man's throat with one slashing pass of his teeth.

The smell of blood hit Sissy, and she instantly shifted. She growled at the new wolf who'd come into her space and threw herself at the bars. In confusing response, the wolf in front of her disappeared and a man stood facing her.

Mostly feral now, Sissy had trouble thinking coherently, but she thought the man's scent was familiar. He was talking, and his soft voice was soothing. She backed away from him and felt herself being pulled back to human form when another larger wolf bounded down the stairs. Her wolf snapped back in charge, taking in the new threat.

The human was still talking to her, unconcerned about the large wolf approaching at his back. Her senses were barraged with sounds and scents. The blood, the sounds of fighting. She was ready to fight anyone, man or wolf, that came near her. But the big chocolate wolf was sending signals that prompted a different response. One that was familiar, something she knew, something she craved. Her mate.

Sissy's wolf went primal. She started to growl, her body demanding that the big male take her and claim her. Her skin felt on fire, and her empty womb throbbed with need. She rubbed her body against the bars to ease the burning, instinctively arching and growling low in the back of her throat to entice the male.

JIM DIDN'T NEED any enticement. The second he hit the room he smelled her need. He stood in front of the barred cell, looking at her emaciated body, her dirty matted fur, but all he could see was his mate. The rational part of his mind knew he needed to stay alert to the danger, but the wolf said to get inside the cell and take her and mark her.

Vaguely, Jim understood that Daniel had set the primer cord on the lock of the cell door and was trying to get Sissy to back away from the bars. He heard the old man tell him to get out of the way, but when Jim didn't respond, Daniel slapped him across the nose.

The whack caught Jim's attention. Daniel said, "I can't blow the lock until she moves away." He pointed to the far side of the cell where the bars met the wall. "Go over there and make her follow you as far into the corner as you can."

Jim rubbed his body along the bars of the cage and howled for her to come to him. Sissy only hesitated for a second. She pressed her body against his, ignoring the barrier between them. He walked her down the line of the bars as far from the cell door as he could get. Even separated by the cold steel and knowing that they might have to fight their way out of there, Sissy's body felt so right next to his. He poked his muzzle in between the bars and licked her face.

The blast stunned him for a second. He shook his head and saw the cell door hanging by one hinge. Sissy was lying at the back of her cell. He rushed past Daniel and into the cell when chaos erupted.

A huge black wolf appeared at the head of the stairs. Jim

instantly recognized Milton. He and his men must have been hiding, maybe on the top floor, waiting to trap them down there. A leaner black wolf just behind Milton was no doubt Jackson.

Milton launched himself at Daniel from high on the stairs. Jim leaped forward to meet him, but Daniel was in the cell's doorway. Milton caught Daniel in human form before he could shift and took him savagely to the floor, ripping at his defenseless body.

Jim sprang onto Milton's back and knocked him away from Daniel. They each sank their teeth in the other and rolled, locked together in a bloody embrace.

chapter twenty-one

Inside the cell, Sissy regained consciousness just as Jax jumped at her. She was still in wolf form and had rolled away from him, but he had her backed against the wall. The adrenaline rush cleared some of the fog from her mind, and she remembered snatches of what she'd been put through by this man and his father—tricked and taken prisoner, Milton threatening her, Jax pleading with her but refusing to help. She remembered the freezing cold and the starvation.

The images slammed into her, and she turned on Jax. Jax was bigger and stronger than she was, but rage filled her and she attacked him.

She sank her teeth into his shoulder and wouldn't let go until she came away with a bloody chunk of fur and muscle. He bit her neck, but she didn't feel the pain. He snapped at her and she caught his lip and ripped a chunk off. Howling in pain, he jerked his head away, and she bit into his front leg, crunching down until she heard the bone snap. His legs went out from under him, and he rolled belly up.

Sissy could have accepted his surrender, but he wouldn't have done the same for her. He would have raped her and forced her into a bond that only death could break.

Jax rolled and knocked her off of him and ran toward the stairs, his broken foreleg hindering his escape. She grabbed on to his retreating haunch and dug into the concrete floor with her claws. With his crippled leg, he couldn't get away.

He spun around to snap at her, but she went down and came up under him, sinking her teeth in his neck. Sissy felt his hot blood fill her mouth, but she didn't let go until he slumped lifeless on top of her.

JIM HEARD SISSY fighting with Jax, and he smelled the blood in the air. He hoped she could hold on, but he had to finish off Milton first or he'd be on both of them. His jaws were embedded deep in Milton's chest, and Milton was locked on Jim's shoulder. They shook their heads, ripping and snarling, but neither let go. They kicked and rolled, locked in a savage embrace. Milton was losing blood, but not fast enough. Jim's shoulder was starting to go numb, and if he lost his footing, Milton would be on him.

Releasing his hold on Milton's chest, Jim twisted like a bucking bull and Milton lost his grip.

They faced off. Blood and saliva dripped from Milton's jaws. Several times they charged, rising up on their back legs, snapping and clawing at each other, but neither gained a good hold on the other.

Milton dove for Jim's injured shoulder, trying to force him to the ground, but Jim leaped into the air and locked his massive jaws on Milton's neck. Jim twisted and he felt a snap, and the black wolf finally fell beneath him.

Jim raised his head and howled, and the answering howls

filled him with power, but there was no returning howl from Sissy. He saw Jax's lifeless body in the cell. *Good for you, Sissy.* He prayed Sissy had escaped upstairs while he was fighting Milton.

He shifted and ran to where Daniel lay on the floor in a pool of his own blood. Too much blood. Deep gouges ran across one side of his face, cutting completely through the skin so his jaw hung loose. One eye was gone, and his arm was almost severed, but he was still breathing—barely.

Then he heard a rustle of movement from inside the cell. He rushed in and pitched Jax's carcass to the side. Sissy, in human form, curled into a shivering ball. He tried to check her, to hold her, but she shied away from him. He couldn't leave her so he bellowed up the stairs for help.

CLINT HAD LANDED the helicopter after one covering pass of the parking lot. He shifted and ran into the fray. He knew they were outnumbered and they'd need every wolf they had. His team was still trading fire across the parking lot, but they were holding their own. Trace was battling with a big wolf on the porch, but he appeared to have the upper hand. The lodge door was shattered and hung open. Clint sprinted past Trace into the hall and ran into another wolf who was heading toward the door. He was inclined to let the retreating wolf go by, but instead the wolf turned on him. They circled like wrestlers, feinting and snapping. Clint looked for an opening and got one. The Missoula wolf rushed in low to take Clint's foreleg, but Clint leaped in the air, twisted and crashed down on the other's back, taking him to the floor. The other wolf surrendered going belly up with his tail between his legs. Trace ran in just then, and they both heard Jim yelling for a medic from downstairs. Clint left Trace to stand over the defeated wolf and headed for the stairs.

From the top of the landing, Clint was shocked by the scene in the room below. The smell of blood and shit and sickness rushed up to him so thick he had to shift. There were three bodies sprawled around the room, two of them dead. The third was Daniel, who'd been like a father to him. He was barely alive. Jim was bloody but upright with Sissy cowering at his feet.

"Get a stretcher down here. Daniel's alive." Clint disappeared through the doorway then reappeared with several more men. One of them had an emergency field kit. They started an IV on Daniel and pushed a liter of fluid as they loaded him on a stretcher.

"You need to let us take a look at you and Sissy," Clint said.

Jim shook his head. "I'm okay. I'll take care of Sissy. Go ahead and take Daniel and anybody else who's in bad shape back in the chopper. The rest of us will head back as soon as we can."

"Okay, Jim. Get some fluids in her and keep her warm. You, too." Clint followed after the men carrying Daniel.

"I will. Tell somebody to get us some clothes."

Two of the Missoula females hurried down the stairs with a stack of sweats, wet towels, and a blanket. Jim recognized Betty, Milton's wife. She looked around at the bodies of her husband and son and rushed back upstairs.

Jim wiped the blood from his face and hands and grabbed a pair of sweatpants for himself. Then he dropped to his knees beside Sissy and whispered, "It's all right, baby. It's all over now. You're safe."

Perhaps she understood, because she let him clean her up with the towel. He dressed her in a smaller set of sweats, pushing her arms and legs into the clothes. He wrapped her in a blanket and picked her up off the floor, cradling her in his arms, and she buried her face in his chest.

Upstairs, the fighting had stopped. Trace came over to Jim

and reported, "There won't be any more trouble. Everybody who could put up a fight is either down or has run off. Clint's team has rounded up what's left of Milton's posse. Some of them may have gotten away, but we'll find them."

Jim asked, "How are our guys?"

"They're mostly okay. You saw Daniel, and they took another guy, Lee, I think, back with them. He was pretty shot up. The others are being looked to now."

"Good. Get my truck up here."

Trace radioed to bring Jim's truck from where it was parked down the road. "They're bringing it up. And, sir, some of the pack is gathered outside and others will be coming. A lot of them didn't have anything to do with this. They're ready to submit to you. What do you want to do?"

Jim looked at Sissy in his arms. "I want to get the hell out of here. I don't give a fuck about this pack. They can all go to hell. Keep a few of my men with you for backup in case anybody tries to start anything, and send the rest home in the vans. You're in charge here now."

"Okay, boss. I'll take care of everything."

The cold air and the bright early morning light hit Jim as he cleared the broken door of the lodge. He hugged Sissy tightly to his chest. Her eyes were open, but they seemed vacant. She'd stopped shaking. He'd seen men go into shock, and he'd watched some of them die, but he wouldn't let that happen to Sissy.

At the foot of the steps, a small crowd of Missoula pack members were waiting. They parted as he started forward. Some of them knelt; others hung their heads as he passed. He smelled their fear. It was within his right to order them killed, but he just wanted to get Sissy away from them.

He met his truck as it was coming up the road. He laid her on the bench seat of his truck and covered her with coats and blankets. She curled into a fetal position and lay still.

Jim's truck roared down the road toward Laramie with the heater blasting. All he could think about was getting her home, tucking her into his big bed, and holding her. He touched her forehead for the hundredth time. She felt warmer, and her eyes had closed again. He hoped she'd fallen asleep.

He didn't know what he'd say to her. *I almost got you killed. I failed you completely. I'm sorry.* Nothing he could say would be enough.

Hours later, he was still beating himself up when he heard her moan. She was awake and moving under the blankets. "Sissy, baby, are you all right?"

Her moans mixed with growls. She began thrashing, throwing off her covers. Jim pulled his truck to the side of the road, just as she punched free of the blankets. She sat up and ripped off her sweatshirt. Her eyes glowed silver in the moonlight.

"Baby, don't do that. You need to stay warm." Even as he said the words, Jim realized she was feeling anything but cold. The scent of her mating heat assaulted his senses. Every cell in his body was programmed to respond to this single scent. This was his female in need, and only he could soothe the burning inside her.

But this was Sissy. And she was drugged. He wouldn't take her like that.

"Sissy, no. They fed you drugs to make you feel like this. I've got to get you home so we can take care of you."

Sissy was beyond listening to reason. A howl left her lips. The sound reverberated through the cab of the truck and called to Jim on his most primal level. His lips pulled back in a snarl as he reached for her.

She was in his arms, and he devoured her mouth. Their tongues and teeth battled. Hips to shoulders, they were melded together, but he wanted her closer. He had to be inside her. His rough hands ran down the soft skin of her back. He shoved at her sweatpants and they slipped off her hips. His fingers sank into the firm flesh of her ass.

Jim pulled away from her swollen lips, and Sissy arched her back and tipped her head back. Jim shuddered. That gesture was a potent sexual symbol. It implied that she was ready to submit to him. He bit her skin from beneath her ear to the dip in her collarbone as she leaned away to give him greater access. The moonlight spilled over her breasts. Her nipples were drawn up into tight buds. The sight of her milky skin in the dim light took his breath away. "Perfect," he murmured. "You're perfect."

One hand cupped a breast while his mouth covered the other. Jim rolled her hard nipple across his tongue and then he claimed it with his teeth, biting down firmly just to the point of pain while his tongue worked over the point. Sissy gasped as her nipple slipped from his mouth into the cold air.

Jim moved to take her other nipple into his mouth when her sharp breath caught his attention. His eyelids heavy with lust, he pulled back and gaped at her beautiful body, exposed there for him. He'd seen her naked before, but this was different. His gaze traveled up her body to her face. "Mine," he growled.

My Sissy. Oh God, this is Sissy.

Slowly, the importance of that distinction dawned on Jim. This was Sissy, whom he'd just rescued from a cage where she was being held until she could be forced to mate with someone against her will. She still had the drugs in her system.

He pulled away from her. He wouldn't take her until she could choose for herself.

Jim tried to lay her down and cover her. "You need to rest, baby," he said. He tried to sound soothing, but his voice was strained with desire.

"*Nooo,*" she wailed, springing up and reaching for him. Jim held her tight to his chest and tried to still her arms as she chanted, "No, no, no!"

"You don't know what you're doing, Sissy."

She broke his hold and launched herself at him. This time Jim felt like he was the one trapped in a cage. Her claws came out and ripped at his sweatshirt. She raked her claws across his chest and drew blood.

The scent of her need mixed with the smell of his blood and filled the cramped space. Jim grappled with her, grabbing her by the shoulders and pushing her away. His control was stretched to the limit.

Finally, Jim jerked away. He found the door latch and stumbled out into the cold.

"I need you," Sissy sobbed as she tried to scramble after him. The dome light revealed her tear-streaked face, and the sight tore at his heart.

Jim stepped back into the open door. "I know, baby. You'll be okay. It's just the drugs. You can ride it out."

"I can't. I'm burning up," she pleaded. "You've got to help me."

"I can't do that, Sissy. God knows I want to, but it wouldn't be right."

"I need you now. I can't stand this," she wailed.

Jim knew the irresistible force of the mating heat. It was strong for the man, but it could be maddening for the woman. She wouldn't settle down until she was satisfied. But he couldn't drive and fight her off at the same time, and they were still three hundred miles from Laramie.

He weighed his options. If he could manage his own desire, he could give her enough relief that she could rest without him violating her. When he got her home, Maggie could take care of her. The women had a hormonal suppressant that wolves took to lessen the pull of the heat. He only had to satisfy her just enough to take the edge off of her pain.

"Okay, Sissy. I'm coming." Jim moved to the passenger side of the truck and climbed into the space. He picked up Sissy and put her on his lap. "Just take it easy," he murmured, nuzzling her neck.

She locked her arms around his neck and slanted her head to meet his mouth. His lips moved hesitantly over hers, but Sissy's tongue aggressively pried at his.

"Oh, hell," Jim muttered. This was not going to be easy. His cock was rock hard under her thighs, and she wiggled her bare bottom against it. He was still wearing his borrowed sweat pants, but they were an ineffective barrier against her heat. "Hold still. Let me take care of you."

Sissy arched in his arms as his hands roamed over her body. Jim cupped and squeezed her breasts until she moaned and writhed against him. He dipped his hand between her legs. Her soft curls snagged at his calloused fingers. Sissy pushed her sex against his hand. He found the hot satin wetness of her center and slid one finger inside smoothly.

Every one of Jim's senses slammed into overdrive. Sissy's sweet clover scent was layered with the smell of her arousal and the tang of blood. Her skin was hot and velvety soft. Even her mewling sounds were driving him crazy.

"Oh Lord, Sissy. I don't know if I can do this." This was everything he wanted, but not like this, in a truck on the side of the road with Sissy half out of her mind. Jim didn't even know if she would remember it later. He hoped that she would, but he prayed that she wouldn't.

"*More.*" Sissy climbed his body. Jim tried to slip in a second finger, but he came up against a barrier of skin. He hadn't known for sure she was a virgin, but here was the proof. He used his thumb to push away what was left of her hymen, then filled her with his fingers.

She ground against each thrust. "Harder," she demanded. "I need more."

Jim worked his fingers rhythmically, and just the touch of his thumb over her swollen clit sent Sissy over the edge. Her nails pierced the skin of Jim's shoulder as she arched and moaned her release.

Sissy rode his hand through her orgasm, but she wasn't satisfied. "Please, more," she pleaded.

Jim dropped his head to her breasts. He suckled the taut nipples, moving from one to the other. His mouth worked feverishly, sucking and teasing while his hand moved inside her again. His fingers pumped inside her as he drew tightening circles around her clit. He finally centered the rough pad of his thumb on the swollen nub, swirling and stroking until she was panting shallow breaths. When she was close, he circled harder and faster. Sissy's body clenched down on his fingers and she arched away from his embrace.

At that point, all he could see were her perfect breasts. His teeth instinctively elongated in his mouth and he bit down on the swell of her breast, marking her as his. Sissy screamed as her body pulsed again and again.

Her sweet essence filled his mouth, and he came with her, his body shuddering his release beneath hers.

chapter Twenty-two

At last, she relaxed in his arms, her eyes closed and her breath-ing returning to normal. Jim laid Sissy carefully on her nest of blankets. He slid into the driver's seat and let his head fall forward onto the steering wheel. He was still uncomfortably erect, but that was the least of his problems.

He counted himself lucky. Some females caught in the throes of a mating heat could go for days before they were sated, but she was too weak for that. He looked at Sissy, sleeping peacefully now, but there was no peace for him.

He'd wronged her. His mark shone livid on her pale breast. He'd claimed her beyond their moment of passion. She was his mate. His body had recognized hers. Her touch, her scent, her taste wrapped around him. He finally understood what he'd been running from for so long. It had always been Sissy. No one else had ever held his heart like she did, and whether she wanted him or not, Jim knew he couldn't bear to see any other male touch her.

Jim was ripped out of his reverie by the muffled ring of his cell phone. He dug into his coat pocket and answered before the sound woke her. "What?" he barked.

"Jim?" Maggie's voice betrayed her worry. "Jim, are you there?"

"Yeah, I'm here. I have Sissy with me. She's all right. She's sleeping right now."

"Thank God." Jim could hear the relief in her voice. "Clint called. The doctor is operating on Daniel. He's hanging on."

"That's good. We're still a few hours away." Jim hesitated. What could he tell her? "Sissy's going to need some help, um, some relief," he stumbled. "They starved her and drugged her. You know," he choked up.

"Oh God, is she in heat?"

"Yes."

"We'll get her through this. I'll get everything ready," Maggie said. "Just bring her home."

It was early morning when Jim pulled up at Maggie's house. She must have been watching for him because she threw open the door as soon as he pulled up. Jim shouldered past her with Sissy in his arms. She was awake again and had begun moaning and thrashing in his grip. Maggie followed as Jim headed to Sissy's bedroom.

He tried to lay her down on her bed but she fought to stay with him. Her arms locked around his neck. He broke her grasp, pulled her arms down and pinned them to the bed, but she continued to kick wildly, growling unintelligibly. Jim threw one leg over her, straddling Sissy's narrow single bed, and sat on her thighs.

Maggie stood nearby, her hand at her mouth, when she saw Sissy's condition. The young woman was growling and moaning.

A gray-haired woman came to Jim's side. He recognized her—SallyAnn, a midwife from the pack—and she had a syringe in her hand.

"Hold her still." She wiped a swab over Sissy's arm and injected what Jim assumed was the hormone suppressor. "I added a strong tranquilizer, so she should be out in a minute."

When Sissy's struggles quieted, Jim released her wrists and lifted himself off the bed. He reached down to pull the covers up and met Maggie's hand as she also moved to cover the girl. Maggie surrendered the blanket, and Jim tucked it around Sissy's shoulders, smoothing her hair away from her face.

Maggie faced Jim across Sissy's bed. He knew he smelled like Sissy and sex, and SallyAnn couldn't have missed his mark on Sissy's breast, but Jim wasn't ready to deal with that yet.

The midwife said, "She'll be out for several hours, but I'll stick around in case she needs another shot." She gently tugged on Maggie's arm. "Come on. I'll make some coffee." The women left Jim alone with Sissy.

He sat on the side of the small bed and pulled Sissy's hand from under the covers and held it in both of his. He looked around. Her room was a mix of the little girl who'd grown up in the room and the woman who inhabited it now. The lavender walls were decorated with framed black and white photographs that she'd taken herself of the countryside around Laramie, and there were bookshelves crammed with a jumble of novels and textbooks and a desk with her computer, but there was also a pile of stuffed animals in the corner topped off with a big brown wolf. She was a grown woman of twenty-four, but she looked so small in her bed. Doubt flooded his mind, and he could barely look at her.

He scanned the room, trying to find something to focus on. Next to Sissy's bed were several photos in silver frames. He picked up the one of him and Lucas standing beside his Black Hawk helicopter. There was another of Maggie and Lucas at their mating ceremony. Jim was standing by Lucas, and Sissy was next to

Maggie. She was about twelve there, looking very pretty with flowers in her long hair. There was also a photo of Sissy as a beautiful wolf, standing in the snow.

He tucked her hand under the covers, kissed her forehead, and quietly breathed, "I love you, Sissy." He'd said those words to her many times before, but never as her mate.

When Jim came into the living room, the midwife went to sit with Sissy and left him alone with Maggie. "I need to see how Daniel's doing," he said. "I'll call and get a female guard over here, and I'll post some men outside. I don't expect any retaliation, but I want you to feel safe."

Maggie glanced at him. "I'll get you a shirt." She came back with what had probably been one of Lucas's old flannel shirts. "Give me a call when you know about Daniel."

He shrugged on the shirt with his head down. He couldn't meet Maggie's eyes, something he'd never experienced as Alpha of the pack. But then she reached over and lifted his chin.

"I should never have let her go." His voice broke.

"There was no way you could have known this would happen."

"But it did, and now I've made it worse." He didn't know how to explain. "She was going crazy. The drugs, the heat. I..."

"You saved her, Jim. You did what you had to do."

"I didn't have to mark her. Lucas would beat the hell out of me for touching his little sister."

"Lucas is gone. He's been gone a long time, and you've lived up to any responsibilities you thought you owed him. Let it go. Sissy is your woman now. This is between you and her."

"I'm not going to push my claim. She didn't have any say in it, and the mating wasn't completed, so she can still get out of it. I'll always take care of her, but she's got to come to me if she wants me."

Maggie slowly shook her head, and he knew what she was leaving unspoken. *She's been coming to you for years, and you've always pushed her away.*

JIM WENT TO the infirmary to check on Daniel. Dr. Lovett was a human doctor who'd married a female from the pack. She was his nurse, and together they ran a private hospital and took care of most of the pack's medical needs as well as seeing local humans. Clint was asleep, sitting up in a waiting room chair.

Jim shook him by the shoulder. "Go on home and get some sleep. I'll stay here with Daniel."

"He was so torn up." Clint was clearly distraught. "I've never seen anyone that bad off and still alive, even in Afghanistan. I should have thought to bring the doctor. We might have been able to save more of him if he'd had treatment sooner."

"You saved him by treating him on the ground and getting him here. Don't feel bad. You did everything you could. Now go on home." Jim helped his nephew to his feet, clasped his shoulders and pointed him to the door.

Jim had to steel himself to see his old friend like this. Daniel was swaddled in bandages over much of his face and body and hooked up to tubes and monitors.

"What are his chances?" Jim asked the doctor.

"It's still too soon to tell. He lost his right arm at the shoulder, and his right eye is gone. I saved his leg, but I doubt he'll have full use of it. Mostly, he lost a lot of blood. Any human with this much damage would have died."

"Has he regained consciousness yet?"

"He came to briefly after his surgery, but I put him in a light medical coma so he could rest. If I think he can take it, I'll wake him up in a few days for the full moon. If he can at least partially shift, his increased metabolism will speed up the healing."

"What about the others who were injured?"

"Everybody but Daniel is out of danger. Dave and Pete had minor gunshot wounds. I patched them up and sent them home. Lee is still here. He took several shots to the chest and abdomen. His injuries would have killed a human, but mostly he's suffering from loss of blood. I've got him on IVs, and I'll watch him for a few days. Everybody should do better after shifting."

Dr. Lovett paused. "Some of your young men may wear scars from this, but they should be proud of them. I haven't had a chance to get away and go check on Sissy, but I talked to Maggie. She said Sissy was doing better. They're keeping her sedated and the hormone suppressants will take the edge off the heat those bastards induced. Other than losing some weight, she should be fine physically. I'm more worried about her psychological recovery. Something like this can be very traumatic. You'll need to watch her for signs of PTSD."

"We will. I know what to look for. Unfortunately, I saw plenty of that in the Army. What about her shifting? Will she be okay?"

"The shift and the run may excite the mating heat. Maggie told me she's wearing your mark but the mating wasn't complete. If you want to mate with her, she should be physically relieved, but I can't say how her mental state would be. If she's not going to mate, I'd suggest she run apart with a pack of strong females, and you keep the males as far away as possible."

"I wouldn't try anything with her so soon. She needs to get over this first, but I'll keep her safe."

Jim felt a little helpless now that everything had settled down. The doctor checked his blood type, and he stayed at the infirmary and let the doctor hook him up for a direct transfusion to Daniel, then left after the relief guard arrived.

When Jim arrived home, he just wanted to fall into his bed, but his body was sticky with dried blood and sweat. He stripped off his bloody clothes. He was going to throw them away, but they smelled of Sissy.

He buried his face in the cloth and breathed in her scent. Despite his fatigue, he instantly went rock hard.

In the shower, he let the hot spray beat down on him. It washed away the dirt and blood, but it couldn't wash away his fears. For years he'd feared that Sissy would want him; now his greatest fear was that she wouldn't. He had to fight his instincts to keep from running to her, but exhaustion gave him a dreamless sleep.

THE NEXT DAY, Jim checked in with Trace in Missoula. The young alpha had gathered his dad and some loyal friends to back him at the pack meeting. He reported he wasn't expecting a challenge. They had Shari and Wade, and what was left of Milton's circle of muscle, in the barred cell or in chains, but he wouldn't deal with them until later.

Trace told Jim that a lot of truths had been unfolding. Originally, Milton had told everyone he'd moved to Missoula because a car dealership there had been for sale. But he'd really moved with the intention of taking over the pack. They found evidence in his papers that he'd scouted several packs until he found one with a weak pack hierarchy and an older Alpha with no heirs.

When Milton had arrived in Missoula, he looked for weaknesses. He had recognized Ray's shady personality and made him his minion. On an icy night, Ray had cut the brake line on their

Alpha's car. After it crashed down a hillside and burned, nobody could tell it wasn't an accident, and Milton had mourned along with the others. At the next pack meeting, it wasn't hard for Milton to beat a weaker challenger and assume total control.

Once established in place, he had demanded absolute loyalty and obedience from the pack, brutally punishing any infractions. He formed a goon squad to intimidate anyone who complained. Privately, he demanded pack members cede parcels of property to the pack while he siphoned off pack money into his private accounts.

Trace said, "He was coming after you too, Jim. That was part of the reason he wanted Sissy for Jackson, so he'd have a legitimate claim to the pack after he had you killed. I'm sorry we let this go on. My dad and some others suspected Milton, but they were afraid to say anything. My dad didn't even tell me because he was afraid I'd go off half-cocked and try to challenge Milton and get myself killed."

"I'm not blaming you, Trace. We'll find out who Milton's accomplices were and get rid of them, and then you can start building the pack again. I'll give you all the help I can."

After talking with Trace, Jim checked in with Dr. Lovett. There wasn't any change in Daniel's condition, but he was still holding on. Jim tried to work on some ranch business, but he couldn't concentrate. Everything inside him said to go to Sissy. He resisted for most of the day, but by late afternoon, he couldn't fight it any longer.

He pulled up in front of Maggie's house and sat in the truck, unable to leave, but unwilling to go inside. Finally, Maggie came out and got in the truck.

In the enclosed space, Jim could smell Sissy's scent on Maggie, and he had to fight to keep from running to her. "Is she awake?"

"She's mostly been sleeping, but when she's awake, she's not really coherent. She tries to fight us, so she's still being sedated. Fortunately, the sedatives keep her from shifting."

"I wanted to see her, but I don't want to upset her or make things worse."

"I know. She wants to see you too, but she's still under the effects of the drugs, and she's so weak. If you can't fully claim her, it's probably better if you stay apart for a while."

Jim gripped the steering wheel, and Maggie stroked his hands. "It's going to get better, you know. She'll come out of this."

"But will she want me? I drove her to Missoula and handed her over to Milton. Can she ever forgive me for that?"

"I don't know," Maggie said. "Are you going to be able to forgive yourself? Right now she just needs your love and your patience. She waited a long time for you. Can you wait for her?"

"There'll never be anybody but her. I'll wait as long as it takes," Jim said.

"We'll all get through this, and pretty soon you can tell her how you feel. How's Daniel? I should go see him, but I don't want to leave Sissy yet."

"Dr. Lovett is keeping him in a coma. It wouldn't do you any good to go over there."

Maggie nodded. "I know. Dr. Lovett explained about the PTSD. He told me what to look for."

"Did he tell you that going on the run might trigger the hormones again? What do you think, Maggie? Should Sissy run tomorrow night?"

She shrugged. "She probably won't want to, but she should try. It would be good for her body to shift. It'll help clear the drugs out of her system. It'll be hard on her, but if we can get her through this one, it'll be better next time."

"I'll set up a separate area for her to run in. Can you call some of her female friends to make a pack with you? If that drug hasn't left her system, she might try to bolt. I'll keep watch, but I'm going to keep my distance."

"I'll make some calls. It should be easy to recruit some of her friends to run with us, and I'll bring along the tranquilizers in case we need them."

"Come out late and keep away from the pack circle," Jim said. "I have to address the pack about what's been happening, then we'll start the run."

Just as Maggie stepped out of Jim's truck, the sound of Sissy's howl filled the air.

chapter Twenty-three

Maggie caught up to Jim at the door and blocked him with her steel gaze.

"Stop, Jim. She's not ready to see you."

"Can you hear her? She needs me. And I need her."

"Randi's sitting with her, and my folks are there. She'll be all right. Give her more time."

Maggie's father appeared at the door. Older, but still solid, his intention to protect Sissy, even from Jim, was clear.

Jim knew it was time to retreat. "I'll leave for now, but I don't know how long I can stay away. She's pulling at me every moment."

"You're reacting to her heat. You're as much a part of this as she is. But her heat is lessening now. It'll be easier on both of you when this is over."

SISSY WAS STRUGGLING with Randi when Maggie came back into the room, but her weakened condition and the tranquilizers made her no match for her friend.

"Where's Jim?" Sissy moaned, rubbing the mating mark on

her breast. "I can smell him. Where is he?"

"He came by to see you, but he had to leave."

Sissy wailed, "He doesn't want me!" She dissolved into tears.

"He wants you, sweetheart, but you've been sick," Maggie soothed. "It'd be better if he stays away for a while."

Sissy's body pulsed with need. The mark on her chest burned. She tried to shift, but nothing happened. It was all so confusing. She growled when she felt the prick of a needle before she faded into sleep again.

THE SMELL OF meat stirred Sissy to wakefulness. Maggie came into Sissy's room, carrying a small steaming bowl of beef stew.

Sissy sniffed. "That smells good," she croaked.

Maggie smiled. "Well, listen to you. You sound pretty clear-headed today."

"Everything's still a little foggy, and I feel like I've been run over by a truck."

"Good."

"How's that good?"

"Because you're talking to me and making some sense. Let's see if you can sit up and eat."

With Maggie's help, Sissy struggled to a sitting position propped up with pillows. The older woman tucked a napkin under Sissy's chin and held the bowl as Sissy spooned the thick broth.

"This is wonderful. I feel like I haven't eaten in weeks."

"From all accounts, you haven't. What do you remember?"

"I don't know. I think I've been dreaming. I get these weird glimpses of myself in a cage, and a fight." Sissy put down the spoon. "It was real, wasn't it?"

"I don't know what you're remembering, but yeah, it's

probably real. Milton and his bunch held you captive for several weeks. Jim and Daniel and Clint's security men went to Missoula to find you. There was a big battle."

"I killed Jax."

Maggie sighed. "Yes, sweetheart, you did. You had to."

"And Daddy? Milton attacked him. Is he okay?"

"He was torn up pretty badly. He's still over at the hospital. They're taking care of him. He wouldn't want you to worry. All he wants is for you to get better, okay?"

Sissy nodded, but tears streamed down her face. "I was so afraid. At first I was sure Jim would come and rescue me, but then days went by. I thought I'd die down there in that cage, and maybe no one would ever know. I would have fought them, even if it killed me. The worst was when I thought Jim didn't care about me anymore." Sissy leaned back and turned her face into a pillow to cry.

Maggie smoothed her hair. "We didn't know. They covered it up and sent me emails from you. It took me a long time to figure it out, but as soon as I told Jim, he went to get you. I'm so sorry we let you suffer."

Sissy pulled open her pajama top and stared at the mark on her breast. "Jim marked me. But I don't feel . . . " Sissy searched for the word, "complete. Did he take me as his mate?"

"You were out of your head with drugs and the mating heat. He did what he had to do to soothe your heat, and he got carried away and marked you, but he didn't complete the mating. He's holding off until you can choose for yourself. With a clear head."

Choose for myself. Sissy didn't welcome the choice. All she felt was rejection, once again. "I'm not hungry anymore. I just want to be alone."

Sissy rested for most of the day, but by mid-afternoon, she

had to get ready for the run.

"We've got to get you dressed," Maggie said.

"I don't want to go."

"You have to. When the moon comes up, you'll shift, and I don't need a full-grown wolf banging around my house."

"Can't we just go out to your folks' place? There's room for us to run, and I don't have the energy to run much more than a few feet anyway."

"You may find that your energy comes back when the moon is up, and Dr. Lovett said your heat may come back too, so I need to know you're in a safe place."

"Then I shouldn't go out to the ranch. That'd just be too much. I don't think I can handle being around other wolves."

"Some of your friends are coming over, and we're going to be an all-girl pack this time. Jim's made a special place for us to run. He and the others will keep away."

He doesn't even want to see me.

"They all want to support you, and it'll do you a lot of good to shift," Maggie said. "You need to exercise and flush the drugs out of your system."

Randi and some of the other women arrived and helped Maggie get Sissy dressed. She was still too weak to do much herself. They carried her out to Maggie's truck, and she fell asleep as the women headed out in their mini-convoy.

JIM USUALLY RELIED on Maggie to take care of a lot of the run day details, and with her and Daniel out, he did the best he could to get everything ready. He called each of the injured pack members to check on them. Everyone but Daniel was well enough to come out for the run. Shifting and being with the pack would help in their healing.

Even though there was no longer a threat, Jim had Clint put on extra security so everyone would feel safe. All the wranglers and ranch staff pitched in to prepare the food and set up the buildings. He expected a big turnout.

Jim steeled himself to face his pack before the run. He stayed apart from them before the gathering at the pack circle so he wouldn't have to field all their questions until then, but he made sure some of the hands were present to welcome them. There hadn't been a war between packs in more than a hundred years, and the members likely didn't know what to expect. They would be looking to him.

Just before moonrise, he stepped up on the Alpha's rock and looked out. Almost every member of the pack faced him. He recognized some of the older folks who hadn't come out in years, and some families had gathered together and even brought their children.

His voice boomed out across the clearing. "You all know by now that our pack went to war against the Missoula pack. We were justified in our actions. It was not that long ago in our history that the packs were ruled by brutality. There were vicious battles to usurp territory and capture females. Pack would make war against pack, and our people lived in fear."

"Not long ago, most of the packs agreed to end the wars and establish rules and protocols for living peacefully. Those who didn't comply were eventually killed or driven out. Today, the laws and traditions that the packs agreed upon keep us safe. They allow us to live productive lives without the fear that everything we work for will be taken away from us. They allow us to raise our families in peace. They allow us to travel and live and work in other pack territories through cooperative agreements. Living our lives in the modern world wouldn't be possible without our laws.

It's hard enough for many of us just living among humans, but there are very few places left where our kind can retreat to the forest and live apart, and most of us wouldn't want that anyway."

Jim took a deep breath. "Missoula violated our laws. We sent one of our own to them by mutual agreement, and their leader guaranteed her safety. But instead of protecting their charge, they attempted to force her to mate with one of their males against her will. They held her prisoner, they starved, tortured, and drugged her, but she didn't submit to them."

Jim felt the anger flow through the pack. There were nervous shuffles and growls.

"We were forced to take action to recover our pack member. Many of us fought, and some were badly wounded. Daniel, our Second, fell protecting me, and his life still hangs in jeopardy, but we didn't leave any of ours behind. Their leader and his son and several others from their pack are dead. More are in custody and will be judged for their actions. I left a good man there, Trace Bridger. Some of you met him while he was here. And I promised him I'd give him whatever help he needs to rebuild his pack. We have nothing to fear from the Missoula pack anymore."

Some cheers broke out in the crowd. Others took the news solemnly. But Jim thought they all were comforted and relieved. He led a howl and all their voices filled the night.

AT THE MAIN compound of the ranch, a group of women surrounded Maggie and Sissy. They'd stayed behind, waiting for the main group to move away. Jim had set aside an area where the women could run without encountering the rest of the pack. He had some of his security people make a perimeter to keep the others out, and the females in the security force were going to be running along with Sissy.

But Sissy had stayed away from the other women. She appreciated what they were doing, but she wasn't ready to talk with them about her experience.

She slept all the way to the ranch, but as soon as she got out of the truck, she sensed Jim all around her. His scent was everywhere, and she felt his close presence. Just having him nearby strengthened her, but she felt her response to him building too quickly.

Sissy was about to tell Maggie that this wasn't a good idea when Jim's howl pierced straight into her womb.

Before the other women could react, Sissy shifted, shredding her clothes, and ran off.

JIM HAD SHIFTED and was set to leap down from the Alpha's rock and lead the pack when he heard Sissy's answering cry. He froze. He nodded for Clint to take the lead, and Clint howled for the pack to follow him.

The others had just left the circle when he saw her. Sissy ran full out into the empty circle. She skidded to a stop at the sight of Jim.

Jim leaped from his rocky perch and landed about ten feet in front of her. He moved toward her slowly. He could smell her need, but he also smelled fear. He wanted to appear as nonthreatening as possible. He brushed his tail casually side to side and kept his steps fluid and easy. He cocked his head and lowered it so he had to look up at her.

She was crouched, ready to spring away, watching every step as he advanced. As he got close, she tensed and took a step back.

Jim quickly plopped down and rolled to his side in front of her.

That seemed to work. She approached him hesitantly,

245

sniffing as if she were bewildered by what she could smell.

Jim wanted to speak. He wanted his human side. He'd tell her how much he loved her and wanted her. He'd take her in his arms and promise to protect her. But he knew Sissy's mind was still muddled and her wolf instincts were confused between the artificial hormones and the real mating urge Jim's mark had provoked.

He lay completely still as she came near, afraid the slightest move would scare her off. She reached her muzzle toward his, sniffed, and darted out her tongue to taste his scent.

Then all of a sudden, the female pack charged into the pack circle to surround Sissy.

Jim snarled a warning for them to back off, but it was too late. Sissy bolted into the woods with Maggie and her guards right behind her.

Jim didn't run with either pack. He waited well away and downwind of the female pack. He followed their progress through the howls, and he was sure they were safe, but he couldn't leave until he saw her again and knew she was all right.

As he heard the small pack approach, he pulled back into the brush. His goal was to watch unseen, but as soon as Sissy came into view, her head came up, sniffing, her eyes searching until they met his.

He stepped out of the brush to show himself to her. The others hung back, uncertain, but Maggie yipped at them to run on. When the clearing was finally quiet, Sissy approached until she was close, then darted off at an angle.

He ran in chase, firing up every instinct. He caught up to her too quickly. Sissy could always give him a good run, but she was still weak. When he bumped her, she stumbled, and she came up snarling with bared teeth.

This time there was no waiting. His need to mate drove him. His teeth clamped onto the back of her neck and forced her head down as he boxed her in under his body. Beneath him, she submitted, turning her head and looking up into his eyes.

This was everything he'd ever wanted. He searched Sissy's eyes. They were full of love, and want—and drugged confusion.

Jim's jaws opened, and he freed her from his grip. She stayed motionless, still framed by his legs, but when he gave her an opening, she shot away without a backward look.

Jim watched her disappear and listened until he heard her rejoin her group, then he shifted and collapsed on the ground, naked and shivering. He couldn't stand to be in his wolf for one second longer. The duality was killing him.

If they could just stay wolf. He could claim his mate and protect her and his young. No moral conflicts, no responsibilities, no one else to consider, just the two of them.

By the time he reached the house, he was freezing. The house was dark and silent. Maggie and Sissy and most of the pack had gone. Daniel was still in the hospital. It was hard to find a time or place to be alone on a large working ranch. There were wranglers, family, and pack around. That was what pack life was about. But as he climbed the stairs to his room, Jim felt more alone than he ever had.

He stood under the steaming shower until his body finally warmed. He'd back off and give Sissy a chance to decide. If she didn't want him, he'd let her go.

Fuck that. I'm going to do whatever it takes to make her mine.

chapter Twenty-four

The next day, with her head clearer, Sissy felt stronger for having shifted, but her emotions were still chaotic. The change should have cleared most of the drugs out of her system, but it was still hard to tell what was real and what was induced. The extreme urges of the mating heat were gone, but she still wanted something or someone. Jim.

Sissy sat at her desk. At the forefront of her mind was Jim. He didn't want her or he would have fully claimed her. He did what he had to do, carried out his responsibility. Nothing had changed.

She had to get through this, and then she'd make some decisions. There was no need to run from him anymore. She had her life. She could finish her graduate studies and get a job or go to work at the gallery full time. There was no rush to make those decisions yet. If nothing else, she had to find out how to make up the time she had lost in her classes.

There were lots of guys in Laramie who'd want her if she decided to stay. Maybe Shari was right. Maybe picking a mate didn't have to be about love.

There were no rules that said she had to mate at all. Maybe she'd take a page from Jim's playbook and only date humans from now on. A lot of wolves weren't all they were cracked up to be.

Maggie broke into Sissy's musing. "Dr. Lovett called," she said. "We can go see your dad."

Sissy looked up. "Yes," she said immediately. Maggie explained as they were on the way that Daniel had been able to partially shift and that had helped to heal some of his wounds. He was awake and out of danger now, but that wouldn't bring back what he'd lost.

Once they got to the infirmary, Maggie and the doctor tried to prepare Sissy, but nothing could come close to the reality of seeing his mangled body.

"Oh, Daddy," she said, her mind clearing. She rushed to his side.

Most of his bandages were gone, and his wounds revealed shiny red scars. His mop of shaggy gray hair had been shaved away. His skin was pale and pasty, similar to the white hospital sheets on his bed, and he looked smaller and older than she'd ever seen him.

His right arm was completely gone, and his skin puckered where the doctor had stitched up his shoulder. His chest bore angry claw marks. A bandage covered the eye that he'd lost, and three scars slashed diagonally from the top of his skull across his cheek to the corner of his mouth, pulling it into a macabre grin. Another cut, where the doctor had reattached his lower jaw, ran from his mouth down his jawline onto his neck.

"I'm not too pretty anymore," he said, trying to smile.

"You were never pretty," she said, laughing between sobs.

"Your momma thought I was quite a looker in my day, but I guess that's been a while."

"Oh, Daddy, I'm so sorry I got you into this," she said, crying. "It was all my fault. If I hadn't demanded to go away, none of this would have happened."

Her father shook his head as much as he could. "Don't go playing that game, sweetheart. None of it was your fault. We lay all this at Milton's feet. That bastard used us all. And he got what was coming to him. Don't you worry about me. Doc says I'll get along just fine. Now, come here. I'll give you a kiss, if this mug of mine doesn't scare you."

"You don't scare me, Dad. I love you so much. You did all this for me."

"I love you too, darling. But don't hug me too hard. I'm still pretty broke up. Doc's got me put together with baling wire, I think. You run along. I know you'll never forget what's happened to you, but you're strong. You put this behind you and go on. Understand?"

"Yes, sir. I will."

Before they left, the doctor performed some blood tests and declared Sissy free of the hormones that had been forced on her.

"At least now I'll know that my reactions are real and not some drug-induced lust."

SISSY STARED AT Jim's name on the screen of her ringing phone. She wasn't going to answer, but her hand overruled her head, hitting the accept icon.

"Hi, baby. How are you feeling?" Jim asked

"I'm fine," Sissy said, hesitantly. "I'm better, you know."

"Yeah," Jim replied. "So, I talked to Dr. Lovett. He said you'd been in to see your dad." He sighed. "That must have been hard. He looks pretty rough."

Sissy fought back tears. "It was terrible seeing him like that.

He said he'd be fine, but he won't, really. He'll never be the same."

"No, but as long as he can sit a horse, I think he'll be okay. We'll get him going again. Ah, the doctor said you were doing good."

"Checking up on me?"

"No." Jim cleared his throat. "Um, well, yes. I had to know if the shifting helped. He said it did, that your blood tests came back clean."

Sissy smiled. "Whatever happened to patient confidentiality?"

"That flew out the window when a big wolf threatened the doctor."

"Oh," Sissy replied. A long moment of silence filled the space between them.

"Look," he said. "This is so hard, baby, but we got started all wrong. I want to take you out, you know, like a date. We've never had that. We could get dressed up, go to dinner, dancing... Anything you want."

She hesitated. "I don't think so."

"We need to talk. I'll wait a little longer if you're not ready, but we're going to do this. You need to give us a chance—the chance I never gave us. I'm so sorry, baby."

"Okay maybe, but nothing too fancy."

"All right. I'll pick you up tomorrow about seven."

SISSY TRIED ON everything she owned, but her clothes all hung from her shrunken frame. Finally, Randi arrived with an armload of garments.

"These ought to fit you. We're about the same size, but I wear my clothes a lot tighter than you do."

"I want to look nice, not trashy."

"Nobody ever said trashy couldn't be nice." Randi smiled.

"Well, maybe they did. But you ought to look like a girl, at least."

They settled for a clingy hunter-green sweater that was low cut enough to satisfy Randi, but covered enough for Sissy. Randi pointed out that it was too tight for her, but it fit Sissy, who was still trying to gain back weight. Paired with dressy black slacks and high-heeled black boots, Sissy looked more sophisticated than she felt.

Randi helped her fix her hair and makeup. "You look beautiful, sweetie," the other woman said, snapping a picture with her phone. "I'm putting this up on Facebook. I've never seen you look this good. On second thought, maybe not. I don't need the competition."

"I'm hardly competition. You can have just about anybody you want."

"Unfortunately, I've had most of them already, and I still haven't found the one I'm looking for. You're lucky. You've known who you wanted all along."

"A lot of good it's done me."

"Well, you've hit some bumps along the way, but it'll be good now."

"I don't know. I'm not the kind of woman he's used to."

"Yeah, but he doesn't want the kind of woman he's used to. He wants you. You look fabulous. Just relax and let whatever happens—happen. Don't overthink it."

JIM ARRIVED RIGHT on time, nervous as a prom date. He knocked and waited at the door until Maggie opened it.

"Don't you look handsome. Come on in. Sissy's almost ready." Maggie was clearly amused at his discomfort. "Do I need to ask you if your intentions are honorable? I could get the shotgun out."

"Oh, shut up. This is hard enough."

"I know, honey. It's just hard to resist. I wish Daniel could be here and see you like this."

"He'd probably punch me out again with his one arm."

Jim's breath caught in his chest when Sissy entered the room. Her long blonde hair was swept up off her neck and her eyes were glowing. "I brought you something. We missed Christmas, but I had this made for you." He handed Sissy a small, flat jewelry box.

Inside was a beautiful pendant, the center a perfect circle of luminous white stone. "Oh, Jim, it's beautiful. I love it." She held it out to him.

He took it and stepped behind her. "It's a Wyoming opal. I saw it in a shop, and it looked like the full moon." When he fastened it around her neck, he couldn't stop himself from sneaking a kiss on her cheek.

Maggie laughed and got in one last shot before they left. "Don't you kids stay out too late."

As he helped Sissy into his truck, she said, "I love how everybody thinks it's so hysterical that we're going out."

"I think they're laughing at the fact that it took us so long."

The problem with living in a small town was that you knew everybody and they knew you. Laramie had the university, with the bars and fast food and coffee shops that the students frequented, and there was Old Laramie with boutiques and antique shops that the tourists loved in the summers, but the real Laramie was still a small town and the locals mostly stuck to their own places like the small Italian café Jim had chosen. He and Sissy greeted many of the other diners as they made their way to their table, but then they fell into an awkward silence. What could they talk about? Being kidnapped. Starting a Werewolf war. Mating?

The waiter took their order and brought them some wine. Sissy took a sip. "I feel like everybody is looking at us."

"That's because they are. Maybe this wasn't such a good idea."
He saw Sissy's face fall. He hadn't meant to disappoint her again.

Jim took her hand and brought it to his lips. "Not us going
out, baby. That's not what I meant. This restaurant. It's just too
public. I want to get you alone."

Sissy's eyes widened. "That's what I want, too. Just you and
me, spending time together. You know."

"Let's get out of here." Jim dropped some money on the table
for the wine and led her out of the restaurant.

He drove them to a drive-in and picked up some food to go
and headed out of town. He pulled down a quiet road until they
were surrounded by snow-covered forest.

"This is better. Do you want the bacon cheeseburger or the
chili dog?"

"Definitely the chili dog, and I want some of those tater tots."

Bundled up in the front seat of the truck, they ate in silence,
but it wasn't awkward any longer. Jim reached over and wiped a
bit of chili from the corner of Sissy's mouth, and then he licked it
from his finger. "You taste good."

"Eat your own food. This is mine."

They each reached for the last tot, but Jim ceded it to Sissy
with a smile as she triumphantly popped it in her mouth. Once
they were done, she stuffed all the wrappings into the sack. Jim
got out of the truck and came around to her side. He kicked the
snow away to clear a spot before he opened the door and leaned
across her and stuck a CD in the stereo system. Then he held out
his hand to help her down. She slid into his arms just as George
Strait's voice filled the air.

"Do you remember the last time we danced?" Jim took her in
his arms and began to move to the music.

"Of course I do." They danced in the pale moonlight,

crunching over the frozen ground. She relaxed in his embrace with her head on his shoulder. As soon as the song ended, it began again.

"I made a whole disc of this song. I didn't want it to end." They danced through the song several more times before he stepped away and took her face in his hands. "I put you through so much. I left you confused. I let you go..." he couldn't finish. "I don't know how I can ever make it up to you, but I want to try."

His lips came down on hers, lightly at first, just nipping at her, then in a solid kiss that joined them head to toe. When her lips parted, he slipped inside to caress her tongue and drink in her sigh. He lingered on the kiss, playing over her mouth with his lips and tongue, relishing the taste and touch of Sissy. As much as it killed him to hold back, he'd let her set the pace.

SISSY SLIPPED HER hands inside Jim's coat and melted into his warmth. Her body followed his as they moved together, not really dancing anymore. When his tongue swiped across hers, her whole body responded. The mark on her chest tingled as if his mouth were there. She pressed against him, suddenly remembering his mouth on her breasts, his fingers inside her.

As the kiss deepened, the mating mark scorched her nerves. Her nipples tightened into hard buds, and heat flooded through her core. It was too much.

She broke the kiss and pulled back. Her breath puffed chilled air between them.

Back in the truck, he took her hand.

"Is it always going to be like this, Jim?"

"I don't know, baby. Tell me what you feel."

"It's so hard and urgent. I just feel overwhelmed. For so long, I thought this was all I ever wanted, but now I don't know. I'm afraid of my feelings. I feel like I'm drowning sometimes. I don't want to lose myself in you."

"I can't imagine you giving up any part of yourself. You're so strong. I'm the big bad Alpha, and I manage a lot of things, but I've never been able to manage you. Baby, you tie me up in knots. I trip over my own big feet whenever I'm around you. I don't ever want you to quit being you. I love you just the way you are."

"You have so much more experience than I do. Was it like this with other women?"

"This is different. I don't have any experience with this. In the past it was all fun and games. I was 'Love 'em and leave 'em Jim,' but not because I wanted it that way. Maybe I did at first, but after a while, I just never found anyone I wanted to stay with. Honestly, I didn't think I ever would.

"I always knew you were special, even when you were a kid. You knew me the way nobody else did. I felt that, but I thought it was just because we were like family. Then I was gone for so long overseas, and Lucas died, and I could hardly face you or Maggie.

"It was only after my dad died and I came back to Laramie to stay that I began to realize that my feelings for you had changed. You were in college, and you were working at the gallery. You'd grown up into a beautiful woman, and it killed me. I was trying so hard to stay away from you when you were all I wanted."

"Why didn't you say anything? Couldn't you see that I wanted you?"

"I saw, and that made it hurt even worse. I didn't deserve you. The things I'd done and the people I'd hurt. You should have had better."

Sissy waited for Jim to finish. This was clearly something he had to get off his chest.

"I haven't been with anybody since I came back to Laramie and took over the pack. God, this sounds stupid." Jim shook his head. "I tried, I really tried. And I kept trying. I thought if I was with somebody, you'd move on, find someone better than me."

"Crystal," Sissy said.

"Yeah. She was using me to get at the pack, but I was using her, too. I wanted to show you how easy it was to just take up with someone else, but it wasn't easy. I tried to feel something, but I couldn't. I didn't want anybody but you."

Sissy took a deep breath. "I don't know what to say."

"Just say you love me."

"I do. I love you, Jim. I always have, and I guess I always will, but I don't know if I can do this."

"You don't have to do anything, except give me a chance to show you I love you. That's all I want. A chance."

chapter Twenty-five

Jim dropped Sissy off with a long kiss at the door. Driving home, he thought about what she'd said. She had good reason to be afraid. For their kind, mating wasn't without risks, and he was sure she'd heard the horror stories.

Occasionally, one or both of a mated couple became lost in their connection. They called it "mating madness." It was rare, and it mostly happened with very young couples or with people who weren't too stable to begin with. They'd become obsessively possessive or they'd merge so deeply with each other they couldn't function alone.

Jim knew Sissy was strong enough to hold her own with him, but she'd also seen a little of what Maggie went through when Lucas died. Sissy had been a teenager, and they'd kept her away from the worst of it, but Jim remembered.

A mated Werewolf pair has a metaphysical joining in which they each became a part of the other. Losing a mate rips away a big part of the heart and mind of the one left behind, and some mates never recover.

Not all mating bonds are equal: the stronger the bond, the deeper the loss. Alphas form stronger links to their mates than the other castes. From the time of mating, they can feel their partner's emotions and physical condition. Most can sense the presence of their partner, wherever they were. Some are capable of reading the other's thoughts and communicating through their bond.

But when that bond is severed, it's a traumatic loss to the survivor, especially if it were sudden. He didn't know how he could ask Sissy to take such a risk.

Jim had pledged to be guardian for Lucas and Maggie when they'd mated, but he never imagined what that would entail. When Lucas was shot down, Maggie felt the loss immediately and went into shock. Jim had taken leave as soon as he could.

When he finally returned, Roy—Jim's father—and Daniel were waiting with Maggie's parents. They'd been keeping Maggie out at the ranch house. Jim heard them talking, but their words barely registered. They were telling him there was little chance that she would recover.

But it was obvious they were keeping something back, and he called them on it.

Jim's father tried to explain. "She wants to die, son, and there's nothing we can do."

Nothing they could have said would have prepared him. He barely recognized Maggie in the wraith he saw chained to the bed in front of him. The room was clean, but he could smell the sickness within her.

Weres rarely became ill, and they recovered quickly from injuries. He'd never seen anyone in this condition. She'd lost a lot of weight. Her skin was pale and dry and hung loosely over her frame. Her hair was matted. She was cut and bruised from struggling against her bonds.

"We had to chain her down to keep her from hurting herself," Roy explained. "She sleeps some, but most of the time she's out of her head, raving and screaming, calling for Lucas."

"Unchain. Her. Now." They did. Jim told them to leave, slammed the door, and locked it.

Jim's howls reverberated through the house for the first twenty-four hours. Sometimes Maggie's weaker howls joined Jim's. After the first day, Jim called out for food—water and meat. After that those who waited outside heard growls and snuffles and sometimes the very human sound of sobbing. At one point the locked room shook with a terrible snarling battle being fought within.

After four days, Jim had carried Maggie out of the room. Their clothing hung in tatters, and they were dirty and covered in scratches and wounds. Maggie was awake, her eyes open, but still.

Jim walked out into the night with her in his arms. Their parents watched their silent procession until the two were lost in the dark.

The next morning, he brought Maggie back to the house. They had washed somewhere along the way, and Maggie was calm and conscious. They slept during the days, and Jim took her out into the wilderness every night. After a week, Maggie could walk out on her own, but she still wouldn't speak. The others left them food and clean clothes, but mostly they left them alone.

It took almost two months before Maggie acknowledged anyone but Jim. One morning after she and Jim came in from their nightly run, Maggie went to the kitchen and sat at the table with Daniel and Roy.

Jim watched from the doorway while his father got up and poured Maggie a cup of coffee. When she took the cup, he went to the stove and filled a plate with eggs and bacon for her. She ate a little, and when she got up, she said, "Thank you," as if it were an ordinary day.

After that, Maggie joined in more. She'd talk and even smile a little. Jim knew he needed to get back to his Army unit, but he hated to leave her.

"I'm okay," she assured him.

"I won't go back if you need me. Just tell me to stay, and it's a done deal."

"I-I want you to go back," she said haltingly. "There's nothing for you to do here except wait on me, and frankly, I'm getting kind of tired of you watching my every move."

"I'll come back as often as I can." Jim hugged Maggie. "Seriously, sweetheart, are you going to be okay? I can't leave until I'm sure."

"I promise you, Jim. I'll be all right. I have to be. I didn't think I could live with such a big hole inside me. I didn't think I'd even want to. At first, it was only your will that kept me alive. But I have Sissy and Daniel and my family."

Jim placed a kiss on the top of her head and answered what he knew she'd been afraid to ask. "I'll be careful. I *will* come back, and I'll always be here for you."

Jim had kept his promise to Maggie, but he didn't know how he could ever put Sissy through that pain.

A FEW DAYS after Jim's date with Sissy, he picked up Daniel from the infirmary and brought him back to the ranch. They got him settled in a deep leather chair next to a roaring fire, and everybody from Clint to the cook came around to welcome him home.

Finally alone, Daniel muttered, "Jim, you're hovering like an old biddy hen. Get me some of that whiskey and then sit down. We need to talk."

Jim brought them each a drink and sank into a chair by the older man and waited for what he had to say.

"You've got to name your new Second."

"You're still my Second."

"Bullshit. I'm not good for anything more than a doorstop now, and that's the truth. It ain't going to hurt my feelings for you to replace me."

Jim took a sip of his whiskey. "I know, but there's no rush. I've still got plenty for you to do. I'm going to need your advice around the ranch. You know more about the day-to-day operations than I do. You're going to have to teach me, so I don't screw everything up. And I still want your help with the pack. Everybody respects you, probably more than they do me. I really need your help with the young wolf corps. I was going to ask you even before this."

The older man shook his head. "Oh Lord, you're going to make me a babysitter to those pups."

"Not a babysitter, a mentor," Jim explained. "You're a hero to those kids. They're already talking about the Christmas War. They think you're a god, except you'll probably scare them to death the way you look right now, but that's okay. You've got more courage and integrity than any man I know. You've got to help me train them, just like you helped bring me up right. I don't know if it's saying much, but I wouldn't be the man I am today without you."

Daniel shook his head. "Your father never saw it. You were too much like him, but I knew what you were made of. I wish Lucas could be here for you now. He'd be so proud of you."

"I don't know, Daniel. I fucked up pretty bad. I put everybody in jeopardy. I was so busy following my dick around that I quit paying attention. I let stalkers and a goddamn genetics researcher get right in the middle of us, and I practically pushed Sissy out of the pack and into Milton's arms. I almost got her killed."

"Sissy was going to do what Sissy was going to do. I should have gone to Missoula and talked to people myself, but I didn't. But we did what we had to do, and we got her back, and we put down that lying dog before he hurt anybody else. Now let's have an end to this pity party you're throwing. You're the Alpha. Act like it. Get Clint in here. I have something to say."

Jim called for Clint, and silence fell between the two men as they sipped their whiskey and waited.

When Clint came in, Daniel addressed them both. "You boys listen to me. I did a lot of thinking while I was laid up for the past few days. You've got to expect a challenge, and soon." He waited. "Even though we beat them in Missoula, there's blood in the water, and some young sharks are gonna come swimming around. You've got no Second, and your position is weak."

Jim said, "I've got Clint."

Daniel shook his head. "Even if you name Clint publicly, folks outside of the pack don't know him. That's okay. He's a secret weapon, but it won't help your position right now. You've got to expect the whole Werewolf community is shook up. There hasn't been a war between packs in most anybody's lifetime. People don't know what to expect, and there are young alphas out there who've just been waiting for an opening. The packs have been settled for so long, challengers haven't had much of a chance."

He pointed to Jim. "You better warn Trace up in Missoula. They're likely to come gunning for him, too. He needs to name himself a strong, older Second, and do it right quick. That's a bad situation waiting to happen all over again."

"I will," Jim said. "I've been talking to him, and he's got some good support up there. Most of the pack was pretty happy to see the end of Milton, but I'll tell him what you said."

"Another thing. It may not just be the solitary alphas you have to worry about. There might be some big guns looking your way, too. Even friendly neighbor packs could be looking to expand their territory, and your ranch is a gold mine none of them would mind having. So you've got to watch your back. Milton took out the Missoula leader so he wouldn't have to face any serious challenge for Alpha. It wasn't the first time an Alpha's been assassinated."

Jim nodded. "We'll keep watch. Clint, you make sure everybody is on the lookout for anybody sniffing around our lands, and as of now, you're Second of this pack. You're a good man, and I'm glad to have you at my back. I'd like to keep you as head of security, so I'll pick out somebody else as foreman of the ranch operations. I'll make the formal announcement at the pack meeting."

"Thank you, Jim," Clint said. He leaned forward. "Daniel, I'll do my best to live up to your reputation. I'll try to make both of you proud."

When Clint left, Jim refreshed their whiskeys. "So you really think this is coming."

"I do."

"The only challenge I ever fought was against you, when I came back after my father died. And I didn't want to do it."

"But you did."

"Yeah, and you didn't make it easy on me. We both came out of it pretty torn up."

Daniel grinned. "I couldn't just let you step in. It was necessary for the pack to see that you could lead them. Now your pack knows it, but the rest of the world doesn't, so you may have to prove it again."

JIM SAT AT Maggie's kitchen table with Maggie and Sissy. He had spent the last hour explaining Daniel's warnings to them. "I want you both to stay at the ranch for a while."

"I can't, Jim," Maggie replied promptly. "I think it's a good idea for Sissy to be out there, but I've got my gallery to run, and with the weather, I can't be driving back and forth every day. Anyway, I'll be fine. I don't have any position in the pack."

Sissy shook off Maggie's idea. "I'm not going off and leaving you here alone. That's not happening, so don't even think about it."

"I can't do what I need to do if I'm worrying about you two all the time," Jim exclaimed.

"Well, quit worrying. I can take care of us if I need to," Sissy said.

"I know you can, baby, but I'd feel so much better if you were someplace I could keep an eye on you. How about if I send somebody to stay with you here? Can we at least compromise? Pretty please?" Jim wasn't the best at begging, but he put on a pleading look and got a smile in return from Sissy.

"Since you asked so nicely, I guess, but we get to pick," Maggie said. "I don't want a bunch of smelly cowboys camping out here."

"Deal. Clint will set something up tomorrow. Now, can we go get some ice cream?"

Sissy laughed, her eyes sparkling. "Ice cream! It's seventeen degrees outside."

"Okay, hot chocolate."

"I can make us some hot chocolate here."

"Only if we can drink it in your room."

"I'm out of here," Maggie said, standing up and covering her ears, and left Jim and Sissy alone at the table.

"Come here." Jim pulled Sissy over so she straddled his lap.

He met her lips in a deep kiss. "Umm. I missed you today. Did you miss me?"

"Not much."

"Liar." Jim stood up and shifted Sissy over his shoulder so her butt was up in the air and her view was looking down his back. "I think you deserve a spanking for lying to me." He gave her a light pop on her bottom.

"You wouldn't dare." Sissy squirmed, but not very much, against his firm grip.

Jim carried her to her bedroom and flopped her onto her bed. "No, I don't think I would dare. I sleep too hard to trust you. You'd probably get me back by supergluing some parts that are important to me."

"That's right, and I'd probably be sorry later, but I'd enjoy it at the time."

"You should be a hard woman to love, but it seems to come real easy to me. Scoot over."

Jim kicked off his boots while Sissy made as much room as she could in her narrow bed.

"You know, this bed is not going to work," he told her.

"Just wait a minute." Sissy threw some quilts and comforters onto the floor and made a comfy pallet. "How's this?"

"Not as good as my king-sized bed out at the ranch, but it'll do." Jim stretched out with his head propped up against Sissy's pile of stuffed animal toys. The big brown wolf toy rolled down the pile between them, and she grabbed it and put it behind her.

"Wait a minute. Let me see that." They wrestled over the toy, but Jim came out the victor and held it up. "This is me, isn't it? I bet you slept with him every night. 'Ooh, Jim. Give me a kiss. I luvvv you.'" Jim made smoochie noises while he "smooched" Sissy with kisses from the stuffed wolf.

"Give me that." Sissy snatched the wolf out of his hand and hugged it to her chest. "And yes, I did get this because it reminded me of you. It was the first time Lucas came back on leave after you guys left. He took me and Maggie to Denver to the natural history museum, and I saw this in the gift shop and begged him to buy it for me. He gave me a hard time about it. He said the same kind of stuff you just did, but, of course, I denied I wanted it because it looked like you. I said I just needed a brown wolf for my collection, but he didn't believe me. He knew I loved you, and he never minded. He didn't ever warn you off about me, did he?"

"No, he never did. He always told me to look out for you, though. I probably would've beat the hell out of him if I'd had a little sister and he tried to put the moves on her. But I was never as understanding as he was."

"He knew, Jim. He knew we'd be together."

"I guess he did. I just didn't see it. I'm pretty blind where you're concerned." Jim sat up and cradled Sissy's face in his hands. "I love you so much."

He smothered her reply with his kiss. Her lips parted and he stroked inside, instantly moving both of them from playful to passionate.

Quickly, Jim's body covered hers as kiss followed breathless kiss. He found the bottom of her sweatshirt and pushed it up so he could caress her silky skin. She arched into his heated touch. His hands skimmed over the smooth expanse of her belly until they met her lacy bra. He traced the edge then moved up to cup her breasts. The hard peaks of her nipples teased his palms.

He was trailing his kisses down to meet his hands when her hand smoothed over his erection. Through the denim, she traced his length from his base to the crown where the tip of his cock nudged uncomfortably against his belt buckle. He froze at the electric connection sparking between them.

When Sissy began to stroke up and down, he rolled back and stilled her hand.

"I guess it's time for that hot chocolate." Sissy snuggled against him.

"I think I'll just take a glass of ice water, then I better get home."

chapter twenty-six

Sissy's head shot up just as the bell on the door of the gallery jingled. She didn't need a bell to tell her there was an alpha Werewolf in the shop. Scenting the intruder from the backroom, Maggie came to the front and stood beside Sissy.

Sissy pushed down her fear. The man standing in the middle of the gallery was big, maybe as big as Jim. He was probably in his early thirties, and he was built. His broad shoulders filled out a fleece-lined leather jacket. He was handsome, tall, and Nordic blonde with sharp blue eyes, but his exuding arrogance overpowered his good looks.

"What are you doing here?" Sissy tried to keep her voice strong as another Were entered, a solid block of muscle. He guarded the door.

"Just visiting," the blonde alpha said. "I heard there was a pretty wolf bitch here in Laramie, and I thought I'd come take a look. I guess the rumors were right. You are pretty, and so's your mom."

"She's not my mother, and you can just back on out of here

before you piss me off," Sissy said with a snarl.

"Ooh-eee." The alpha took off his cowboy hat and dusted it across his knee. "Pretty and sassy."

"And taken. I can smell somebody's mark on her," said the guard Were.

"That doesn't mean anything. You're not mated yet, are you, darlin'?"

Maggie brought up the shotgun she kept under the counter and aimed it at the larger wolf. "I've got two barrels, aimed low, that say you aren't going to be in any shape to mate with anybody."

The blonde alpha appeared to be amused. "You don't have to get so defensive, ma'am. I've just come a-courting. That's all. We came all the way from Reno just to meet you. My name's Wyatt, and you'd be Sissy Hunt, no doubt. I'll be Alpha out there soon, and I've been looking for a strong woman to stand by my side. You're all that and damn fine looking, too."

"Well, if that's all you've got, get out. The last man who came courting me without my permission is dead," Sissy growled. "I ripped out his throat and left him bleeding on the floor. If that's not what you're looking for, you'd better turn around and get out while you still can."

"Yeah, I heard what you did to Jackson Simmons, but I figure he wasn't man enough for you. I am, but I don't want to fight with you. You consider what I said. Reno's a strong pack. We've got lots of land. Mineral and oil rights, too. Hell, I even own a silver mine," he added, as though that would be the deciding factor.

"You'd be the female Alpha of an important pack, one of the biggest and richest in the West. You'd have everything you could ever want, and nobody'd ever mess with you again. If you were with me, there wouldn't be anybody who'd dare come challenging. I can give you all that." He swept his arms open to indicate himself.

"You think on it. I'll come back for your answer."

"Do you have a death wish?" Sissy shouted. "My answer is no, and you're on Laramie pack lands, I assume without permission. If I were you, I'd head on home before you get yourself and your buddy killed."

"I'm not afraid of your Alpha, but I'll be going for now. Believe me, you'll be hearing from me again. Soon."

Sissy stared at them, her growl soft but menacing. The big blonde man turned his back to her and walked away, stopping to shoot her a broad smile before he ducked out the door. Less confident, the guard wolf backed away, never taking his eyes off the women.

Maggie picked up her cell phone as soon as the two men left. She put the call on speaker. "Jim. Two wolves, outsiders, just now in the shop."

"Are they gone?"

"Yes, they just left."

"Are you and Sissy all right?"

"We're fine. Just a little shaken up," Maggie answered.

"Lock up. Clint's in town. I'll send him right over, and I'll be there as soon as I can."

Sissy sank onto the stool behind the counter. She didn't want to show how scared she'd been, but her trembling hands gave her away.

By the time Jim arrived, Clint and his men had come by and secured the shop and scoured the downtown area, but other than scent traces they didn't find any sign of the wolves. Sissy and Maggie had already given Clint a description, and he had done a little intel.

"My best guess is the dominant one is the son of the Reno pack's Second," Clint reported to Jim. "Reno's Alpha is older and doesn't have an heir, so I'd say this guy's looking to make a challenge and take over the pack there. I couldn't tell you if he has any intentions toward challenging you. He might just want to take a strong outside mate to shore up his position, but he might use a challenge here as a stepping-stone to taking over the Reno pack, or even both packs."

"Shit. This is the last thing I need," Sissy heard Jim say.

Maggie had made some tea, but it wasn't coming close to calming their nerves, and Jim's overbearing manner wasn't helping.

"That's it. You're closing the gallery, and you're both coming out to the ranch," he said.

That's it. Sissy stood up. "I don't like being bullied, remember? I held my own against them, and it's not likely they'll be back."

Jim frowned. "That may be, but I'm not taking any chances. I won't have you taken again."

Sissy shot daggers at him, but she knew he was right. As fierce a fighter as she was, she and Maggie were too vulnerable, and she knew from experience that there wasn't much you could do if the other side decided to fight dirty.

"Look. It's less than a week until the full moon, and if there's going to be a challenge, and it looks like there will be, we've got to be ready. I don't want to split up my men. We need to circle the wagons and get ready for whatever's coming."

When he was right, he was right. While Maggie made a special closed sign for the gallery, Jim wrapped a reluctant Sissy in his arms.

"Don't fight me on this," he told her. "I need to feel you safe in my arms. My heart dropped into my boots when Maggie called. I don't think I could live if anything happened to you now."

"Nothing's going to happen. We'll keep each other safe."

"I hope you're right, baby doll."

They made a stop by Maggie's house and packed some bags, then Jim drove them back to the ranch with Clint following behind.

Clint and Daniel joined them for dinner, but they were a pretty solemn bunch that night. Jim had already told the older man about the day's events, and nobody felt like going over it again.

After dinner, Maggie was the first to excuse herself. "I'm going to go up and get settled. I need to unpack and take a long hot bath."

"I think I'll go up, too." Sissy started to follow, but Jim caught her wrist.

"Wait a minute for me." The look in his eyes said whatever was happening between them would take longer than a minute.

She waited at the base of the stairs until he said good night to the men. Jim took her hand, and they went up the stairs together.

When they reached her room, she turned to kiss him, but he shook his head. He walked her down the hall to his rooms and pulled her inside and into his arms. He shut the door.

"I'm making you mine tonight."

"You want to mate tonight? I don't think I'm ready." Sissy started to pull away.

"Not mating, just making love. A man and a woman. I want you, Sissy, like I've never wanted anyone else." He covered her lips with his and swept inside her mouth hungrily.

Her arms came up around his neck and she matched his kiss.

Jim slowly peeled her clothes away, kissing every inch of exposed skin. He pulled her sweater over her head and dropped it to the floor. When he unhooked her bra, she instinctively covered her breasts with her hands.

"No, baby, let me do that," he said, his hands replacing hers.

His calloused fingers played across the tips until he dipped his head and took first one then the other between his lips.

Sissy arched her back and moaned.

Jim trailed kisses back up her neck. "Now me."

She took her time opening his shirt button by button, tugging his shirttails out of his jeans. She pushed the shirt off his shoulders to expose his heavily muscled chest. A sprinkling of dark hair dusted his pecs and trailed down beneath his belt. She flicked his tight nipples with her tongue.

"My turn. Let's get those boots off." Jim backed Sissy to the bed and guided her down onto her back. He pulled off her boots and socks, licking up her instep, then he smoothly stripped away her jeans, leaving her in a tiny scrap of pink lace.

"God, you're so beautiful. I don't know where to start." Jim knelt over her and kissed her belly, dipping into her belly button with his tongue. He trailed his kisses down until he met with lace, then breathed across the thin barrier, bringing a shiver.

"This is it, Jim. I've never been this far, except, you know." Sissy's face flushed. Jim remembered how she'd begged him to satisfy her in her heat.

"I know, baby. Don't worry about that. This is the first time for us." He peeled her panties down her long legs, then reversed the trip, smoothing up the insides of her calves then her thighs to ruffle through the blonde down between her legs. His finger easily slipped inside her tight, slick channel.

Jim laid his body alongside hers and kissed her. He'd lost his boots, but he still wore his jeans. Sissy opened his belt and the button of his jeans, then tugged down the zipper. His erection, still wrapped in white cotton, sprang free. He helped her shimmy his jeans off, then held his breath as her warm hand reached inside his briefs. Her fingers barely circled him.

274

"It's bigger than I thought," she breathed.

"It'll be okay. I promise. It might hurt a little."

"I know. I'm not afraid," she said as she pulled him free and explored the silken steel of his shaft.

They kissed and stroked as he prepared her to take him. A rush of hot wetness told him she was ready.

"My mark is burning. I need you." Sissy pulled at Jim to cover her.

"Easy, baby." He licked over her mating mark. "I know it's hard, but no biting. The mating will come later. For now, just try to relax and let me love you."

Jim pushed into her slowly, rocking forward gently before retreating as she adjusted to his size. Only part of the way in, he said, "Wrap your legs around me."

Sissy's long legs rode his hips as he lifted her butt. He entered her in one hard thrust, seating himself fully.

Sissy's inarticulate scream cut through the quiet. When she opened her eyes, Jim was looking down at her, grinning.

"Did I scream?"

"Yeah. Just a little. I don't think they heard you in Idaho."

"Oh, God."

"Are you okay?"

"More than okay. It didn't really hurt, it was just the feeling...It was so amazing."

"Are you ready for some more?"

"Oh yeah."

Jim stroked in and out, with Sissy countering every move as they drove each other higher.

"Now, Jim."

Jim adjusted his angle so each thrust worked across the bundle of nerves at the top of her cleft. Sissy ground against him harder and faster until she screamed her release. Her muscles gripped him, milking his response as he followed her over the edge.

Later, they lay spooned together on a sheepskin rug in front of a blazing fire. Jim tucked a soft throw over their legs. Sissy's skin shimmered in the flickering golden light. The second time had been easier, and when Jim had put his mouth on her, she'd come apart for him again and again.

"That was wonderful," she whispered. "More than I ever imagined. I do love you, Jim, and I'm not afraid anymore. If you want to complete the mating, I will."

"We will, baby, but first I want to deal with this full moon. I don't want anything between us when we begin our lives together."

NO ONE HAD seen the Reno wolves again, but over the next days there were several reports of outsider wolves showing up around town. One Werewolf had supposedly been hanging around on the sidewalk outside of another pack member's shop. Two more had been seen at a local restaurant. A few folks from the pack called in to say they had scented unfamiliar wolves at various spots around town. Rumors were flying.

Sheriff Murray had called Jim. "I've been hearing there were some strangers in town, and I know some of your fellows have been sniffing around."

"There were some folks in from out of town." Jim adopted the sheriff's euphemisms. "I expect they'll be leaving soon and every-thing will be back to normal."

"From what I hear, things haven't been normal for a while. I caught wind of some serious problems in Missoula. I don't want that sort of thing happening around here. It's not going to make the locals any friendlier to your kind." He dropped any pretense of friendly concern.

"I take care of *my kind*, Frank. And I'm taking care of this."

"I'm sorry about Daniel, but I'm glad Sissy is all right." The sheriff hung up and left Jim wondering where he was getting his information.

Clint came in right after the call. Jim had sent him out to follow up on the reports, but he had no luck. By the time he arrived at any of the locations, there was no trail left to follow, and the nervous pack members who called in weren't able to give useful descriptions.

"I'm not getting anywhere with this," Clint told him. "I can't tell what's real or not. It's like chasing ghosts."

"Well, we know that the wolves that Maggie and Sissy saw were real."

"Yeah, but once people heard about that incident, coupled with our recent trouble, it may just be some kind of hysteria, people seeing trouble on every corner."

"Or trouble may already be here. I have a feeling about this. I expect a challenge, but I don't know if it's coming from inside the pack or out. And I don't know how those Reno wolves figure into it."

Sissy and Maggie were sitting in the great room. Jim called them into the study. "I want to get a call out to everybody in the pack. Anyone who's worried can come stay out at the ranch until after the full moon run tomorrow, and everybody else stays close to home. I don't want folks going to the bar tonight or off on dates. Everybody who doesn't have to work should stay home. If anyone feels scared, they should call and Clint and some of the security team will come to them. Here's the pack roster. It's got all the contact numbers. Can you split it up and start making calls?"

"Sure, we can take care of it." Sissy came behind the desk and cradled Jim's head against her breast. "You're really worried about this, aren't you? Do you think we're going to be attacked?"

"I don't know, baby, but I can't take that chance. We're just going to play it safe. And I don't want you out of my sight, even here on the ranch. I want you inside the house unless you're with me or Clint. We don't know what your Reno boyfriend is up to."

"He's going to *be* my Reno boyfriend if you try to put a collar on me. I hear it's real nice there." Sissy ruffled his hair and planted a kiss on the top of his head.

Jim swatted her on the butt. "Call the folks, but don't scare them. Reassure them that we'll keep them safe."

LATER, JIM WAS happy to snag a few minutes alone in the afternoon with Sissy. He'd just dropped down beside her on one of the deep leather couches in the great room when his phone buzzed. With a sigh of frustration, he pulled it out, surprised to see Crystal's name on the readout. He started to switch it off, but instead he answered and waited.

"Jim? It's Crystal." When he didn't say anything she continued hesitantly, "I heard about what happened. I'm glad you got Sissy back."

"Did you call to tell me that?"

"No, I wanted to apologize."

"There's no need. We said everything that needed to be said."

"I didn't. I'm so ashamed. I'm sorry I deceived you. You deserved better than that. I let my emotions take over. I got caught up in the excitement of meeting you, and I lost touch with the project and everything I'd come to Laramie to do."

"Like experiment with Werewolves."

"I wish I could make you see how important this research will be. Maybe sometime in the future you'll let me explain, but that's not why I called. I'm back in Seattle, but I was talking to a colleague at the University of Nevada in Reno. He was asking about your pack."

"Why?"

"Don't worry. I didn't tell him anything. He was asking because he'd heard that a group of young alphas—he described it as a war party—was headed your way. He assumed they meant to challenge you."

"Yeah, we've seen a couple of them already. Did he say how many were coming?"

"He thought there were five or six. Are you going to be okay?"

"I can handle it."

"I know you can. I just wanted to give you a heads up. I thought I owed you that much."

"You don't owe me anything."

"I do. I abused your trust and your pack. I am sorry." Again silence. "Are you and Sissy together now?"

"We're working on it."

"I know it will work out. She's a lucky girl. I wish you both the best. I really do. Good-bye, Jim."

"Thank you for the warning, Crystal. Good-bye." He hung up.

Sissy arched her brow. "What was that about?"

"She was calling to warn us. Said a 'war party' from Reno was going to pay us a visit."

"So it's official."

"I guess so."

That evening, there were two more wolf sightings in town, but again Clint's security team didn't find anything when they investigated.

Later that night, Sissy curled close to Jim in his bed. He laced his fingers with hers. "You aren't scared, are you, baby?"

"Not scared. Worried."

"We'll face this, whatever it is, and then we'll have our whole lives. I want to marry you. Not just a mating ceremony, but a real wedding, with the dress and everything. I want to watch you come down the stairs and stand beside me. Will you marry me, Sissy?"

"Yes, I'll marry you. I want forever with you."

"I'll do everything I can to make that happen."

chapter twenty-seven

By late afternoon of the next day, several nervous families had
taken Jim up on his offer. Maggie got them settled in the pack
cabins on the ranch and made sure there was plenty of food for the
hands and the visitors. Clint doubled up the patrols. The
wranglers were busy securing the livestock and preparing the
outbuildings. Jim was out supervising everything.

Everybody was busy except Sissy. Cooped up in the house on
Jim's orders, she paced and fidgeted. Trying to calm herself, she
finally settled on the sofa in Jim's study with a romance novel.

"You've been reading that same page for five minutes."

Sissy looked up to see Daniel standing in the doorway. "Have
you been watching me, Daddy?"

"Yeah, I guess we're in the same boat. Nothing much for
either of us to do." He crossed over and sat beside her. "I've been
doing some figuring, though, and I think I've come up with a plan."

HOURS LATER, JIM came into the study and found Sissy curled up
and dozing on his couch, looking all warm and soft under a woolen

throw.

"Baby doll, wake up," he breathed in her ear.

She stirred. "Oh, hi." She turned her face to his.

"You sleepy?"

"Bored, mostly. I haven't done anything all day."

"I'm sorry. It's just until all this is over. I can't take the chance of anything happening to you." He pulled her against him and breathed in her scent, like sweet clover and warm sunshine. "Come on." He tugged at her. "I want to show you something."

She took his hand and barely suppressed a laugh when he stopped her at the doorway and did a quick check to make sure the coast was clear. He didn't want to get caught up in any pack business, she guessed. They darted across the great room and up the stairs. He pulled her into his room and as he pinned her up against the door, she heard him click the lock into place.

He pressed into her as his lips came down in a surprisingly soft kiss. "I've been so busy all day, and all I wanted was to be with you."

"I missed you, too." She pulled his head down for a deep kiss that had the mark on her breast burning for more. She palmed his erection through his jeans. "Is this what you wanted to show me? Because I'd be glad to take a good, long look."

Jim hissed at her touch. "That's nice, but no, actually I had something else in mind." He pulled away to reveal a blanket spread before the fireplace. A warm fire blazed, and a picnic was laid out on the blanket.

There was a platter with sliced roast beef, cheeses, and pickles. A small wicker basket held warm, sliced bread, and there were two big wedges of gooey chocolate cake.

Sissy grinned. "Did you do this all yourself?"

Jim poured Sissy a cup of coffee from a Thermos as she

admired the feast. "I had a little help from the kitchen, but I set it up. I had to have you to myself for a few minutes. Come on. Get something to eat." He pulled her down next to him and tucked her under his arm.

They picked at the food. Jim knew that with so much weighing on their minds, neither of them had much of an appetite. Sissy fed him some bites of the chocolate cake, and he licked at her fingers and smiled, but he was clearly distracted. Finally, she said, "Just go ahead and say what you need to say."

"I'm sorry. I didn't want to spoil this."

"It's okay."

"It's liable to get crazy tonight. I want you to stay by your father. I need to know you'll be safe."

"I've already talked to him. You don't need to worry."

"I can't help but worry. I almost lost you once. I won't risk that again."

"Daddy will be right there."

They both fell silent.

"What are you going to do if..." Sissy trailed off.

"Shush. I don't want to talk about that now. The moon will be full in about an hour. Lay here with me for a little while." He pressed his fingertips to her lips. "I want to talk about your lips. I love your bottom lip." He nipped it between his teeth and gently tugged. "And your eyes... I love this one." He dropped a kiss on one eyelid. "And this one." Another kiss. "And I love this little spot underneath your ear." His mouth drifted down her neck before coming back to her mouth.

He stretched and cradled her head with his arm. Gently pushing her hair from her forehead, he dropped soft kisses on her lips. "I want you to know that this is the best time of my life."

Sissy swallowed a sob, but couldn't stop the tears from

running down her face.

"Don't cry, baby."

"You sound like you're saying good-bye."

"No. Never. This is the best time of my life. Finally being with you. Every day is better than the last. And there are so many more ahead of us. I don't plan on missing a single one." He kissed away her tears. "Tonight, after the run, I'm going to make you my mate. Forever, baby doll."

"I'll love you forever."

After a last long kiss, he pulled her to her feet. "Now, come on. Let's get this done."

ALMOST EVERYONE FROM the pack had come out, but there was none of the usual fun, family atmosphere. Armed guards were all around. Even the children, tucked away in the big hall, were quiet. Everyone felt the tension, the feeling that something was coming.

Jim and Sissy and Maggie moved among those who came out, smiling and calming fears. When it came time to move to the pack circle, Jim took Sissy's hand, and they led the way to the snow-covered clearing.

The moon rose above the trees. Jim took his place on the Alpha's rock and looked over his pack. If anything was going to happen, it would happen now.

A disturbance at the edge of the woods caught his attention, and the pack parted. Adam came forward, followed closely by four large unfamiliar Weres. Jim figured the big blonde to Adam's left had to be Wyatt, the Reno wolf who'd paid the visit to Sissy. The others were also alphas, and they looked like seasoned enforcers, probably ex-military, not the gangly kids Adam had gathered around himself before.

Jim let them come into the circle before he called down to

Adam. "You were banished. You have no right to be on these lands."

"I'm here to claim my right. I challenge you for this pack and this land." Adam stepped toward Jim. "You're weak. You willingly traded away your female, and you almost got your Second killed. You put the whole pack in danger. The way I hear it, you guys took quite a beating in Missoula, and you wouldn't have won if you hadn't surprised them. You don't deserve to be Alpha of this pack."

Jim ignored him and addressed the Reno wolf. "Are you also challenging for leadership, or are you here to back up Adam's challenge?"

"I don't have any interest in this pack beyond a personal matter. I'm here to back Adam's challenge."

"Are those your goons?" Jim indicated the other three.

"They came with me, but they've agreed to side with Adam and stay for a while after the challenge to help him get this pack in shape."

"And what do you get out of it?"

"I plan to take your female. Hopefully, after you're out of the picture, she'll see the advantages of accepting my suit."

"You realize that'll be over my dead body."

"Enough talk." Adam stepped forward, clearly annoyed at being ignored. "What assurance do we have that this will be a fair challenge? We came to fight you and an equal number who might want to stand with you, not the whole pack."

Jim jumped down from the Alpha's rock and advanced on the small group of challengers.

"There are no assurances. You forfeited any rights by returning. You issued the challenge. Stand by it or get out."

Adam addressed the whole pack. "You deserve an Alpha who isn't afraid to be a wolf. Anyone who sides with me will be rewarded when this is all over. If you stay out of it, I won't hold it against you, but if you come in against me, you can expect to go down with Jim. He doesn't even have a Second to help protect you."

"Yes, he does." Clint took his place beside Jim. "I'm the Second of this pack."

"So it's you two against us five?"

"No. It'll be five against five." Sissy stepped forward with two of Clint's security men, both of them strong and well-trained.

"Keep her out of this, Winter," Wyatt snapped at Jim. "I don't want my female harmed."

"Sissy, get back. You don't have any part in this." Jim shot her a look and held up his hand.

"Seriously?" Sissy moved up next to Jim and faced Wyatt. "The only reason Adam has anybody to stand with him at all is because this yahoo wants to cart me off like some prize. I'm either going to stand by your side in this pack or not at all."

The strength in her voice melted Jim's thunderous heart. As much as he feared for her, he knew she was right. He flashed her a smile full of pride and love and turned to face their enemies.

"You heard the lady." Jim shifted first, and he instantly took Adam to the ground. Jim's jaws covered Adam's neck and drove his head down while the trapped wolf's rear legs scrambled for purchase in the soft earth. Around him he heard the others engage, but he couldn't see much through the thick dust and snow in the air.

He had a good grip and could keep Adam down, but he couldn't inflict much damage from his position. When he opened his jaws to get a better advantage, he was hit from behind. One of the Reno wolves powered him to the ground, but Jim quickly rolled out of his grip.

He turned on the new attacker and found himself facing both Adam and the second wolf. Adam went in high, while the other ducked low in a coordinated attack. Jim and Adam each snapped at the other's shoulders, but the second wolf sunk his teeth in Jim's flank, just where it joined his belly, and Jim couldn't maneuver without risking a tear that would cripple him. The best he could do was to keep tearing at Adam until the other wolf lost his hold.

Out of the corner of his eye, Jim knew that Clint had taken on the largest of the Reno enforcer wolves, and they rolled in the snow, fangs and claws slashing at each other.

The smell of blood and the savagery of the fight prompted the rest of the pack to shift, and they crowded around the combatants in a tight circle, howling and snarling. The snow-packed ground was quickly drenched with blood.

One of the Reno wolves lunged at Sissy, but Wyatt cut him off. He'd shifted into a huge golden wolf. He was bigger and more powerful than Jax had been, but she was stronger than when she'd fought before, and she was counting on the fact that Wyatt wouldn't want her too badly hurt.

Now she was face to face with the snarling giant. She snapped at him, but because of his size, she didn't want to give him the opening to come over her and take her down. She'd be helpless under his weight. When he rose up to lunge at her, she sprang up gracefully and sailed over his back, tearing a piece of his ear away in her mouth. He howled and turned on her, but not before she got her teeth deeply embedded in his rear haunch. He couldn't get to her from that position, but he thrashed from side to side, whipping her behind him like a rag doll.

Don't let go. Don't let go. Just hold on until Jim gets here. Sissy felt her clenched jaws weakening. She couldn't hold on much longer.

She released her grip just enough so the force of Wyatt's thrashing would throw her off, but not without leaving a good chunk of his skin and muscle in her fangs. She landed a few feet away and was on her feet before he could turn around.

The golden giant bled profusely, and Sissy was aware that her own silver fur was streaked with blood as they circled, neither taking their eyes off the other. Wyatt was bleeding freely, but his muscles were taut and his fangs were bared. He still had plenty of fight.

Sissy hoped he remembered that he'd wanted her as a mate. If he intended to kill her, there wasn't much she could do to stop him.

Except fight.

JIM FEARED THE hold the younger wolf had on him would weaken him, so he let himself be taken to the ground. Each of the attacking wolves let go in order to dive in for the kill, but Jim twisted so the second wolf's body blocked Adam's attack.

Facing the Reno wolf, Jim lunged up underneath his attacker and ripped a bite out of his groin. The wounded wolf rolled away, bleeding and howling in pain and was immediately set on by one of Clint's men.

Adam jumped in and tore at Jim's chest. The two wolves rolled and scrambled, locked in combat, until Jim got his teeth into the side of Adam's throat. The other wolf thrashed against the hold, blood spurting as Jim's fangs severed Adam's jugular vein. Jim felt the hot blood pumping into his mouth until the younger wolf stopped struggling and he let him slip from his jaws.

His fight was over. Jim looked around and saw Clint had his opponent down by the throat. The Reno wolf fought for air as Clint clamped down on his windpipe and kept hold. The two other Reno enforcers were also down.

Only Wyatt and Sissy's battle was unresolved.

Sissy backed up as Wyatt advanced. As Wyatt's muscles

bunched to spring, Jim jumped between Wyatt and Sissy and bared his teeth at the attacking wolf. A glance around showed what he and the others had done: Wyatt was the only one of the challengers left standing. He lay down and lowered his head to the ground.

Jim shifted back to human form and towered over the prostrate wolf. "It's over," he called out. "Shift back now."

Clint let go of the dying wolf he had by the throat, and the fighters all shifted back, except for Adam, whose body lay motionless at the edge of the circle. The rest of the pack kept still, not shifting yet.

"I'll let you live because I don't want war with Reno or any of the other packs," Jim told Wyatt. "Tell them we'll fight to keep what's ours, but we won't retaliate further. I'll have my men escort those of you who are still alive to the infirmary. Our doctor will see to your wounds, but one way or another, I want you all out of my territory by morning."

The security team surrounded the four wounded men. They tied a tourniquet around Wyatt's thigh to stop his bleeding, and one of his men pulled him to his feet and supported him out of the pack circle. Another of the Reno pack helped the bloody wolf Jim had taken down, and they shuffled off after Wyatt. One of Clint's men hefted Adam's body onto his shoulder and carried him away.

The pack, still in wolf form, pressed closer. Jim put his arm out for Sissy to come to his side. "Are you hurt?" he asked.

"No, I'm fine, just a little beat up, but you're bleeding."

"I'll be okay. We'll all be okay now."

The fighters all shifted back to wolf form. Clint came before them first. When Clint rolled his head and bared his neck, Jim took Clint's throat in his teeth. He bore down only hard enough to draw blood, then let go and rubbed his muzzle against Clint's.

Then Clint offered the same obeisance to Sissy. She took his throat gently before she licked his face.

Next Maggie came to them. Jim accepted her gesture, but when she showed her neck to Sissy, Sissy shook her head, hesitant to dominate the sister-in-law who'd practically raised her. Jim nodded at her, letting her know it was the right thing to do. There was a growl and they turned to see Daniel, gray and shaggy, standing proudly behind her on the three legs he had remaining. So she tenderly bit down on Maggie's throat.

In ones and twos, the pack wolves came forward to acknowledge Jim and Sissy as the Alpha couple. They crouched low as they approached and kept their eyes down. Some bared their necks and others rolled to show their bellies. Each one got a bite and a lick or a rub from both of their Alphas.

When the pack had all submitted to them, Jim raised his head in a howl, and he and Sissy took off at the head of the pack. The pack followed their lead, howling into the still night.

Fresh snow began to fall as they ran, adding to the thick white covering already on the ground. It would blanket the ground reddened by the battle. They cut through the pristine drifts, the glistening snow adorning the tips of their fur. The pack startled a young bull elk, and Jim and Clint ran it down, efficiently tearing out its throat. Jim stood aside with Sissy, panting frosty breaths in the cold, watching the pack feed. After a while the pack ran on, and Jim and Sissy broke for home.

They shifted on the run, and they raced naked into the ranch house. They'd been running so hard they hadn't had a chance to get cold. Sissy beat Jim to the bedroom, but he took her down in front of the fire on the sheepskin rug.

Jim pinned her under his body, her back hot against his chest. She squirmed beneath him, rubbing her bottom against his rigid cock. He growled low in his throat. With an arm under her hips, he pulled her to her knees and entered her with one thrust. From behind, he drove into her hard and fast, and she responded, rocking into every move.

Jim hooked his arms under her shoulders and pulled her body up against his chest. He felt his teeth reforming in his mouth, growing longer and sharper. Sissy turned her head to look at him over her shoulder. When she saw the light glint off his canines, she tossed her hair to the side and bared her neck to him.

Jim bit into the soft flesh where her shoulder met her neck. Sissy uttered a cry of pain and ecstasy. Her blood rushed into his mouth, and his saliva flowed into her wound. He took her into himself. He felt her consciousness pushing at his, unable to fully connect. They were joined in an unbreakable bond, but it wasn't yet complete.

When Jim released her, he let her pull away. She sank down onto the soft rug on her back and pulled him down to her. He entered her again, this time more tenderly, with a smooth and steady tempo.

SISSY FELT HER fangs emerging. She ran her tongue over the sharp tips and smiled up at Jim.

"Baby doll. Do it. I want to be yours," Jim whispered.

Sissy clamped onto the thick muscle on the side of Jim's neck. The first taste of his blood sent a hot rush pulsing to all her nerve endings. She sensed him inside and all around her. She felt the urgency of the orgasm he was barely holding back. More than that, she experienced his passion, and she knew the depth of his love and the fear he suffered for her.

I love you, Sissy. I always will. His words sounded clearly in her mind as his mouth came down on hers. Their passions coiled around each other and spiraled into a mutual orgasm that surged between them, leaving them shaking and breathless.

JIM STROKED SISSY'S hip, admiring her golden skin, burnished by the fire's glow. "You know, joining the challenge, that was amazingly brave and amazingly stupid. You planned to do that, didn't you?"

"If I'd told you, you would have locked me in the safe room." She brought her arms around his neck.

"Yes, I would." He trailed kisses down her jaw. "Promise me you'll never do anything like that again."

Her hands stroked down his back. "I can't promise you that." She arched her neck, and he nipped and licked her throat.

"You were so fierce. Every one of the pack submitted to you."

"Not you."

"Only with my heart. I gave that to you a long time ago."

chapter twenty-eight

The entire pack gathered. The ranch had been chaotic for days. Trucks with food and flowers had formed a caravan between town and the ranch, and Maggie had commandeered the whole downstairs of Jim's house, directing caterers, cooks, and decorators.

Jim had hardly seen Sissy for weeks. She and Maggie had moved back to Maggie's house in town, and Sissy and her girlfriends had been running back and forth to Denver, picking out dresses and shoes. They'd managed to steal a few quiet hours together here and there, but Jim was more than ready for them to begin their lives together.

Now, he stood in front of the big fireplace in the great room. He knew he looked good in his western-cut tux and shiny new black boots. He hated the nervous anticipation. He'd hardly been able to speak coherently to anybody all day. But he was glad it was finally time.

Guests filled the room and overflowed out onto the porch. The door to Jim's study opened and out came Clint and Maggie, arm in arm. She was beautiful in a burgundy gown. The Second kissed her cheek and left her standing across from Jim on the other side of the broad hearth. As he crossed to take his place as best man, he gave Jim a wink.

Sissy's best friend Randi came next. She was paired with Trace, who'd come down from Missoula for the occasion. She looked particularly predatory in a slinky fuchsia gown, and Trace's shy smile said he had no problem being her prey. Three other couples followed arm in arm, the women all dressed in shades of pink.

With the wedding party assembled around the fireplace, everyone's attention turned to the long staircase. Jim held his breath as Sissy appeared at the top of the stairs. Her blonde hair was swept up off her neck, and her creamy shoulders were bare. The opal pendant he'd given her hung from her neck. Her new mating mark showed faintly, provoking a lusty growl from Jim as his matching mark, hidden under his now too-tight collar, burned in response.

He'd never seen anyone so beautiful. Her eyes found his, and she smiled a smile he knew was for him alone. He held his breath as she appeared to float down the stairs in a cloud of ivory silk and sparkling beads. Her hands held a bouquet of roses that were the same shade of pink as the blush on her cheeks.

Daniel waited at the base of the stairs. He wrapped Sissy's arm in his and led her to Jim's side. As he handed his daughter over, he said, "I'm counting on you to take care of her now."

"I'll do my best, but I believe she can take care of herself." Jim took her hand and whispered, "Baby doll, you take my breath away."

The officiant was an elderly pack member who'd been performing weddings for the pack as long as anyone could remember. "This is both a mating ceremony and a wedding where we are gathered to join our Alphas, Jim and Sissy, as lifelong mates and as husband and wife.

"Who will stand as guardian for this couple?"

"I will," Clint responded solemnly.

"Do you pledge to protect and support this couple and the children of their union?"

"I do."

"You are so bound." The old man turned his attention back to the wedding couple. "There is always joy among us when two people find their true mates, and there is also trepidation because we know the pain that can come from the severance of that bond. Jim, Sissy, I've watched you both grow up. You've faced your troubles and come out stronger together. I've never seen a better match.

"Sissy, do you accept Jim as the mate of your heart, as your partner in life, and as your husband?"

"I do." Sissy turned to face Jim. "I am yours forever. I'll stand by your side and share your joys and sorrows. I'll love you with my last heartbeat."

"Jim, do you accept Sissy as the mate of your heart, as your partner in life, and as your wife?"

"I do." His voice was thick with emotion. "Baby, you are my heart. You have all of me. I'll proudly stand by your side and share your joys and do what I can to see that you don't have many sorrows. I love you now and always."

"As you have accepted each other and vowed your love, I now pronounce you married in the eyes of the state of Wyoming and mates according to the tradition of the packs. You may kiss your mate."

Jim breathed in Sissy's scent, and the crowded room faded

away. He leaned in and took her lips with his. The mating mark Sissy had given him tingled with the kiss. He sensed her mark respond. He felt her heartbeat matching his, and he knew her joy. It would always be like this for them. Their bond would only grow deeper with time.

Clint gave Jim a little nudge and brought him back to the moment. Clint whispered, "Better stand down, buddy, before you set off the whole pack."

Jim broke the kiss, but he couldn't drag his eyes away from Sissy's.

The old man gently turned them to face the assembled crowd. "Friends, I'd like to present your Alphas, Jim and Sissy Winter, and offer them our traditional blessing."

The whole pack spoke the words together. "May you live long together and die in each other's arms."

As their friends and family applauded the union, Jim pulled Sissy into his arms again. "You're everything I ever wanted. I'm sorry it took me so long to see it, but I want you to know, when we joined, everything that came before was wiped away. Today we begin forever."

Dear Reader,

I hope you enjoyed Jim and Sissy's story. Here's the story behind the story. I got the idea for *Laramie Moon* when I was traveling around Montana and Wyoming. Since wolves have been reintroduced into the wild throughout the West, many ranchers view them as nuisance predators who prey on their livestock, and federal and state regulations have left ranchers with few legal options. I saw bumper stickers on trucks with slogans like "Shoot, shovel, and shut up." That made we wonder what it would be like to be a Werewolf living in the middle of ranching country where turning furry and running around the countryside would be dangerous, and coming out to the public in a community already hostile to wolves would open up an ugly can of worms. My solution to this dilemma was to create a Werewolf rancher and give him the biggest ranch around where he could hide and protect his pack. And that's how Jim was born.

I explored Laramie, with its historic downtown district of bars, bookstores, galleries and shops in buildings dating back to the 1860's (where Maggie's art gallery is located) and visited the beautiful University of Wyoming Campus. To become more familiar with ranch life, I spent some time at the wonderful CM Ranch, near Dubois, Wyoming. I got to ride and watch the wranglers handle the horses and cattle and get a feel for the rhythm of the place. I also loved the town of Dubois. Although it's quite a bit smaller than Laramie, it has the same Western character. The Rustic Pine Tavern is a community center, and I had it in mind when I wrote the bar scene at the beginning of the story. Wyoming was a wonderful experience, and all I'd seen and learned helped me bring life to *Laramie Moon*.

While I was back home finishing the book, I listened to a lot of country music and found songs that fit right in with the story. I picked George Strait's "I Get Carried Away," one of my favorites, to be Jim and Sissy's love song. Jim wants to maintain control and do what he thinks is the right thing, but when he's near Sissy, he can't help but be swept away. I also love Josh Turner's "I Wouldn't Be a Man." Jim finally has to admit, "I wouldn't be a man if a woman like you was anything I could resist," and I'm so glad he quit resisting! I hope you'll give the songs a listen.

Thank you for reading *Laramie Moon*. If you want to become a part of Jim and Sissy's world, visit www.claremckay.com/contact to sign up for my newsletter. You'll hear from me about once a month for big news, sales, new releases, contests, giveaways, signings and more. Check out my website claremckay.com or follow me on Facebook - ClareMcKayAuthor - or Twitter - @Clare_McKay. I'd love to hear from you.

Thank you for reading.

- Clare

ACKNOWLEDGEMENTS

For a first time author, there are so many people to thank. This book wouldn't be in anybody's hands if I hadn't had the support of these folks, so bear with me.

First, I need to thank my Trifecta Publishing House team. Lori Lyn, thank you for hearing my pitch and sending me to Diana Ballew who read *Laramie Moon* and wanted it. Thank you, Diana, for loving my book. And special kudos to my awesome editor (and I mean that in the sense of shock and awe) Eilis Flynn, who caught every weak point and made me make the story better.

I also need to thank my professional support. My writing chapters GSRWA and EVRWA have given me so much over the years with workshops, conferences, write-a-thons, and happy hours, and lots and lots of creative and supportive friends. The amazing Cherry Adair and her challenge made me "Finish the Damn Book." Dr. Cynthia Grace led me through the contract process and made sure my book and my interests were protected. Dr. J gave me deadlines and encouraged me to push on. Volya Dzemka, my talented photographer, made me look good in my headshots. The Art Institute of Seattle awarded me a four-month sabbatical to go to Wyoming and write, and the folks at the CM Ranch in Dubois, Wyoming graciously helped me experience the ranch life I was writing about. Thank you all.

My writing partners, Josie Malone and Skip Ferderber, have been there for me from brainstorming sessions to revisions. They give me the honest feedback I need, they offer suggestions when I'm stuck, they encourage me when I'm down, and they remind me to do what I love. I can never thank you enough.

Love and thanks to my good friends – Jim and Marion who gave me a retreat when I needed the quiet. Lonnie who always listens, Pam who cheers, and Jim G who was always sure this book was about him.

Finally, my family deserves more than thanks. My husband Pat never complained when I closed the door and wrote all night. My daughter Camilla brought home the first paranormal romance I ever read (and got me hooked). My son Lee gave me the sights and locales of Laramie that got me started on this book. Phaedra and David are the best daughter- and son-in-law I could ever ask for and completely backed their crazy mother-in-law. And my sister Becca is my first and best reader, always. You believed in me even when I wasn't so sure. I love you all.

ABOUT THE AUTHOR

Clare McKay always knew she wanted to write. From her first taste of historical novels in the dusty stacks of the public library, she devoured worlds populated by heroes, knights, warriors, and brave heroines. Excursions into the realms of sci-fi and fantasy, from H.G. Wells and H.P. Lovecraft to Star Trek and Star Wars, all opened her to supernatural alternatives to the romantic past.

While she's never lost her love of history, Clare writes contemporary paranormal romance and fantasy. She loves to tuck in her supernatural elements alongside the unsuspecting everyday world of cowboys, ranchers, small town sheriffs, and big city detectives. "I like the idea that there are other worlds and magickal creatures living alongside us, rarely glimpsed until some event brings them into our lives and changes everything."

Clare migrated from Austin, Texas to the Pacific Northwest with her husband some twenty years ago. She teaches at an art college, keeps up with her kids and grandkids, roots for the Mariners and the Seahawks, gardens whenever the sun is out, and travels when she can. But nothing thrills her like seeing her characters come to life, overcome their challenges together, and find their own happily-ever-afters.

Follow Clare on Facebook: Clare.McKay.94 and Twitter: @Clare_McKay or visit her website: www.claremckay.com.

Made in the USA
Charleston, SC
29 September 2016